ALSO BY RAY BRADBURY

A Graveyard for Lunatics

The Toynbee Convector

Death Is a Lonely Business

Something Wicked This Way Comes

The Haunted Computer and the Android Pope

The Stories of Ray Bradbury

*Where Robot Mice and Robot Men Run Round
in Robot Towns*

Long After Midnight

Dandelion Wine

When Elephants Last in the Dooryard Bloomed

The Halloween Tree

The October Country

I Sing the Body Electric!

Switch on the Night

The Illustrated Man

The Martian Chronicles

R Is for Rocket

Dark Carnival

The Machineries of Joy

The Anthem Sprinters

A Medicine for Melancholy

Moby Dick (screenplay)

Fahrenheit 451

Golden Apples of the Sun

S Is for Space

GREEN SHADOWS, WHITE WHALE

GREEN SHADOWS, WHITE WHALE

A NOVEL BY

RAY
BRADBURY

WITH DRAWINGS BY
EDWARD SOREL

ALFRED A. KNOPF

NEW YORK · 1992

THIS IS A BORZOI BOOK
PUBLISHED BY ALFRED A. KNOPF, INC.

The following chapters were previously published in different
form: 4, under the title "The Great Collision of Monday Last";
12, "The Terrible Conflagration up at the Place"; 13, "The
Beggar on O'Connell Bridge"; 15, "The Haunting of the New";
18, "One for His Lordship, and One for the Road"; 21, "Getting Through Sunday Somehow"; 22, "The First Night of
Lent"; 23, "McGillahee's Brat"; 27, "Banshee"; 28, "The Cold
Wind and the Warm"; 29, "The Anthem Sprinters."

Chapter 9 appears in the May 1992 issue of *The American
Way* under the title "The Hunt Wedding."

Library of Congress
Cataloging-in-Publication Data

Bradbury, Ray.
    Green shadows, white whale : a novel by Ray Bradbury.—
1st ed.
    p.   cm.
    ISBN 0-394-57878-3
    I. Title.
PS3503.R167G75   1992
813'.54—dc20   91-58552
                                                           CIP

Manufactured in the United States of America
First Edition

WITH LOVE AND GRATITUDE
TO KATHY HOURIGAN,
WHO HELPED MAP DUBLIN
AND BEYOND

AND TO REGINA FERGUSON,
WHO SHEPHERDED MY FAMILY
THROUGH THAT COLD IRISH WINTER

AND TO THE MEMORY OF
HEEBER FINN, NICK (MIKE) MY TAXI
DRIVER, AND ALL THE BOYOS IN THE PUB,
AND TO THE PROPRIETOR OF THE
ROYAL HIBERNIAN HOTEL, HECTOR FABRON,
AND PADDY THE MAÎTRE D'
AND ALL THE HOTEL STAFF,
THIS BOUQUET
LONG IN COMING

GREEN SHADOWS,
WHITE WHALE

1

I looked out from the deck of the Dún Laoghaire ferry and saw Ireland.

The land was green.

Not just one ordinary sort of green, but every shade and variation. Even the shadows were green, and the light that played on the Dún Laoghaire wharf and on the faces of the customs inspectors. Down into the green I stepped, an American young man, just beyond thirty, suffering two sorts of depression, lugging a typewriter and little else.

Noticing the light, the grass, the hills, the shadows, I cried out: "Green! Just like the travel posters. Ireland *is* green. I'll be damned! Green!"

Lightning! Thunder! The sun hid. The green vanished. Shadow-rains curtained the vast sky. Bewildered, I felt my smile collapse. A gray and bristly customs official beckoned.

"Here! Customs inspection!"

"Where did it go?" I cried. "The green! It was just here! Now it's—"

"The green, you say?"

The inspector stared at his watch. "It'll be along when the sun comes out!" he said.

"When will that be?"

The old man riffled a customs index. "Well, there's nothing in the damn government pamphlets to show when, where, or *if* the sun comes out in Ireland!" He pointed with his nose. "There's a church down there—you might ask!"

"I'll be here six months. Maybe—"

"—you'll see the sun and the green again? Chances are. But in '28, two hundred days of rain. It was the year we raised more mushrooms than children."

"Is that a fact?"

"No, hearsay. But that's all you need in Ireland, someone to hear, someone to say, and you're in business! Is that *all* your luggage?"

I set my typewriter forth, along with the flimsiest suitcase. "I'm traveling light. This all came up fast. My big luggage comes next week."

"Is this your first trip here?"

"No. I was here, poor and unpublished, off a freighter in 1939, just eighteen."

"Your reason for being in Ireland?" The inspector licked his pencil and indelibled his pad.

"Reason has nothing to do with it," I blurted.

His pencil stayed, while his gaze lifted.

"That's a grand start, but what does it mean?"

"Madness."

He leaned forward, pleased, as if a riot had surfed at his feet.

"What kind would that be?" he asked politely.

"Two kinds. Literary and psychological. I am here to flense and render down the White Whale."

"Flense." He scribbled. "Render down. White Whale. That would be *Moby Dick,* then?"

"You read!" I cried, taking that same book from under my arm.

"When the mood is on me." He underlined his scribbles. "We've had the Beast in the house some twenty years. I fought it twice. It is overweight in pages and the author's intent."

"It is," I agreed. "I picked it up and laid it down ten times until last month, when a movie studio signed me to it. Now I must win out for keeps."

The customs inspector nodded, took my measurements, and declared: "So you're here to write a *screenplay*! There's only *one* other cinema fellow in all Ireland. *Whatsis*name. Tall, with a kind of beat-up monkey face, talked fine. Said 'Never again.' Took the ferry to find what the Irish Sea was like. Found out and delivered forth both lunch and breakfast. Pale he was. Barely able to lug the Whale book under one arm. 'Never again,' he yelled. And you, lad. Will you ever lick the book?"

"Haven't you?"

"The Whale has not docked here, no. So much for literature. What's the *psychological* thing you said? Are you here to observe the Catholics lying about everything and the Unitarians baring their breasts?"

"No, no," I said hastily, remembering my one visit here, when the weather was dreadful. "Now between lowerings for the Whale, I will study the *Irish*."

"God has gone blind at that. Can you outlast Him? Why try?" He poised his pencil.

"Well . . . ," I said, putting the black sack over my head, fastening the noose about my neck, and yanking the lever to drop the trapdoor, "excuse me, but this is the last place in the world I'd dream of landing. It's all such a mystery. When I was a kid and passed the Irish neighborhood on one side of town, the Micks beat the hell out of me. And when they ran through *our* neighborhood, we beat *them*. It has bothered me half a lifetime why we did what we did. I grew up non-plussed—"

"Nonplussed? Is *that* all?" cried the Official.

"—with the Irish. I do not dislike them so much as I am uncomfortable with my past. I do not much care for Irish whiskey or Irish tenors. Irish coffee, too, is not my cup of tea. The list is long. Having lived with these terrible prejudices, I must fight free of them. And since the studio assigned me to chase the Whale in Ireland, my God, I thought, I'll compare reality with my hand-me-down suspicions. I must lay the ghost forever. You might say," I ended lamely, "I've come to *see* the Irish."

"No! *Hear* us, yes. But our tongue's not connected to our brain. *See* us? Why, lad, we're not *here*. We're over there or just beyond. Lend me those glasses."

He reached gently to take the spectacles from my nose.

"Ah, God." He slipped them on. "These are twenty-twenty!"

"Yes."

"No, no! The focus is too exact. You want something that bends the light and makes a kind of mist or fog, not quite rain. It's then you'll see us floating, almost drowned, on our backs, like that *Hamlet* girl . . . ?"

"Ophelia?"

"*That's* her, poor lass. Well!" He perched the glasses on my nose. "When you want a fix on the mob, take these off or you'll see us marching left when we should be lurching right. Still, you will never probe, find, discover, or in any way solve the Irish. We are not so much a race as a weather. X-ray us, yank our skeletons out by the roots, and by morn we've regrown the lot. You're right, with all you've said!"

"*Am* I?" I said, astonished.

The inspector drew up his own list behind his eyelids:

"Coffee? We do not roast the bean—we set fire to it! Economics? Music? They go *together* here. For there are beggars playing unstrung banjos on O'Connell Bridge; beggars trudging Pianolas about St. Stephen's Green, sounding like cement mixers full of razor blades. Irish women? All three feet high, with runty legs and pig noses. Lean on them, sure, use them for cover against the rain, but you wouldn't seriously chase them through the bog. And Ireland itself? Is the largest open-air penal colony in history . . . a great racetrack where the priests lay odds, take bets, and pay off on Doomsday. Go home, lad. You'll dislike the lot of us!"

"I don't dislike *you*—"

"But you *will*! Listen!" the old man whispered. "See that clump of Irishmen hurrying to get off the island before it sinks? They're bound for Paris, Australia, Boston, until the Second Coming.

"Why all the riot to get out of Eire, you ask? Well, if you got your choice Saturday night of, one, seeing a 1931 Greta Garbo fillum at the Joyous Cinema; or, two, making water off the poet's statue near the Gate Theatre; or, three, throwing yourself in the River Liffey for entertainment, with the happy thought of drowning uppermost, you might as well get out of Ireland, which people have done at the rate of a mob a day since Lincoln was shot. The population has dropped from eight million to less than three. One more potato famine or one more heavy fog that lasts long enough for everyone to pack up and tiptoe across the channel to disguise themselves as Philadelphia police, and Ireland is a desert. You've told me *nothing* about Ireland I don't already *know*!"

I hesitated. "I hope I haven't offended you."

"It's been a pleasure, hearing your mind! Now, this book you'll be writing. It's . . . pornographic?"

"I will not study the sex habits of the Irish, no."

"Pity. They are in dire need. Well, there's Dublin, straight on! Good luck, lad!"

"Goodbye . . . and thanks!"

The old man, incredulous, stared at the sky. "Did you *hear* him? Thanks! he said."

I ran to vanish in lightning, thunder, darkness. Somewhere in the noon twilight, a harp played off key.

2

On and off the boat train and along the rainy streets by taxi, I finally signed in at the Royal Hibernian Hotel and telephoned Kilcock to see how I might find the Devil Himself, as the reception clerk put it while handing my luggage to the bellboy, who shuddered me by elevator up to my room to plant my luggage where it wouldn't take root, as he said, and backed off from me as if he had searched a mirror and found no image.

"Sir," he said. "Well, are you some sort of famous author?"

"Sort of," I said.

"Well." The bellboy scratched his head. "I been asking around the pub and the lobby and the kitchen, and no one ever *heard* of you."

At the door, he turned.

"But don't worry," he said. "Your secret's safe with *me*."

The door shut quietly.

I was suddenly mad for Ireland or the Whale. Not knowing which, I grabbed a cab that veered through streets filled with tens of thousands of bicycles. We headed west along the Liffey.

"Is it the long or short you'd want?" asked my driver. "The long way around or the short arrival?"

"Short—"

"*That's* expensive," interrupted my driver. "Long is cheaper. Conversation! Do you *talk*? By trip's end, I am so relaxed I forget the tip. Besides, it's a map, chart, and atlas of Liffey and beyond that I am. Well?"

"The *long* way around."

"Long it *is*!" He kicked the gas as if it needed awakening, skinned a dozen bicyclists, and sailed out to snake the Liffey and mind the air. Only to hear the motor cough and roll over dead, just short of Kilcock.

We peered in at an engine long gone in mystery and leaning toward the tomb. My driver hefted a large hammer, decided against giving the engine a coup de grace, slung the hammer aside, and walked to the rear of the taxi to detach a bike and hand it over. I let it fall.

"Now, now." He reinstalled the vehicle in my hands. "Your destination's but a short drive down this road." He shook the bike. "Climb on."

"It's been a few years..."

"Your hands will remember and your ass will learn. Hop."

I hopped to straddle and stare at the dead car and the easy man. "You don't seem upset..."

"Cars are like women, once you learn their starters. Off with you. Downhill. Careful. There's few brakes on the vehicle."

"Thanks," I yelled as the vehicle rolled me away.

3

Ten minutes later, I stopped at the top of a rise, listening.

Someone was whistling and singing "Molly Malone." Up the hill, wobbling badly, pedaled an old man on a bike no better than mine. At the top he fell off and let it lie at his feet.

"Old man, you're not what you once was!" he cried, and kicked the tires. "Ah, lay there, beast that you are!"

Ignoring me, he took out a bottle. He downed it philosophically, then held it up to let the last drop fall on his tongue.

I spoke at last. "We both seem to be having trouble. Is anything wrong?"

The old man blinked. "Is that an American voice I hear?"

"Yes. May I be of assistance . . . ?"

The old man showed his empty bottle.

"Well, there's assistance *and* assistance. It came over me as I pumped up the hill, me and the damned vehicle"— here he kicked the bike gently—"is both seventy years old."

"Congratulations."

"For what? Breathing? That's a habit, not a virtue. Why, may I ask, are you *staring* at me like that?"

I pulled back. "Well . . . do you have a relative in customs down at the docks?"

"Which of us hasn't?" Gasping, he reached for his bike. "Ah, well, a moment's rest, and me and the brute will be on our way. We don't know where we're going, Sally and me— that's the damn bike's name, ya see—but we pick a road each day and give it a try."

I tried a small joke.

"Does your mother know you're out?"

The old man seemed stunned.

"Strange you say that! She *does*! Ninety-five she is, back there in the cot! Mother, I said, I'll be gone the day; leave the whiskey alone. I never married, you know."

"I'm sorry."

"First you congratulate me for being old, and now you're sorry I've no wife. It's sure you don't know Ireland. Being old and having no wives is one of our principal industries! You see, a man can't marry without property. You bide your time till your mother and father are called Beyond. Then, when their property's yours, you look for a wife. It's a waiting game. I'll marry yet."

"At *seventy*!?"

The old man stiffened.

"I'd get twenty good years of marriage out of a fine woman even this late—do you *doubt* it?!" He glared.

"I do not."

The old man relaxed.

"Well, then. What are *you* up to in Ireland?"

I was suddenly all flame and fire.

"I've been advised at customs to look sharp at this pov-
erty-stricken, priest-ridden, rain-filled, sleet-worn country,
this—"

"Good God," the old man interjected. "You're a writer!"

"How did you guess?"

The old man snorted, gesturing.

"The country's overrun. There's writers turning over rocks
in Cork and writers trudging through bogs at Killashandra.
The day will come, mark me, when there will be five writers
for every human being in the world!"

"Well, writer I am. I've been here only a few hours now
and it feels like a thousand years of no sun, only rain, cold,
and getting lost on roads. My director will be waiting for me
somewhere if I can find the place, but my legs are dead."

The old man leaned at me.

"Have you begun to dislike your visit? Look *down* on?"

"Well..."

The old man patted the air.

"Why not? Every man needs to look down on someone.
You look down on the Irish, the Irish look down on the
English, and the English look down on everyone else in the
world. It all comes right in the end. Do you think I'm bothered
by the look on your face, you've come to weigh our breath
and find it sour, measure our shadows and find us short? *No!*
In fact, I'll help you solve this dreadful place. Come along
where you can witness an awful event. A dread scene. A
meeting of Fates, *that's* it. The true birthplace of the Irish...
Ah, God, how you'll *hate* it! And yet..."

"Yet?"

"Before you leave us, you'll love us all. We're irresistible.
And we know it. More's the pity. For knowing it makes us

all the more deplorable, which means we must work harder to become irresistible again. So we chase our own behinds about the country, never winning and never quite losing. There! Do you see that parade of unemployed men marching on the road in holes and tatters?"

"Yes!"

"That's the First Ring of Hell! Do you see them young fellows on bikes with flat tires and no spokes, pumping barefoot in the rain?"

"Yes!"

"That's the Second Ring of Hell!"

The old man stopped. "And here ... can you read? The Third Ring!"

I read the sign. " 'Heeber Finn's' ... why, it's a *pub*."

The old man pretended surprise. "By God, now, I think you're right. Come meet my ... family!"

"Family? You said you weren't *married*!"

"I'm not. But—in we go!"

The old man gave a great knock on the backside of the door. And there was the bar, all bright spigots and alarmed faces as the dozen or so customers whirled.

"It's *me*, boys!" the old man cried.

"Mike! Ya gave us a start!" said one.

"We thought it was—a crisis!" said another.

"Well, maybe it is ... for *him* anyway." He jabbed my elbow. "What'll ya have, lad?"

I scanned the lot, tried to say wine, but quit.

"A whiskey, please," I said.

"Make mine a Guinness," said Mike. "Now, introductions all around. That there is Heeber Finn, who owns the pub."

Finn handed over the whiskey. "The third and fourth mortgage, that is."

Mike moved on, pointing.

"This is O'Gavin, who has the finest bogs in all Kilcock and cuts peat turf out of it to stoke the hearths of Ireland. Also a fine hunter and fisher, in or out of season!"

O'Gavin nodded. "I poach game and steal fish."

"You're an honest man, Mr. O'Gavin," I said.

"No. As soon as I find a job," said O'Gavin, "I'll deny the whole thing."

Mike led me along. "This next is Casey, who will fix the hoof of your horse."

"Blacksmith," said Casey.

"The spokes of your bike."

"Velocipede repair," said Casey.

"Or the spark plugs on any damn car."

"Auto-moe-beel renovation," said Casey.

Mike moved again. "Now, this is Kelly, our turf accountant!"

"Mr. Kelly," I said, "do you count the turf that Mr. O'Gavin cuts out of his bog?"

As everyone laughed, Kelly said: "That is a common tourist's error. I am an expert on the races. I breed a few horses—"

"He sells Irish Sweepstakes tickets," said someone.

"A bookie," said Finn.

"But 'turf accountant' has a gentler air, does it not?" said Kelly.

"It does!" I said.

"And here's Timulty, our art connoisseur."

I shook hands with Timulty. "Art connoisseur?"

"It's from looking at the *stamps* I have the eye for paintings," Timulty explained. "If it goes at all, I run the post office."

"And this is Carmichael, who took over the village telephone exchange last year."

Carmichael, who knitted as he spoke, replied: "My wife got the uneasies and she ain't come right since, God help her. I'm on duty next door."

"But now tell us, lad," said Finn, "what's your crisis?"

"A whale. And..." I paused. "Ireland!"

"Ireland?!" everyone cried.

Mike explained. "He's a writer who's trapped in Ireland and misunderstands the Irish."

After a beat of silence someone said: "Don't we *all*!"

To much laughter, Mr. O'Gavin leaned forward. "What do you misunderstand, specific like?"

Mike intervened to prevent chaos. "Underestimates is more the word. Confused might be the sum! So I'm taking him on a Grand Tour of the Worst Sights and the Most Dreadful Truths." He stopped and turned. "Well, that's the lot, lad."

"Mike, there's one you missed." I nodded to a partition at the far end of the bar. "You didn't introduce me to... *him*."

Mike peered and said, "O'Gavin, Timulty, Kelly, do you *see* someone there?"

Kelly glanced down the line. "We do not."

I pointed. "Why, it's plain as my nose! A man—"

Timulty cut in. "Now, Yank, don't go upsetting the order of the universe. Do you see that partition? It is an irrevocable law that any man seeking a bit of peace and quiet is automatically gone, invisible, null and void when he steps into that cubby."

"Is that a fact?"

"Or as close as you'll ever get to one in Ireland. That area, no more than two feet wide by one deep, is more private than the confessional. It's where a man can duck, in need of feeding his soul without converse or commotion. So for all intents and purposes, that space, until he breaks the spell of silence himself, is uninhabited and *no one's there*!"

Everyone nodded, proud of Timulty.

"Fine, Timulty, and now—drink your drink, lad, stand alert, be ready, watch!" said Mike.

I looked at the mist curling through the door. "Alert for what?"

"Why, there's always Great Events preparing themselves out in that fog." Mike became mysterious. "As a student of Ireland, let nothing pass unquestioned." He peered out at the night. "*Anything* can happen ... and always *does*." He inhaled the fog, then froze. "Sssst! Did you *hear*?"

Beyond, there was a blind stagger of feet, heavy panting coming near, near, near!

"What ... ?" I said.

Mike shut his eyes. "Sssst! Listen! ... *Yes!*"

4

Shoes pounded the outside steps, drunkenly. The double wing doors slammed wide. A battered man lunged in, reeling, holding his bloody head with bloody hands. His moan froze every customer at the bar. For a time you heard only the soft foam popping in the lacy mugs, as the customers turned, some faces pale, some pink, some veined and wattle red. Every eyelid down the line gave a blink.

The stranger swayed in his ruined clothes, eyes wide, lips trembling. The drinkers clenched their fists. Yes! they cried silently. Go on, man! What *happened*?

The stranger leaned far out on the air.

"Collision," he cried. "Collision on the road."

Then, chopped at the knees, he fell.

"Collision!" A dozen men rushed at the body.

"Kelly!" Heeber Finn vaulted the bar. "Get to the road! Mind the victim—easy does it! Joe, run for the Doc!"

"Wait!" said a quiet voice.

From the private stall at the end of the pub, the cubby where a philosopher might brood, a dark man blinked out at the crowd.

"Doc!" cried Heeber Finn. "Was you there all the *time?*"

"Ah, shut up!" cried the Doc as he and the men hustled out into the night.

"Collision . . . " The man on the floor twitched his lips.

"Softly, boys." Heeber Finn and two others gentled the victim atop the bar. He looked handsome as death on the fine inlaid wood, with the prismed mirror making him two dread calamities for the price of one.

Outside on the steps, the crowd halted, shocked as if an ocean had sunk Ireland in the dusk and now bulked all about them. Fog in fifty-foot rollers and breakers put out the moon and stars. Blinking, cursing, the men leaped out, to vanish in the deeps.

Behind, in the bright doorframe, I stood, dreading to inter-fere with what seemed village ritual. Since arriving in Ireland, I could not shake the feeling that at all times I was living stage center of the Abbey Theatre. Now, not knowing my lines, I could only stare after the rushing men.

"But," I protested weakly, "I didn't hear any cars on the road."

"You did not!" said Mike, almost pridefully. Arthritis lim-ited him to the top step, where he teetered, shouting at the white tides where his friends had submerged. "Try the cross-road, boys! That's where it most often does!"

"The crossroad!" Far and near, footsteps rang.

"Nor," I said, "did I hear a collision."

Mike snorted with contempt. "Ah, we're not great ones for commotion, or great crashing sounds. But collision you'll see if you step on out there. Walk, now, don't run! It's the devil's own night. Running blind you might hit into Kelly, beyond, who's fevered up with pumping just to squash his lungs. Or you might head-on with Feeney, too drunk to find any road, never mind what's *on* it! Finn, you got a torch, a flash? Blind you'll be, lad, but use it. Walk now, you *hear?*"

I groped through the fog and, immersed in the night beyond Heeber Finn's, made direction by the heavy clubbing of shoes and a rally of voices ahead. A hundred yards off in eternity, the men approached, grunting whispers: "Easy now!" "Ah, the shameful blight!" "Hold on, don't jiggle him!"

I was flung aside by a steaming lump of men who swept suddenly from the fog, bearing atop themselves a crumpled object. I glimpsed a bloodstained and livid face high up there, then someone cracked my flashlight down.

By instinct, sensing the far whiskey-colored light of Heeber Finn's, the catafalque surged on toward that fixed and familiar harbor.

Behind came dim shapes and a chilling insect rattle.

"Who's that!" I cried.

"Us, with the vehicles," someone husked. "You might say we got the collision."

The flashlight fixed them. I gasped. A moment later, the battery failed.

But not before I had seen two village lads jogging along with no trouble at all, easily, lightly, toting under their arms two ancient black bicycles minus front and tail lights.

"What . . . ?" I said.

But the lads trotted off, the accident with them. The fog closed in. I stood abandoned on an empty road, my flashlight dead in my hand.

By the time I opened the door at Heeber Finn's, both "bodies," as they called them, had been stretched on the bar.

And there was the crowd lined up, not for drinks, but

blocking the way so the Doc had to shove sidewise from one to another of these relics of blind driving by night on the misty roads.

"One's Pat Nolan," whispered Mike. "Not working at the moment. The other's Mr. Peevey from Maynooth, in candy and cigarettes mostly." Raising his voice: "Are they dead, now, Doc?"

"Ah, be still, won't you?" The Doc resembled a sculptor troubled at finding some way to finish up two full-length marble statues at once. "Here, let's put one victim on the floor!"

"The floor's a tomb," said Heeber Finn. "He'll catch his death down there. Best leave him up where the warm air gathers from our talk."

"But," I said quietly, confused, "I've never heard of an accident like this in all my life. Are you sure there were absolutely no cars? Only these two men on their *bikes*?"

"Only?" Mike shouted. "Great God, man, a fellow working up a drizzling sweat can pump along at sixty kilometers. With a long downhill glide his bike hits ninety or ninety-five! So here they come, these two, no front or tail lights—"

"Isn't there a law against that?"

"To hell with government interference! So here the two come, no lights, flying home from one town to the next. Thrashing like Sin Himself's at their behinds! Both going opposite ways but both on the same side of the road. Always ride the wrong side of the road, it's safer, they say. But look on these lads, fair destroyed by all that official palaver. Why? Don't you see? One remembered it, but the other didn't! Better if the officials kept their mouths shut! For here the two be, dying."

"Dying?" I stared.

"Well, think on it, man! What stands between two able-bodied hell-bent fellas jumping along the path from Kilcock to Maynooth? Fog! Fog is all! Only fog to keep their skulls from bashing together. Why, look, when two chaps hit at a cross like that, it's like a strike in bowling alleys, tenpins flying! Bang! There go your friends, nine feet up, heads together like dear chums met, flailing the air, their bikes clenched like two tomcats. Then they all fall down and just lay there, feeling around for the Dark Angel."

"Surely these men won't . . ."

"Oh, won't they? Why, last year alone in all the Free State no night passed some soul did not meet in fatal collision with another!"

"You mean to say over three hundred Irish bicyclists die every year, hitting each other?"

"God's truth and a pity."

"I never ride my bike nights." Heeber Finn eyed the bodies. "I walk."

"But still then the damn bikes run you down!" said Mike. "Awheel or afoot, some idiot's always panting up doom the other way. They'd sooner split you down the seam than wave hello. Oh, the brave men I've seen ruined or half ruined or worse, and headaches their lifetimes after." Mike trembled his eyelids shut. "You might almost think, mightn't you, that human beings was not made to handle such delicate instruments of power."

"Three hundred dead each *year*?" I was dazed.

"And that don't count the 'walking wounded' by the thousands every fortnight who, cursing, throw their bikes in the bog forever and take government pensions to salve their all-but-murdered bodies."

"Should we stand here talking?" I gestured helplessly toward the victims. "Is there a hospital?"

"On a night with no moon," Heeber Finn continued, "best

walk out through the middle of fields, and be damned to the evil roads! That's how I have survived into this my fifth decade."

"Ah . . ." The men stirred restlessly.

The Doc, sensing he had withheld information too long, feeling his audience drift away, now snatched their attention back by straightening up briskly and exhaling.

"Well!"

The pub quickened into silence.

"This chap here . . ." The Doc pointed. "Bruises, lacerations, and agonizing backaches for two weeks running. As for the other lad, however . . ." And here the Doc let himself scowl for a long moment at the paler one there, looking rouged, waxed, and ready for final rites. "Concussion."

"Concussion!"

The quiet wind rose and fell in the silence.

"He'll survive if we run him quick now to Maynooth Clinic. So whose car will volunteer?"

The crowd turned as a body toward Timulty. I stared, remembering the front of Heeber Finn's pub, where seventeen bicycles and one automobile were parked. "Mine!" cried Timulty. "Since it's the only vehicle!"

"There! A volunteer! Quick now, hustle this victim— gently!—to Timulty's wreck!"

The men reached out to lift the body, but froze when I coughed. I circled my hand to all and tipped my cupped fingers to my lips. All gasped in soft surprise. The gesture was hardly done when drinks foamed down the bar.

"For the road!"

And now even the luckier victim, suddenly revived, face like cheese, found a mug gentled to his hand with whispers.

"Here, lad, here. Tell us . . ."

"What happened, eh? Eh?"

"Send," gasped the victim. "Send for Father Leary. I need the Extreme Unction!"

"Father Leary it is!" Nolan jumped and ran.

"Get my wife," husked the victim, "to call me three uncles and four nephews and my grandfather and Timothy Doolin, and you're *all* invited to my wake!"

"You was always a good sort, Peevey!"

"There's two gold coins put by in my best shoes at home. For me eyelids! There's a third gold coin; buy me a fine black suit!"

"It's good as done!"

"Be sure there's plenty of whiskey. I'll buy it meself!"

There was a stir at the door.

"Thank God," cried Timulty. "It's you, Father Leary. Father, quickly, you must give the Extremest form of Unction you ever gave!"

"Don't tell me my business!" said the priest in the door. "I got the Unctions, you provide the victim! On the double!"

There was a cheer from the men as the victim was held high and run for the door where the priest directed traffic, then fled.

With one body gone off the bar, the potential wake was over, the room empty save for myself, the Doc, the revived lad, and two softly cudgeling friends. Outside, you could hear the crowd putting the one serious result of the great collision into Timulty's car.

"Finish your drink," the Doc advised.

But I stood, looking numbly around at the pub: at the recovered bicyclist, seated, waiting for the crowd to come back and mill about him; seeing the blood-spotted floor, the two bicycles tilted near the door like props from a vaudeville turn, the dark night waiting outside with its improbable fog; listening to the roll and cadence and gentle equilibrium of these voices, balanced each in its own throat and environment.

"Doctor," I heard myself say as I placed the money on the bar, "do you often have auto wrecks—collisions between people in *cars*?"

"Not in our town!" The Doc nodded scornfully east. "If you like that sort of thing, now, Dublin's the very place!"

Crossing the pub, the Doc took my arm as if to impart some secret which would change my fate. Thus steered, I found the stout inside me a shifting weight I must accommodate from side to side as the Doc breathed softly in my ear.

"Look here now, son, admit it, you've traveled little in Ireland, right? Then listen! Biking to Maynooth, fog and all, you'd best take it fast! Raise a din! Why? Scare the other cyclists and cows off the path, both sides! If you pump slow, why, you'll creep up on and do away with dozens before they know what took them off! And another thing: when a bike approaches, douse your light—that is, if it's working. Pass each other, lights out, in safety. Them devil's own lights have put out more eyes and demolished more innocents than all of seeing's worth. Is it clear now? Two things: speed, and douse your lights when bikes loom up!"

At the door, I nodded. Behind me I heard the one victim, settled easy in his chair, working the stout around on his tongue, thinking, preparing, beginning his tale:

"Well, I'm on me way home, blithe as you please, asailing downhill near the cross, when . . ."

Outside, the Doc offered final advice.

"Always wear a cap, lad, if you want to walk nights ever— on the roads, that is. A cap'll save you the frightful migraines should you meet Kelly or Moran or anyone else hurtling full tilt the other way, full of fiery moss and hard-skulled from birth. Even on foot, these men are dangerous. So you see, there's rules for pedestrians, too, in Ireland, and wear a cap at night is number one!" He handed me a cap.

Without thinking, I took the brown tweed cap and put it

on. Adjusting it, I looked out at the dark mist boiling across the night. I listened to the empty highway waiting for me ahead, quiet, quiet, quiet, but not quiet somehow. For hundreds of long strange miles up and down all of Ireland, I saw a thousand crossroads covered with a thousand fogs through which one thousand tweed-capped, gray-mufflered phantoms wheeled along in midair, singing, shouting, and smelling of Guinness stout.

I blinked. The phantoms shadowed off. The road lay empty and dark and waiting.

Taking a deep breath, I straddled my bike, pulled my cap down over my ears, shut my eyes, and pumped down the wrong side of the road toward some sanity never to be found.

5

The door swung wide at my knock.

My director stood there in boots and riding pants and a silk shirt open at the neck to reveal an ascot tie. His eyes bulged like eggs to see me here. His chimpanzee mouth fell down a few inches, and the air came out of his lungs in an alcohol-tinged rush.

"I'll be damned!" he cried. "It's you!"

"Me," I admitted meekly.

"You're late! You okay? What delayed you?"

I waved behind me, up the road.

"Ireland," I said.

"Christ, that explains it. Welcome!"

He pulled me in. The door slammed.

"You need a drink?"

"Ah, God," I said. Then hearing my newly acquired brogue, I spoke meticulously.

"Yes, sir," I said.

As John, his wife Ricki, and I sat down to dinner, I gazed long and hard at the wee dead birds on a warm plate, their heads awry, their beady eyes half shut, and said:

"Can I make a suggestion?"

"Make it, kid."

"It's about the Parsee Fedallah who runs as a character through the whole book. He ruins *Moby Dick*."

"Fedallah? *That* one? Well?"

"Do you mind if right now, over our wine, we give all the best lines and acts to Ahab? And throw Fedallah overboard?"

My director lifted his glass. "He's *thrown!*"

The weather outside was beginning to clear, the grass was lush and green in the dark beyond the French windows, and I was blushing warmly all over to think I was really here, doing this work, beholding my hero, imagining an incredible future as screenwriter for a genius.

Somewhere along in the dinner the subject of Spain came up, almost casually, or perhaps John brought it up himself.

I saw Ricki stiffen and pause in her eating, and then continue picking at her food as John went on about Hemingway and the bullfights and Franco and traveling to and from Madrid and Barcelona.

"We were there just a month ago," said John. "You really ought to go there sometime, kid," he said. "Beautiful country. Wonderful people, it's been a bad twenty years, but they're getting back on their feet. Anyway, we had a little event there, didn't we, Ricki? A small thing got out of hand."

Ricki started to rise, her plate in her hand, and the knife fell clattering to the table.

"Why don't you tell us about it, dear," said John.

"No, I—" said Ricki.

"Tell us what happened at the border," said John.

His words were so heavy that, weighted, Ricki sat back

down and after a pause to regain her breath, held for a long moment, let it out, "We were driving back up from Barcelona and there was this Spaniard wanted to get into France without papers and John wanted us to smuggle him across the border in our car under a rug in the back seat and John said it was okay and the Spaniard said please and I said my God, if they found out, the border guards, if they caught us we'd be held, put in jail maybe, and you know what Spanish jails are like, in there for days or weeks or forever, so I said no, no way, and the Spaniard pleaded and John said it was a matter of honor, we had to do it, we had to help this poor man and I said I was sorry but I wouldn't endanger the children. What if I was in jail and the kids would be in the hands of others too many hours and days and who would explain to them and John insisted and there was a big row—"

"Very simply," said John, "you were a coward."

"No, I wasn't," said Ricki, looking up from her food.

"You were yellow," said John, "pure yellow, and we had to leave the poor son of a bitch behind because my wife didn't have enough guts to let us get him across."

"How do we know he wasn't a criminal, John," said Ricki. "Some sort of political fugitive, and then we would have been in jail forever—"

"Just yellow is all." John lit a cigarillo and leaned forward to stare at his wife at the far end, miles away down the table. "I really hate to think I am married to a woman with no guts, who wears a yellow stripe down her back. Wouldn't you hate to be married to that kind of woman, kid?"

I sat back in my chair, my mouth full of food I could not chew nor swallow.

I looked at my genius employer and then at his wife then back to John and then back to Ricki.

Her head was bent.

"Yellow," said John, a final time, and blew smoke.

As I looked down at the dead bird on my plate, I recalled a scene that now seemed so long ago.

In August, I had wandered, stunned, into a bookstore in Beverly Hills looking for a small, comfortable-sized copy of *Moby Dick*. The copy I had at home was too large to travel. I needed something compact. I shared with the proprietor my excitement about writing the screenplay and traveling overseas.

Even as I spoke, astonished, a woman in the far corner of the shop turned and said, very clearly:

"Don't go on that journey."

It was Elijah, at the foot of the *Pequod's* gangplank, warning Queequeg and Ishmael not to follow Ahab off 'round the world: it was a dread mission and a lost cause from which no man might return.

"Don't go," said the strange woman again.

I recovered and said, "Who *are* you?"

"A former friend of the director's and the former wife of one of his screenwriters. I know them both. God, I wish I didn't. They're *both* monsters, but your director's the worst. He'll eat you and spit out your bones. So—"

She stared at me.

"—what ever you do, *don't* go."

Ricki's eyes were shut, but tears were leaking out of the lashes and running down to the tip of her nose where they fell, one by one, onto her plate.

My God, I thought, this is my first day in Ireland, my first day at work for my hero.

6

The next day after lunch, we circled Courtown House, the old mansion where my director stayed. There was a large meadow and a forest beyond and another meadow and forest beyond that.

In the middle of the meadow we met a rather large black bull.

"Huh!" cried John, and whipped off his coat.

He charged the bull, shouting:

"Ha, *Toro*! *Toro*, ha!"

One minute from now, I thought, *one* of us will be dead. *Me?*

"John!" I cried quietly, if such is possible, "please, put on your coat!"

"Huh, *Toro*!" my director yelled. "Ho!"

The bull stared at us, motionless.

John shrugged his coat back on.

I ran ahead of him to toss Fedallah overboard, assemble the crew, bid Elijah to warn Ishmael not to go, then launch the *Pequod* to sail off and around the world.

So it went, day on day, week on week, as I killed the Whale each night, but to see him reborn each dawn, while I was lost in Dublin, where the weather struck from its bleak quarters in the sea and came searching with sheets of rain and gusts of cold and still more sheets of rain.

I went to bed and woke in the middle of the night thinking I heard someone cry, thinking I myself was weeping, and I felt my face and found it dry.

Then I looked at the window and thought: Why, yes, it's just the rain, the rain, always the rain, and turned over, sadder still, and fumbled about for my dripping sleep and tried to slip it back on.

Then, late each afternoon, I taxied out amidst Kilcock's gray stone with green beards on it, a rock town, and the rain falling down for weeks as I worked on a script that was to be shot in the hot sun of the Canary Isles sometime next year. The pages of the script were full of hot suns and burning days as I typed in Dublin or Kilcock, with the weather a beast at the windows.

On the thirty-first night, a knock at the door of my hotel room revealed Mike, shuffling.

"There you are!" he exclaimed. "I been thinking on what you said. You to find the Irish, me to help. I got me a car! So would you get the hell out to find some wild life in our land? And forget this damn rain on the double?"

"Double!" I said gladly.

And we blew along the road to Kilcock in a dark that rocked us like a boat on a black flood until, sweating rain, faces pearled, we struck through the pub doors and it was warm as a sheepfold because there were the townsmen pressed in a great compost heap at the bar and Heeber Finn yelling jokes and foaming up drinks.

"Heeber!" cried Mike. "We're here for that wild night!"

"A wild night it is!"

Whereupon Heeber whipped off his apron, shrugged his meat-cleaver shoulders into a tweed coat, jumped up in the air and slid down inside his raincoat, slung on his beardy cap, and thrust us at the door.

"Nail everything down till I get back!" he advised his crew. "I'm taking these gents to the damnedest evening ever! Little do they know what waits for them beyond!"

He opened the door. The wind threw half a ton of ice water on him. Taking this as a spur to rhetoric, Heeber added in a roar, "Out with you! On!"

"Do you think we should?" I wondered.

"What do you mean?" cried Mike. "Would you freeze in your room? Rewrite the dead Whale?"

"Well...," I said, and slung on my cap.

Then, like Ahab, I thought on my bed, a damp box with its pale cool winding sheets and the window dripping next to it like a conscience all night through. I groaned. I opened the door of Mike's car, took my legs apart to get in, and in no time we shot down the town like a ball in a bowling alley.

Finn at the wheel talked fierce, half hilarity, half sobering King Lear.

"A wild night? Ahead! You'd never guess, would you, to walk through Ireland, so much could go on under the skin?"

"I knew there must be an outlet somewhere," I yelled.

The speedometer was up to one hundred kilometers. Stone walls raced by on the right, stone walls raced by on the left. It was raining the entire dark sky down on the entire dark land.

"Outlet indeed!" said Finn. "If the Church only knew, or maybe it figures: The poor buggers! and lets us be!"

"Where?"

"There!" cried Finn.

The speedometer read 110. My stomach was stone like the stone walls rushing left and right. Up over a hill, down into a valley. "Can't we go a bit faster?" I asked, hoping for the opposite.

"Done!" said Finn, and made it 120.

"That will do it nicely," I said, in a faint voice, wondering what lay ahead. Behind all the slate-stone weeping walls of Ireland, what happened? Somewhere in this drizzling land were there hearth-fleshed peach-fuzz Renoir women bright as lamps you could hold your hands out to and warm your palms? Beneath the rain-drenched sod, the flinty rock, at the numbed core of living, was there one small seed of fire which, fanned, might break volcanoes free and boil the rains to steam? Was there then somewhere a Baghdad harem, nests awriggle and aslither with silk and tassel, the absolute perfect tint of women unadorned? We passed a church. No. We passed a convent. No. We passed a village slouched under its old-men's thatch. No. Yet...

I glanced over at Heeber Finn. We could have switched off the lights and driven by the steady piercing beams of his forward-directed eyes snatching at the dark, flicking away the rain.

Wife, I thought to myself, children, forgive me for what I do this night, terrible as it may be, for this is Ireland in the rain of an ungodly time and way out in Galway, where the dead must go to die.

The brakes were hit. We slid a good ninety feet; my nose mashed on the windshield. Heeber Finn was out of the car.

"We're here!" He sounded like a man drowned deep in rain.

I saw a hole in the wall, a tiny gate flung wide.

Mike and I followed at a plunge. I saw other cars in the dark and many bikes. But not a light. Oh, it *must* be wild to be *this* secret, I thought. I yanked my cap tight, as rain crawled down my neck.

Through the hole in the wall we stumbled, Heeber clenching our elbows. "Here!" he husked. "Hold on. Swig on this to keep your blood high!"

I felt a flask knock my fingers. I poured its contents into my boilers to let the steam up my flues.

"It's a lovely rain," I said.

"The man's mad." Finn drank after Mike, a shadow among shadows.

I squinted about. I had an impression of midnight sea upon which men like little boats passed on the murmurous tides, heads down, muttering, in twos and threes.

Good God, what's it all mean? I asked myself, incredibly curious now.

"Wait!" whispered Heeber. "This is *it!*"

What did I expect? Perhaps some scene like those old movies where innocent sailing ships suddenly flap down their cabin walls and guns appear like magic to fire on the foe. Or a farmhouse falls apart like a cereal box, Long Tom rears up to blast a projectile five hundred miles to crack Paris. So here, I thought, will these stones spill away, that house open wide, rosy lights flash on, so that from a monstrous cannon ten dozen pink women, not dwarf Irish but willowy French, will be shot out and down into the waving arms of this grateful multitude?

The lights came on.

I blinked.

For there was the entire unholy thing, laid out for me in the drizzle.

The lights flickered. The men quickened.

A mechanical rabbit popped out of a little box at the far end of the stony yard and ran.

Eight dogs, let free from gates, yelping, ran after in a great circle. There was not one yell or a murmur from the crowd of men. Their heads turned slowly, watching. The rain rained down on the half-lit scene. The rain fell on tweed caps and thin cloth coats. The rain dripped off thick eyebrows and sharp noses. The rain hammered hunched shoulders. The rabbit ran. The dogs loped. The rabbit popped into its electric kennel. The dogs collided, yiping. The lights went out.

In the dark I turned to stare at Heeber Finn, stunned.

"Now!" he shouted. "Place your bets!"

We were back in Kilcock, speeding, at ten o'clock.

The rain was still raining, like an ocean smashing the road with titanic fists, as we drew up in a great tidal spray before the pub.

"Well, now!" said Heeber Finn, looking not at us but at the windshield wiper palpitating before us. "Well!"

Mike and I had bet on five races and had lost, between us, two or three pounds.

"I won," Finn said, "and some of it I put down in your names, both of you. That last race, I swear to God, won for all of us. Let me pay!"

"It's all right, Heeber," I said, my numb lips moving.

Finn pressed two shillings into my hand. I didn't fight him. "That's better!" he said. "Now, one last drink on me!"

Mike drove me back to Dublin.

Wringing out his cap in the hotel lobby he looked at me and said, "It *was* a wild Irish night for sure!"

"A wild night," I said.

I hated to go up to my room. So I sat for another hour in the reading lounge of the damp hotel and took the traveler's privilege, a glass and a bottle provided by the dazed hall porter. I sat alone listening to the rain and the rain on the cold hotel roof, thinking of Ahab's coffin-bed waiting for me up there under the drumbeat weather. I thought of the only warm thing in the hotel, in the town, in all the land of Eire this night, the script in my typewriter with its sun of the South Pacific, its hot winds blowing the *Pequod* toward its doom, but along the way fiery sands and its women with dark charcoal-burning eyes.

And I thought of the darkness beyond the city, the lights flashing, the electric rabbit running, the dogs yiping, the rabbit gone, the lights out, and the rain flailing the dank shoulders and soaked caps and ice-watering the noses and seeping through the sheep-smelling tweeds.

Going upstairs, I glanced out a streaming window. There, on the street, riding by under a lamp, was a man on a bike. He was terribly drunk. The bike weaved back and forth across the bricks, as the man vomited. He did not stop the bike to do this. He kept pumping unsteadily, blearily, as he threw up. I watched him go off in the dark rain.

Then I groped up to find and die in my room.

7

On Grafton Street just halfway between The Four Provinces pub and the cinema stood the best, or so John said, Gentleman Riders to Hound emporium in all Dublin, if not Ireland, and perhaps one half of Bond Street in London.

It was Tyson's, and to speak the name was to see the front windows with their hacking coats and foulards and pale yellow silk shirts and velvet hunting caps and twill pants and shining boots. If you stood there long enough you could hear the horses fribbling their lips and snorting their laughter and twitching their skin to jerk the flies off, and you could hear the hounds whining and barking and running in happy circles (dogs are always happy and thus their smiles, unless they are miserable because their master crossed his eyes at them); but as I say, if you stood there long enough waiting for someone to hand you the reins, the owner of the shop, seeing you as one of the blindfolded hypnotics wandered out of Huston's Barn, might come out and lead-kindly-light your way into the smell of leather and boot cream and wool; and buckle on your new trenchcoat for you and fit on a tweed cap abristle for a thousand rains within the month and measure your pigfoot and wonder how in hell to shove it into a boot and all the while around you Anglo-Irish gents being similarly whisper-murmured at by lilting tongues; and the weather turned bad outside within thirty seconds after you set foot within, that you linger and buy more than your intent.

Where was I? Oh, yes. I stood out in front of Tyson's on three separate nights.

Looking at the wax model, as tall as Huston and as strideful and arrogant in all his Kilcock Hunt finery, I thought: How long before I dress like that?

"How do I look, John?" I cried, three days later.

I spun about on the front steps of Courtown House smelling of wool, boot leather, and silk.

John stared at my tweed cap and twill pants.

"I'll be goddamned," he gasped.

8

"You know anything about hypnotism, kid?"

"Some," I said.

"Ever been hypnotized?"

"Once," I said.

We were sitting by the fire after midnight with a bottle of Scotch now half empty between us. I hated Scotch, but since John relished it, I drank.

"Well, you haven't been in the hands of a real pro," said John, languidly, sipping at his drink.

"Which means you," I said.

John nodded. "That's it. I'm the best. You want to go under, son? I'll put you there."

"I had my teeth filled that one time, my dentist, a hypnodontist, he—"

"To hell with your teeth, H.G." H.G. was for H. G. Wells, the author of *Things to Come*, *The Time Machine*, and *The Invisible Man*. "It's not what comes out in teeth, it's what goes on in your head. Swallow your drink and give me your paw."

I swallowed my drink and held out my hands. John grabbed them.

"Okay, H.G., shut your eyes and relax, total relaxation, easy does it, easy, easy, nice and soft and slow and easy," he murmured, as my eyes shut and my head lolled. He kept speaking and I kept listening, nodding my head gently and he talked on, holding my hands and breathing his mellow Scotch in my face and I felt my bones go loose in my flesh and my flesh lounge out under my skin and it was easy and nice and sleepy and at last John said: "Are you under, kid?"

"Way under, John," I whispered.

"That's the way. Good. Fine. Now listen here, H.G., while you're there and relaxed, is there any one message you want to tell me so I can tell yourself? Give instructions, as it were, for self-improvement or behavior tomorrow? Spit it out. Tell me. And I'll instruct you. But easy does it. Well ... ?"

I thought. My head swayed. My eyelids were heavy.

"Just one thing," I said.

"And what's that, kid?"

"Tell me—"

"Yes?"

"Instruct me to—"

"What, kid?"

"Write the greatest, most wonderful, finest screenplay in the history of the world."

"I'll be damned."

"Tell me that, John, and I'll be happy ... ," I said, asleep, deep under, waiting.

"Well," said John. He leaned close. His breath was like an aftershave on my cheeks and chin. "Here's what you do, kid."

"Yes?" I said.

"Write the damnedest, finest, most wonderful screenplay ever to be written or seen."

"I will, John," I said.

9

It's not often in the life of a writer lightning truly strikes. And I mean, there he is on the steeple, begging for creative annihilation, and the heavens save up spit and let him have it. In one great hot flash, the lightning strikes. And you have an unbelievable tale delivered in one beauteous blow and are never so blessed again.

And here's how the lightning struck.

I had been hard at it with harpoon and typewriter for three hours out at Courtown House when the telephone rang. John, Ricki, and I had gathered for lunch and another try at trapping the pale flesh of the great Beast. We looked up, glad for the interruption.

John seized the phone, listened, and gave a great gasping cry.

"Well, I'll be goddamned!"

Each word was exquisitely pronounced—no, not pronounced: yelled—into the telephone.

"Well, I'll be absolutely and completely goddamned!"

It seemed that John had to shout all the way to New York City and beyond. Now, gripping the phone, he looked out across the green meadows in December light as if somehow, too, he might stare long distance at that man he was yelling at so far away.

"Tom, is it really *you?*" he cried.

The phone buzzed: yes, it was *really* Tom.

John held the phone down and shouted the same way at

Ricki, at the far end of the dining room table. I sat between,
half buttering my toast.

"It's Tom Hurley, calling from Hollywood!"

Ricki gave him one of her elusive, haunted smiles and
looked down again at her scrambled eggs.

"Well, for God's sake, Tom!" said John. "What are you *up*
to? What are you *doing?*"

The phone buzzed.

"Uh-huh," said John, emphatically, listening. "Uh-huh!
Uh-huh!" He nodded. "Good, Tom. Fine. Fine. Lisa, yes, I
remember Lisa. Lovely girl. When? Well, that's *wonderful*,
Tom, for *both* of you!"

The telephone talked for a long moment. John looked at
me and winked.

"Well, it's the hunt season here, Tom, yes, great fox-
hunting country. Ireland's the best in the world. Fine jumps,
Tom, you'd love it!"

Ricki looked up again at this. John glanced away from her,
out at the swelling green hills.

"It's the loveliest land in creation, Tom. I'm going to live
here forever!"

Ricki started eating rapidly, looking down.

"They have great horses here, Tom," said John. "And you
know horses better than I do. Well, you ought to come over
and just lay your eyes on the beauties!"

I heard the voice on the phone say it wished it could.

John gazed at the green fields. "I'm riding with the Waterford Hunt Thursday, Tom. What the hell . . . hell, why don't
you just fly over to hunt *with* me?"

The voice on the phone laughed.

Ricki let her fork drop. "Christ," she muttered. "Here it
comes!"

John ignored her, gazed at the hills and said:

"I *mean* it, be our houseguest, bring Lisa too!"

The voice on the phone laughed, not so loud this time.

"Tom, look," John pursued, "I need to buy one or two more horses to race or maybe breed, you could help me pick. Or—"

John stared out the window. Beyond, a hound trotted by on the green field. John sat up suddenly, as if the animal were inspiration.

"Tom, I've just got the damnedest wildest idea. Listen, you *do* want to bring Lisa along, yes? Okay, pile her into a plane tomorrow, fly to Shannon—Shannon, Tom—and I'll come to Shannon myself to drive you here to Kilcock. But listen, Tom, after you've been here a week we'll have a *hunt wedding*!"

I heard the voice on the phone say, "What?"

"Haven't you ever heard of a hunt wedding, Tom?" cried John exuberantly. He stood up now and put one foot on the chair and leaned toward the window to see if the hound was still trotting across the field. "Tom, it's just the best damn kind of wedding for a man like you and a woman like Lisa. *She* rides, doesn't she? And sits a horse well, as I recall. Well, then, damn it, think how it would be, Tom! You're getting married anyway, so why not you two pagans here in Catholic Ireland? Out here at *my* place . . ." He cast a quick glance at Ricki. "*Our* place. We'd call in every horse in ninety miles around and every decent hunter, and the lovely hounds, the loveliest hounds and bitches you ever saw, Tom, and everyone in their pink coats—what *color*, Tom—and the women in great-fitting black coats, and after the marriage service you and Lisa and I would go to hunt the finest fox you ever saw, Tom! What do you *say*? Is Lisa there? Put her on!" A pause. "Lisa? Lisa, you sound great! Lisa, *talk* to that bastard! No arguments! I'll expect you here day after tomorrow for the Waterford Hunt! Tell Tom I won't accept the charges if he calls back. God love you, Lisa. So long." John hung up.

He looked at me with a chimpanzee smile of immense satisfaction.

"By God now! What *have* I done? Did you *hear* that? Will you help out, kid?"

"What about *Moby Dick*, John?"

"Oh, hell, the Whale will survive. God, I can just see the parish priest's eyebrows burning. I can hear the rouse in the pubs when they *hear*!"

"I can watch myself cutting my throat in the bathtub." Ricki headed for the door. It was always the horses to be ridden or tubs soaked in up to her mouth at a time like this, which was usually twice a week, living with a power unit like John. "So long, lousy husband. Goodbye, cruel world."

The door slammed.

Not waiting to hear the fierce douse of water above in the giant bathroom, John grabbed my knee.

"God almighty, it'll be a time!" he cried. "Ever *seen* a hunt wedding?"

"Afraid not."

"Christ, it's *beautiful*! Damn! Beyond belief!"

I looked at the door through which Ricki had gone.

"Will Tom and Lisa come, just like *that*?"

"They're both sports."

"Am I supposed to interpret that as positive assurance we'll see them this week?"

"We'll go to Shannon and drive them here, won't we, kid?"

"I thought I was supposed to rewrite the solid-gold-doubloon-on-the-mast scene, John."

"Oh, hell, we both need a few days off. Ricki!"

Ricki reappeared in the door, her face the color of snow and lilacs. She had been waiting for the call she knew would come.

"Ricki," said John, beaming at her as on one of his children. "Goddamn, listen—here's the *plan*!"

Tom and Lisa got off the plane fighting. They fought inside the door of the plane. They fought coming out the door. They yelled at each other on the top step. They shouted coming down the steps.

John and I just looked up, aghast. I was glad Ricki was off somewhere, shopping until suppertime.

"Tom!" cried John. "Lisa!"

Halfway down the steps, Lisa turned and ran back up, raving. She was going back to the States *now*! The pilot, on his way out, told her there was a rather slender chance of this, for the plane was not going back immediately. Why not? she demanded. By this time Tom had bounded back up to her side, yelling at the pilot that he should indeed turn the damn ship round and fly this madwoman back, he would pay double, triple, and if he could manage to crash on the way, fine.

John, listening, sat down on the steps of the unloading platform, shut his eyes, shook his head, and bellowed with laughter.

Hearing this, Tom came to the rail above and looked down sharply. "Jesus Christ, John!"

John went up and hugged and kissed Lisa a lot, which *did* it. We finally saw them through customs, packed them into the Jaguar, and tooled across the vast green pool table of Ireland.

"Beautiful! Beautiful!" cried Lisa, as the hills rushed by.

"What *weather*!" said Tom.

"Don't let it fool you," John announced. "Looks lovely, but it rains twelve days out of ten. You'll soon be at the whiskey, like me!"

"Is that possible?" Tom laughed, and I laughed with him, looking over. What I saw was what I had seen for years around Hollywood, a man lean as whipcord and leather; hard riding, tennis every day, swimming, yachting, and mountain climbing had fined him down to this. Tom was fifty-three, with a thick shock of iron-gray hair. His face was unlined, deeply tanned, his jaw was beautifully sharp, his teeth were all there and white, his nose was a hawk's nose, exquisitely prowed in any wind anywhere in the world. His eyes were blue, water bright and intensely burning. The fire in him was a young man's fire, and it would never go out: he would never let it go out himself, and there was no man with an ego powerful enough to kill it. Nor, for that matter, was there a woman in the world whose flesh could smother Tom. There never had been, and now, this late, there never could be. Tom was his own mount and saddle, he rode himself and did so with masculine beauty. I could see by the way Lisa held his arm that she both angrily and happily accepted him for what he was, a single-minded man who had roamed the world and done what he wanted to do when he wanted to do it, without asking anyone and without apologies. Any woman who tried to lay tracks down for Tom, why, he would simply laugh and walk away. Now, this day, he had decided to come to Ireland. Tomorrow he might be with the Aga Khan in Paris and the day after in Rome, but Lisa would be there, and it would go on that way until someday, many years from now, he fell from a mountain, a horse, or another woman, and died at the base of that mountain, horse, or woman, showing his teeth. He was everything men would like to be if they were honest with themselves, everything John wanted to be and couldn't quite live up to, and a hopeless and crazily reckless ideal for someone like me to admire from a distance, having been born and bred of reluctance, second thoughts, premonitions, depressions, and lack of will.

"Mr. Hurley," I couldn't help asking, "why *have* you come to Ireland?"

"Tom is the name. And . . . John *ordered* me here! When John speaks, I *come*!" said Tom, laughing.

"Damn right!" said John.

"*You* called *him*, remember, Tom?" Lisa punched his arm.

"So I did." Tom was not in the least perturbed. "I figured it had been too long since we saw each other. Years go by. So I pick up the phone and call the son of a bitch and he says, Tom, come! And we'll have a wild week and I'll go on my way and another two years will pass. That's how it is with John and me, great when we're together, no regrets apart! This hunt wedding, now . . ."

"Don't look at me," I said. "My ignorance is total."

"Lisa, here, didn't quite warm up to it," Tom admitted.

"No!" cried John, swiveling to burn her with one eye.

"Nonsense," said Lisa, quickly. "I brought my hunt wardrobe from West Virginia. It's packed. I'm *happy*! A hunt wedding—*think*!"

"I am," said John, driving. "And if I know me, it might just as easily be a hunt funeral!"

"John would love that!" said Tom, talking to me as if John were not present, riding through green and green again. "Then he could come to our wake and get drunk and weep and tell all our grand times. You ever notice—things happen for *his* convenience? People are born for him, live for him, and die so he can put coins on their eyelids and cry over them. Is there anything *isn't* convenient or fun for John?"

"Only one thing," Tom added after a pause.

John pretended not to hear.

"What's that?" I asked.

"Being alone." Tom was suddenly serious. "John doesn't like being alone, ever. You must never leave John alone, remember that, no matter what." Tom looked at me with his keen, clear, bright-water eyes. "John once said to me, Tom, the loneliest time in a man's day is the time between when he stops work and starts dinner. That single hour is as desolate as three in the morning of a long night, he said. *Then* is when a man needs friends."

"I said *that* to you?" said John in fake astonishment.

Tom nodded. "I got a letter from you last year. You must have written it at five, some afternoon. You sounded alone. That's why I call once in a while. That's why I'm here. Jealous, Lisa?"

"I think I am," said Lisa.

Tom looked at her steadily.

"No," said Lisa, "I'm *not*."

Tom patted her leg. "Good girl." He nodded up at John. "How about giving us a road test?"

"Road test it *is*!"

We drove the rest of the way to Kilcock at eighty miles an hour. Lisa blinked quite often. Tom didn't blink at all, watching Ireland loom at him in landfalls of green.

I kept my eyes shut most of the way.

There was a problem having to do with a hunt wedding. Quite suddenly we discovered that none had been held in Ireland for years. How many years, we never found out.

The second and greatest problem was the Church.

No self-respecting priest was about to show up to fuse the lusts of two Hollywood characters, although Lisa Helm was from Boston and a thoroughly nice lady, but Tom Hurley was from all the points of Hell, a cross-country horseman who played destructive tennis with Darryl Zanuck and advised the Aga Khan on the insemination of thoroughbreds.

No matter. For the Church, it was out of the question. Besides which (John had never bothered to ask), neither Tom, despite his Irish background, nor Lisa was Catholic.

What to do? There were no other churches near Kilcock.

Not even a paltry small Protestant chapel you might sleepwalk in for a long Sunday noon.

So it finally fell to me to inquire of the local Unitarian church in Dublin. What's worse than a Protestant? A Unitarian! It was no church and no faith at all. But its keeper, the Reverend Mr. Hicks, agreed, in a rather hyperventilated exchange on the phone, to assume the task because he was promised his rewards on Earth by John Huston rather than in Heaven by a God who was rarely named, so as to save embarrassment.

"Have they been living in sin?" asked the Reverend Mr. Hicks abruptly.

I was shocked. I had never heard such talk before.

"Well . . ." I said.

"*Have* they?"

I shut my eyes to focus the bridal pair, loud in the Dublin streets noon and night.

They had had a fight about one wedding ring, then another, a fight about possible flowers, a fight about the day and date, a fight about the minister, a fight about the location of the ceremony, a fight about the size of the wedding cake, with or without brandy, a fight about the horses and hounds, and even a fight with the master of the hunt, a fight with his assistant, a fight with the Courtown butler, an altercation with a maid, a carousal with the pub owner about liquor, another brannigan with the liquor merchant in town for not giving a markdown on three cases of not very excellent champagne, plus fights in restaurants and pubs. If you wanted to keep a record of the fights in one week, the best way to imprint it on the calendar was with a shotgun.

John loved it all.

"Always like a good scrap!" he exclaimed, his grin so wide it needed sewing. "My cash is on the lady's nose. Tom may

ride the days, but she'll win the nights. Besides, everyone has
his foibles. Tom drinks too much Old Peculiar—"

"Is that a real name?"

"An English ale, uh-huh. Old Peculiar. But that's Tom. A
pal, nevertheless. They'll finish the fights and settle in for a
soft marriage, you wait and see."

"Reverend Hicks," I said over the phone, "Tom and Lisa
fight a lot."

"Then they've *sinned* a lot!" the reverend mourned. "You'd
best send them round."

Tom and Lisa fought about going to see Mr. Hicks.

They fought going in.

They argued in front of him.

They yelled coming out.

If a voice can be pale, the reverend's voice was pale describ-
ing the pair.

"This is not a marriage," he protested. "It is a rematch!"

"Exactly my sentiments, Reverend," I agreed, "but will
you advise them of the boxing rules and send them to their
corners?"

"If they'll promise to stay there four days out of five. Is
there a Bible chapter, I wonder? Futilities, verse four, para-
graph two?"

"There *will* be."

"And will I write it?"

"I have faith in you, Father!"

"Reverend!" he cried.

"Reverend," I said.

"Well, how in hell we got into this mess is what I'd like to
know!" Ricki said into the phone.

John's voice barked back from Paris, where he was interviewing actors for our film. I could hear him loud and clear as I helped lug in the flowers and place the table for the wedding cake and count the cheap champagne in cases along the wall.

"Mess!" John yelled. "It's no mess, by God; it's going to be the greatest goddamn event in Irish history. They'll start the uprising over. Are the flowers there?"

"The damn flowers are!"

"Has the cake been ordered?"

"You know it has!"

"And the champagne?"

"The worst, but it's here."

"Better get hold of Heeber at his pub. Tell him to bring in the best. God, *I'll* pay for it. It's time Tom scared the moths out of his wallet, but *hell*! Call Heeber!"

"The alien from Mars just did that—"

"Is *he* there? Put him on!"

Ricki threw the phone at me. I dodged but caught.

"John, I've finished the Saint Elmo's fire scene and—"

"To hell with that, kid. I've fallen—"

"With *whom*?" I said automatically.

"No, no, for Christ's sake, no *woman*! This is more important. Off a *horse*!"

"*Fell* off?"

"Shh! Don't let Ricki hear! She'd cancel the hunt! I'm okay. Just some pulled ligaments. Unconscious five minutes and limping like mad. The Gimp, by God, the Gimp. But I'll be home late today. Check the last flight from London. I rode at Longchamps at dawn two days ago."

"I thought you were casting—"

"Sure! But the damn horse jumped when some car horn blew. I flew a mile high. I'm okay now. With a slight tendency, without warning, to fall down and writhe in agony when my back gives. Don't let me scare you, kid."

"I'm scared, John. If you die, *I'm* dead!"

"Nice sentiment. You're the screwed-tight optimist. Just tell me I won't fall down and writhe with Saint Vitus at the wedding."

"Heck, you'd do it just to steal the show."

"Why *not?* Hire a cab, pick me up at the airport tonight, tell me the Saint Elmo's fire scene on the way. Can I stay in your room at the Royal Hibernian overnight? I should be walking without crutches by morning."

"Holy God, John, *crutches?*"

"Pipe down! Is Ricki in the room, for Christ's sake?"

"She went to answer the door. Wait . . ."

Ricki stood in the hall looking at a piece of paper in her hand. Her face was a fall of snow and her eyes were beginning to drop tears. She came and handed me the paper.

John's voice said, "I hear someone crying."

"They *are,* John."

I read from the scribbled note.

" 'Alma Kimball O'Rourke fell under her horse today. She was killed instantly and the horse was destroyed.' "

"Omigod," said John, five hundred miles away in Paris.

"She was the wife of the Kildare Hunt's captain, wasn't she?" I asked.

"Jesus, yes," said John quietly.

I finished reading the note. " 'The funeral's day after to-morrow. The entire hunt will be there.' "

"My God," murmured John, growing quieter still.

"That means . . . ?" I said.

"The hunt wedding," Ricki said, "must be called off."

John heard and said, "No, no. Only *delayed*."

Mike drove me into Dublin to find Tom, who had taken a room at the Russell Hotel. He and Lisa had fought about that too. He wanted to stay at Huston's with her. But the Catholics *and* the Protestants, she pointed out, were both watching. So it was the hotel for Tom until the ceremony. Besides, he could play the stock market better, alone in his Dublin hotel room. That cinched it. Tom checked in.

I found Tom in the lobby of the hotel, mailing some letters. I handed him the note and said nothing.

There was a long pause, and then I could see the thin transparent inner lids of Tom's eyes, his eagle's eyes or his lizard's eyes or his cat's eyes, slide down between us. They did not slam like the great gates of Kiev, but it was just as final, just as definite, just as complete. The noise his eyelids made closing, while he continued to stare at me, was awful in its silence. I was outside in my world, if my world existed at all, and Tom was inside his.

"She's dead, Tom," I said, but that was useless. Tom had switched off whatever batteries kept him tuned to the audible universe, to any air that held words and phrases. I said it again "She's dead."

Tom turned and strode up the stairs.

I spoke to Mike at the door. "The minister? The Unitarian. We'd better go tell him."

Behind me, I heard the elevator door open.

Tom was there in the doorway. He did not step out. I hurried over.

"Yes, Tom?"

"I was just thinking," said Tom. "Someone should cancel the wedding cake."

"Too late. It arrived as I was leaving Courtown."

"Christ," Tom said.

The elevator door shut.

Tom ascended.

* * *

The plane from London was late getting into Shannon. By the time it arrived, I had made three trips to the Gents', which shows you how much ale I had downed, waiting.

John waved his crutches from the top of the landing steps and almost fell the length in his eagerness to get down to me. I tried to help, but he all but struck me with his implements, hurrying along in giant bounds like someone who was born and raised an athlete on crutches. With every great jump forward, favoring one leg, he cried out half in pain, half in elation:

"Jesus, God, there's always something new. I mean, when you're not looking, God gives you a tumble. I never fell like this. It was like slow motion, or going over a waterfall or shooting the rapids just before you wake—you know how it is, every frame of film stops for a moment so you can look at it: now your ass is in the air, now your spine, vertebra by vertebra, now your neckbone, collarbone, top of your head, and you can see it all rotating, and there's the horse down there, you can see him too, frame by frame, like you're taking a picture of the whole damn thing with a box Brownie working away thirty frames a second, but all perfectly clear and held in the second, which expands to hold it, so you can see yourself and the horse, waltzing, you might say, on the air. And the whole thing takes half an hour in seconds. The only thing that speeds up the frames is when you hit the turf. Christ. Then, one by one, you can hear your suspenders snapping, your tendons, that is, your muscles.

"You ever walk out at night in winter and listen? Damn! The branches so loaded with snow they might burst! The whole tree's a skeleton, you hear the sap bend and the wood creak. I thought all my bones would shatter, shale, and flake down inside my skin. Wham! Next thing I know, they run me to the morgue. Not *that* way, I yelled. Turned out it was an ambulance, and I only *thought* it was the coroner!

"Hurry up, for Christ's sake—I'm running faster than you are. I hope I don't fall down right now and have one of my convulsions. You'd really see something. Flat on my back like a Holy Roller, talking in tongues, blind with pain. Wham! Where's Tom?"

Tom was waiting for us in the Buttery of the Royal Hibernian Hotel. John insisted on crutch-vaulting down to find the American Irishman.

"Tom, by God, *there* you are!" said John.

Tom turned and looked at us with that clear cold sky-blue winter-morning gaze.

"Jesus," gasped John. "You look *mad*. What are you so mad *about*, Tom?"

"She was riding sidesaddle," said Tom evenly. "She should not have been riding sidesaddle, damn her."

"Now, who would *that* be?" asked John, with that oiled and easy polite but false voice of his. "What woman is *that*?"

At noon the next day, Mike and I drove John out to Kilcock. He had practiced some great healthy crutch bounds and was apishly exuberant at his prowess, and when we reached Courtown he was out of the car ahead of us and half across the bricks when Ricki came running down the steps.

"My God! Where *were* you! Be careful! What *happened*?"

At which point John dropped his crutches and fell writhing in the drive.

Which, of course, shut Ricki up.

We all half-lifted, half-carried John into the house.

Ricki opened her trembling mouth, but John lifted his great glovelike hand and, eyes shut, husked:

"Only brandy will kill the pain!"

She brought the brandy, and over her shoulder he spied Tom's champagne cases in the corridor.

"Is that crud still here?" he said. "Where's the Dom Perignon?"

"Where's *Tom*?" Ricki countered.

The wedding was delayed for more than a week out of respect for the lady, who, as it turned out, had *not* ridden sidesaddle but whose misfortune it was to be a small object under a more than substantial burden.

On the day of her memorial service, Tom spoke seriously of going home.

A fight ensued.

When Lisa finally convinced Tom to stay, *she* fell into a depression and warned of a similar trip, because Tom insisted on not ordering a fresh wedding cake and on keeping the old one as a dust-catcher for more than a full week of mourning.

Only John's intervention stopped the fights. Only a long and inebriated dinner at Jammet's, the best French restaurant in Ireland, restored their humor.

"Quiet!" said John as we dined. "The kitchen door as it opens and shuts, opens, shuts! *Listen!*"

We listened.

As the door squealed wide on its hinges, the voice of the chef could be heard shrieking in frenzies at his cooks.

Open:

A shriek!

Shut:

Silence.

Open:

A scream!

Shut:

Silence.

"You *hear* that?" whispered John.

Open. Shriek!

"That's *you,* Tom."

Shut, silence. Open, scream.

"That's *you,* Lisa."

Open, shut, open, shut.

Scream, shriek, shriek, scream.

"Tom, Lisa, Lisa, Tom!"

"My God!" cried Lisa.

"Dear Jesus!" said Tom.

Scream, silence, scream.

"Is that *us?*" both said.

"Or an approximation," said John, his cigarillo smoking in his languid mouth. "Give or take a decibel. Champagne?"

John refilled our glasses and ordered more.

Tom and Lisa laughed so much they had to grab each other, and then their heads fell to each other's shoulders, choking and breathless.

Very late, John called the chef out to stand in the kitchen door.

Wild applause greeted him. Amazed, he shrugged, nodded, and vanished.

As John paid the bill, Tom said, very slowly, "Okay. She was *not* riding sidesaddle."

"I was hoping you'd say that, Tom." John exhaled a long slow stream of cigarillo smoke, laying out the tip. "I was *hoping* you would."

Mike and I picked up the Unitarian minister, the Reverend Mr. Hicks, the night before the great hunt wedding and drove him to Kilcock.

On his way to the car he had something fine to say about Dublin. As we drove from Dublin he had something truly excellent to say about the outskirts and the River Liffey, and when we hit the green countryside he was most effusive of all. It seemed there was no speck or seam visible on, in, or through this county or the next. Or if flaws were there, he chose to ignore them for the virtues. Given time, he would speak the list. Meanwhile, the hunt wedding lay like white lace on the morning shore ahead and he focused on it, with his pursed mouth, his red pointy nose, and his flushed eyeballs.

As we churned gravel in the yard, he gasped, "Thank God, there's no moon! The less seen of me arriving, the better!"

"The whole town will see you through the windows tomorrow," I observed, dryly, "holding the pagan service and fluting the blasphemous oration."

The Reverend Mr. Hicks turned to a shape carved from a moonstone. "Find me a bottle," he husked, "and put me to bed."

I awoke just before dawn in a high attic servant's room and lay conjuring the great day in the morning this was promised to be.

The theater of Ireland waited.

I thought I heard brogues below, going home late from Finn's or arriving early for the Protestant Embarrassment.

I thought I heard the huntsman's horn, practicing on the green rim of the world.

I imagined I heard a fox yipping in response.

There was a small shadow on the edge of the land; the hunted beast, I was sure, arriving to be first onstage.

Then, sprawled in bed, eyes shut, I conjured up the arrival of hounds in tumult and then horses, shivering their skin over their flesh, in bad need of psychologists' advice, and none here. That was silly, of course. Horses and hounds do not arrive first. The kennelmaster must lead one and the various bluebloods rein and reassure the others. Yet I did hear blood cries and yawps somewhere in my half sleep, and the jingling of accoutrements galloped to a halt.

Not wishing to be stage director to it all, I churned over into a whimpering and talkative sleep, warning myself to burrow deep and listen not.

Only to hear John's voice at the door to my room, as he stirred the parquetry with his crutches. "No use, kid. Time to get up."

And the real hounds and horses arrived below.

All was in readiness. The stale wedding cake, growing more ancient by the hour, awaited. The tooth-aching and tongue-blistering champagne was laid by.

The horses were steaming the air and smiling derisive smiles in the courtyard.

The hounds were padding in circles, wetting bricks, hooves, and boots.

The lords and ladies and the owners of liquor shops all across Eire had arrived, of course, and dismounted to the nibbling smiles of horses and the suspicious protests of the hounds.

"Stirrup cups for all!" someone cried.

"That's *before* we ride," a lady corrected. "And it's just for the groom."

"What I meant to say is, is the *bar* open?"

"There *is* no bar," announced the Reverend Mr. Hicks, standing so straight and correct it was obvious he had just been there, "but there *is* champagne, good silver buckets and bad. Beware of the shilling poison up front. Demand the pound sterling Mumm's."

The horses were quickly abandoned and the hounds left to harass the kennelmaster and water the yard.

The guests booted up the steps, making hollow clubbing sounds on the concrete, their faces distorted not by fun house mirrors but by ancestry alone. Time and the patient chromosome had worked their clay, bucking the teeth, rheuming the eye, elongating the lip, beaking the nose, cleaving the chin, hollowing the cheek, jugging the ears, eroding the hair, tufting the eyebrows, bleaching the eyelids, waxing the complexion, pocking the brow, and knobbing the elbows, wrists, and fingers. Some looked as if they had stood too many years inside and looking out from stable doors.

My God, I thought, what a jumble sale of skulls and ears, lower lips and high-flung eyebrows. Here danced the spider, there thundered the hippo, here the spaniel eye wet itself with Irish sunlight, there the hound mouth drooped into despairs of days when no sun rose. Not quite crayfish, a fiddle-crab liquor salesman sidled up the steps, bringing with him the eyes of Adonis locked in a face so crimson he might have parboiled himself for breakfast. Here they all came, in pink or black coats, with bloated brows, insucked nostrils, and wharf-piling jaws.

I reeled back and drifted with the clamor of boots to see elbows shoving about in the rummage for Mumm's as against Twelvetrees bubbly.

"Who put the poison above and the remedy below?"

Instant silence followed as they beheld Tom Himself nodding his face toward the obscure-and-terrible as against the famed-and-fabulous.

"Let's have a tasting," someone said. "Compare old Sour Ditch to Kingsblood Royal."

Tom could not prevent as several dozen hands emptied the tooth-destroyer to make way for Mumm's mouthwash.

All was *almost* in readiness. Along with the killing wine and its cure, to one side were a few caviar sticks and cheese biscuits that Tom had laid on, while farther on, an ice floe frozen forever, the bridal cake waited for eternity.

Since it had already stalled eight days, its mesa and sides stalwart in the hours and quarter month just passed, the cake had an air of Miss Havisham about it, which, spied, was declared *sotto voce* innumerable times in earshot of the butlers and maids, who adjusted their ties and aprons and searched the ceiling for deliverance.

There was a sneeze.

Lisa appeared at the top of the stairs, only to sneeze again, spin about, and run back up. There was a sound of nose-blowing: the faintest whiff of hunting horn. Lisa returned, steadied herself, and sneezed on the way down.

"I wonder if this is a Freudian cold," she said beneath the Kleenex over her nose.

"What in hell do you mean by *that*?" Tom scowled.

"Maybe my nose doesn't *want* to get married." Lisa followed this with a quick laugh.

"Very funny. Very, very funny. Well, if your nose wants to call off the wedding, let it speak." Tom showed his teeth, nibbling the air much like the courtyard horses, to prove his humor.

Lisa half turned to flee, but another sneeze froze her in place. Any further retreat ceased when several crutches punched down the stairs, swinging between them in his pink coat the director as clown, the happy huntsman as lunatic gymnast. Taking the steps two at a time and swinging his long booted legs as if to project himself over our heads, John descended, talking over his shoulder and not minding where he fiddled his supports.

"It took an hour for the damned ambulance to get there;

meanwhile, I twitched and snaked around and screamed so loud that windows slammed a hundred yards off. Six shots didn't stop my yells. At the hospital, the Doc took one look, turned me over, and—*crack*! like a kick in the spine—the pain stopped, as did my screams. Then, by God, I began to laugh."

Turning from John, I plowed through the champagne mob. "Get me one of those," called John. "Make it two. Hello, Lisa, don't you look fine, just *fine*!"

Lisa sneezed.

"My God, look at your nose, Lisa," John commiserated. "So damn red it looks as if you'd been up five nights boozing!"

Lisa held to her stomach with one hand, her nose with the other, and ran upstairs.

"Thanks a *lot*," said Ricki, halfway down.

"What'd *I* do?" John protested. "Where's she going?"

"To powder her nose, dimwit."

"Where's Mr. Hicks?" said John, escaping swiftly in leap-frog vaults.

"Hello, hello!" He stopped in midhop to wave at all the windows along the back of the dining room, where two dozen or so local noses imprinted the panes.

The villagers, mad, angry, or irritated housewives, hesitated, not knowing how to swallow John's happy salute.

A few waved back. The rest pulled off, not taken in by his apish Protestant amiability.

"Welcome, welcome!" John called, knowing they could not hear. "It's the Hollywood sinner here, born in sin, living in sin, and soon to die, writhing, in sin. Hello!"

Some must have read his lips, for no fewer than a half dozen indignant villagers leaped back as if he had leavened the air with brimstone.

"Drink this against the day." I arrived with the champagne.

"But will it cure at noon?" John drank.

"One hour at a time," I said. "Where's the reverend? Oh, *there* he is. Reverend!"

The reverend came from the hall, smelling of hounds and horses. "I have been out commiserating with them for partaking in this wicked enterprise," he said, and added quickly, "Oh, *not* the wedding, for sure. But the hunt. Everyone seems happy. But no one has invited the fox."

"We asked, but he pleaded business." John smiled. "Are we ready?"

The Reverend Mr. Hicks grabbed a champagne from a tray as it passed, gulped it, and said, "As we'll *ever* be."

The lords and ladies and liquor merchants gathered, simmering with the good drinks, hiccuping with the bad—a medley of pink coats, celebrating joy; and black, promising unfaithful husbands and mournful wives.

The Reverend Mr. Hicks positioned himself in front of the glare of Tom and the dabbed-at and snuffling nose of Lisa, who peered around as if blind.

"Shouldn't there be a Bible?" she wondered.

A Bible, the reverend almost cried out, as he searched his empty hands.

Tom scowled but said:

"Yes. While Unitarian, we *are* Protestants. A Bible!"

The reverend looked around for someone to fill his hands with such a useful tool, which Ricki did in great haste, wondering if it was proper.

Off balance in two ways, the weight of the thing being one, Unitarian practice another, the reverend clenched the book but did not open it, fearing that some lost chapter or verse might leap to disquiet his mind and capsize the ceremony. Placing the Bible like a brick on the lectern, an ignored cornerstone to his peroration, he lit out:

"Have you been living in sin?" he cried.

There was a still moment. I saw the muscles under Tom's

pink riding coat flex and tear themselves in several directions; one to punch, one to pray.

I saw the clear crystal lid come down over one of Tom's blazing eyes, in profile, shutting out the dear minister.

Lisa's tongue wandered along her upper lip, seeking a response, and, finding none, slipped back to neutral.

"What was that *again*?" Tom's eyes were burning lenses. If they'd been out in the sun, the Reverend Mr. Hicks would long since have gone up in smoke.

"Sin," said the Reverend Hicks. "Have you been *living* in it?"

Silence.

Tom said, "As a matter of fact, we *have*."

Lisa jabbed his elbow and stared at the floor. There was an outbreak of muffled coughing.

"Oh," said the Reverend Mr. Hicks. "*Well,* then."

What followed was not a ceremony but a sermon and not a sermon but a lecture. Sin was the subject, and the bridal couple the object. Without actual circling and sniffing their hems and cuffs, the reverend managed to make everyone in the room acutely aware of underwear and of ties that choked. He wandered off the subject and then wandered back. It was sin this and sin that, sins of the lovers and future husbands, sins of the put-upon and not always guaranteed brides. Somewhere along in the hour he mislaid the ceremony. Finding it in the corners of his eyes, and in Tom's concentrated glare, Mr. Hicks hesitated and was about to ricochet back to pure sin, if sin ever *was* pure, when John shortened the hour.

He let one crutch slip. It slammed the floor with a fine crack and rebounding clatter.

"Tom and Lisa, do you take each other as man and wife!" cried the Reverend Mr. Hicks.

It was over! No one heard the shots or saw wounds or blood. There was a shared gasp from three dozen throats.

The reverend slapped his revised Unitarian Bible shut on mostly empty pages, and the locals from the pub and the town villagers, pressed to the windows, leaped back as if caught by lightning, to avoid the direct-current gaze of Tom, and at his elbow the downcast eyes of Lisa, still recirculating her blush. The reverend ran for the champagne. By some accident never to be explained in Ireland, some of the cheap had risen to spoil the best.

"Not *that*." The reverend swallowed, grimaced, and gestured his goblet. "The *other,* for goodness' sake!"

Only when he had rinsed his mouth and swallowed to improve the hour did color tint his cheek and spark his eyes.

"Man!" he shouted at Tom. "That was *work*. Refills!"

There was a show of hands waving goblets.

"Gentlemen, ladies!" John reminded them of their manners. "Cake to go with the champagne!"

"John!" Ricki jerked her head. "*No!*"

But it was too late. All turned to focus their lust on a bridal confection which had waited, gathering dust, for eight days.

Smiling like an executioner, John brandished the knife. Lisa took it as if she had just pulled it from her breast and desired to shove it back in. Instead she turned to bend over the lonely and waiting cake. I crowded near to watch the speckles of dust flurry up from frosting stirred by Lisa's breath.

She stabbed the cake.

Silent, the cake was obdurate.

It did not cut, it did not slice, and it gave only faint tendencies to flake or chip.

Lisa struck again and a fine powder puffed up on the air. Lisa sneezed and struck again. She managed to dent the target in four places. Then she started the assassination. With a furious red face above and the knife gripped in both hands, she wrought havoc. More powder, more flakes.

"Is the damn cake *fresh*?" someone said.

"Who *said* that?" said Tom.

"Not me," said several people.

"*Give* me that!" Tom seized the knife from Lisa's hands. "*There!*"

This time, shrapnel. The cake cracked under his blows and had to be shoveled onto the plates with a dreadful clatter.

As the plates were handed round, the men in their pink coats and the women in their smart black stared at the broken teeth strewn there, the smile of a once great beauty laid to ruin by time.

Some sniffed, but no aroma or scent arose from the powdered frost and the slain brandy cake beneath. Its life had long since fled.

Which left the good souls with a confectioner's corpse in one hand and a bad vintage in the other, until someone rediscovered the rare vintages stashed against the wall and the stampede for the saviors' refreshment began. What had been a moment of statues-in-panic wondering how to be rid of two handfuls of failed appetite became a wonder of imbibation and loosened tongues. All babbled, churning around and about every few minutes for a refulfillment of Mumm's while Tom, suffering the rejection of a lost salesman, slugged back brandies to relight the fury in his eyes.

John stomped through the crowd, not hearing but laughing at jokes.

"Pour some on my crutches," he cried, "so I can move!"

Someone did.

It would have been pitiful had it not been ludicrous to see the gentry wandering with platefuls of hard rock-shrapnel cake, picking at it with forks, saying how delicious and demanding more.

On the third go-round the crowd turned brave, abandoned

the vitrified cake, and filled their empty glasses with Scotch. Whereupon there was a general exodus toward the yard, with people feverishly seeking places to hide the last of the concrete cake fragments.

The hounds in the yard leaped, barking, and horses reared, and the Reverend Mr. Hicks hurried out ahead with what looked to be a double double in his fist, garrulous and cheerful, waving to what he thought were village Catholics near the hounds and Protestants by the horses. The villagers, stunned, waved back, in pretense of a religion they despaired of to the point of contempt.

"Did he . . . ," said Tom, behind me.

"Did he *what?*" Lisa sneezed.

"Did Mr. Hicks . . . *did* you hear him say, 'I pronounce you man and wife'?"

"I *think* so."

"What do you mean? Did he or *didn't* he?"

"Something like."

"Something *like?*" cried Tom. "Reverend . . . ? Toward the end of the ceremony . . ."

"Sorry about the living-in-sin bit," said the reverend.

"Reverend Hicks, did you or did you *not* say 'I now pronounce you man and wife'?"

"Ah, yes." The Reverend wrinkled his brow and took another snort. "Easily fixed. I now pronounce you man and wife. Go thou and sin some more."

"And sin *no* more!" corrected Tom.

"Ah, yes," said the Reverend Mr. Hicks, and wove himself into the crowd.

"I rather *like* that." Lisa sneezed happily. "Go thou and sin some more. I hope you'll be back early. I sent someone to dope the fox in hopes of an early night. Are you really going to climb on that silly horse with all those drinks?"

"I have only had six," said Tom.

"Shit," said Lisa. "I guessed it at eight. Can you really mount that damn horse drunk?"

"I'm in fighting trim. And I've never heard you swear. Why *today*?"

"The Reverend Hicks, in his sermon, said it was the end of the world. Can I help you up on the funny-looking steed?"

"No, my dear," Tom said and laughed, because people were listening.

With great dignity he strode to his horse and propelled himself into the saddle. Through gritted teeth he said, "The stirrup cup!"

"Oh, yeah." Lisa turned to find Ricki with the silver wine-filled goblet.

"Attention!" Ricki called. "The bride will now give the stirrup cup to the groom."

Lisa wafted the cup up so swiftly the wine spilled on Tom's breeches. He stared down, his face by degrees suffusing to a scarlet not unlike his jacket's, grabbed the cup and slugged it back. The guests applauded and leaped unsteadily into their saddles. John threw his crutches at me and manhandled his horse, which flinched.

"John, you're *not* going on the hunt!" cried Ricki.

"Damn right. When I get up, kid, hand me the crutches!"

"What good are crutches up there?" I said.

"It's for when I fall *off*, kid." And John laughed a great guffaw as the horse reared, terrified of clowns.

"John, for God's sake!" said Ricki.

John lurched again. The thing that saved him from his death ride was a muscle spasm that shot him in the back. He fell and writhed. We all gathered to watch. Seeing our faces, John lectured:

"This is how I was in Paris. Pretty bad, eh? Pretty bad?"

"Huntsman!" shouted Tom. The huntsman blew his horn.

Far off on a hill I thought I saw the fox, tired but waiting.

"Goodbye, my dear," said Tom.

Lisa sneezed and waved her wet hankie.

The horses charged off with the hounds, baying.

"Kid," said John, on the ground, "call *two* doctors. One for Lisa's throat, one for my backside. And get us up to bed."

"Oh, *no* you don't!" said Ricki.

"Not the *same* bed, of course." John smiled.

The Reverend Mr. Hicks watched the horses and hounds diminish in the distance, then spoke to Lisa.

"Your husband asked a question. What . . . ?"

"*Are* we married? *Did* you legally marry us?"

The reverend searched his coat to turn some papers end over end. "No." He handed the papers to Lisa. "Not until you've both signed *these*."

Lisa blew her nose and said, "Does anyone have a *pen?*"

Mr. Hicks patted his pockets and shook his head.

Back at the Royal Hibernian Hotel, the next morning I awoke early, for no reason except perhaps too much bad rather than good wine.

Then, for no reason, save intuition, I peered out at the constant, ever-falling, and eternal rain and thought I saw a lean man in a svelte raincoat, with no umbrella but a tweed Grafton Street cap pulled down over his iron-gray hair and hawk's nose, striding by so quickly I almost said his name. My mouth moved to whisper it.

I plunged into bed to drown in tides of coverlet until nine, when the phone rang twenty times, forcing me to reach out blindly to find the damned thing.

"You're *up?*" said Ricki's voice.

"No, still deep under."

"Shall I call later?"

"No, no. It sounds like you need to talk now."

"How did you guess? Well, here's the dope. In the confusion someone invited Heeber Finn's pub friends into the house, which was like a riot of hounds and horses. They rid the place of Tom's poor booze and overloaded on John's, vanquished the brandy, debilitated the sherry, and invited all the lords and ladies down to Finn's to improve the talk. Along the line, the Reverend Mr. Hicks vanished. We found him out in the stables just now. He's refused to get up unless we put him on the Belfast train. The cake was shaken down with the stove clinkers and removed as shale for the garden path. The horses, waiting last night, ran home alone. Some of the hounds are out in the stable, asleep with the reverend. I think I saw the fox at the kitchen door at dawn, lapping cream with the cats, who, seeing his exhaustion, let him. John is in bed writhing in pain *or* exercising. At least he has stopped shrieking descriptions of both. I will now go to sleep for the weekend. You are to rewrite the Whale Chase whether it needs chasing or not, says John. Lisa has pleaded, then demanded, air tickets for Rome and—oh, here she *is*."

"Hello," said a frail far voice.

"Lisa!" I called with false bravado.

"There's only one thing I want to say."

"Say it, Lisa."

She sneezed.

"Where—" she said and stopped. Then she finished it. "Where's *Tom?*"

10

It was Christmas noon and I had been invited out to Courtown for a turkey dinner plus gift-giving; John had asked in a few huntsmen and their wives and Betty Malone, who took fine care of his horses, and a writer and his mistress from Paris. We had the turkey and gave all the gifts save one.

"Now," announced John, "for Ricki. The big event. Outside, everyone!"

We went outside, and at a fairly loud whistle from John, Betty came running around the side of the house leading a black mare with a Christmas wreath encircling its neck.

Ricki shouted with delight and embraced John and then the horse. John hefted her up into the saddle and she sat there, laughing with joy and petting the lovely beast.

"Okay," said John. "Go!"

Ricki gave the mare the peremptory kicks and took off, once around the front yard and then over a fence. On the way over and down, she fell off. We all yelled and ran forward. I had never seen anyone, in person, fall off a horse, so I groaned and felt kicked in the stomach.

John reached Ricki first and stood over her. He didn't touch her or help her to her feet. He didn't examine her legs or arms or body, he just leaned down at her and yelled, "You bitch, get back on that horse!"

Which froze us all in place.

John stood between so we could not reach or touch Ricki.

Unaided, shaking her head, Ricki got to her feet.

"Damn you," cried Huston, "back on that horse!"

She tried to climb back up, but she was dizzy. Huston shoved her up in place. She looked around at the green grass, the fence, her husband and, finally, at the horse under her, and at me.

I felt my mouth move. It made no sound but it shaped two words:

Merry Christmas.

Merry Christmas, her mouth said, silently, back to me.

Merry Christmas.

11

I had now read *Moby Dick* all the way through three times. That's three times eight hundred–odd pages. Some parts I had read ten times. Some scenes as much as twenty. And along the way, throwing out the junk, getting rid of the fat to X-ray the bones and the marrow in the bones.

I was and remained a pursuer of the Whale. I was a small ahab, with no capital up front. For I felt that as fast as I swam, the Whiteness outpaced my poor strokes and my inadequate boat: a portable typewriter and great white pages waiting to be covered with blood.

Himself and I put our blood on it, but that was not enough. It must be Melville's blood and tears. He was Hamlet come alive on the castle wall and Lear on the moor. Sometimes we heard him cry most clearly. The rest of the time, his voice was drowned in salt tides that by arriving and leaving put us off balance. There were days when My Leader, for all his talent for massaging actors into shapes and editing their shadows into recognizable parades, could not help me, nor I him.

There were days, in sum, when we stared at each other, shrugged, and then began to laugh. We had bitten off a minnow and discovered it was Leviathan in all its biblical size and maniac fury. Laughter was the only release from our dumbness, which could become stupidity if we dared put down some of the ideas that had crossed our lips, to be buried in whiskey.

One day, in the midst of our Melvillean ignorance, I suddenly leapt to my feet and cried, "I'm gone!"

"Where to?" said the monster from the Directors Guild.

"Heeber Finn's."

"To do what?"

"Cram the Whale in a large mug to *drown* him."

"Can I come along?" said the Beast.

12

"And even further back," said Finn, in the midst of yet another monologue behind the bar, "there was a terrible event, best remembered and not seen."

"What year was that?" asked my director.

"Around about the Easter uprising," said Finn. "And the big houses beyond burned to ruins, knocked flat in their tracks. You've seen the remains?"

"I have," said John.

"The patriots did that when they was mobs," said Finn. "My father was one."

"And so was mine," said Doone.

"And mine, and mine," said all.

"A sad time."

"Not all sad, thank God. For once in a while, God lets go a laugh. And it had to do with me father and the father of our own Lord Kilgotten. Shall I tell you the start, go, and *finis*?"

"Tell," I said.

"Well," said Finn, "in the midst of the Troubles, in the cold snows of late winter that took Easter by surprise, my father, and all the fathers of all the dimwit boys you see leaning here, holding up the bar, stumbled upon an idea that lit, or you might say ignited, a plan that—"

"What was the plan, Finn, what *was* the plan?" said all, though they had heard the tale before.

"The plan was this . . ." whispered Finn, leaning across the bar to tell his winter secret.

The men had been hiding down by the gatekeeper's lodge for half an hour or so, passing a bottle of the best between, and then, the gatekeeper having been carried off to bed, they dodged up the path at six in the evening and looked at the great house with the warm lights lit in each window.

"That's the place," said Riordan.

"Hell, what do you mean, 'that's the place'?" cried Casey, then softly added, "We seen it all our lives."

"Sure," said Kelly, "but with the Troubles over and around us, sudden like a place looks *different*. It's quite a toy, lying there in the snow."

And that's what it seemed to the fourteen of them, a grand playhouse laid out in the softly falling feathers of a spring night.

"Did you bring the matches?" asked Kelly.

"Did I bring the . . . what do you think I *am*!"

"Well, *did* you, is all I ask."

Casey searched himself. When his pockets hung from his suit he swore and said, "I did not."

"Ah, what the hell," said Nolan. "They'll have matches inside. We'll borrow a few. Come on."

Going up the road, Timulty tripped and fell.

"For God's sake, Timulty," said Nolan, "where's your sense of romance? In the midst of a big Easter Rebellion we want to do everything just so. Years from now we want to go into a pub and tell about the Terrible Conflagration up at the Place, do we not? If it's all mucked up with the sight of you landing on your ass in the snow, that makes no fit picture of the Rebellion we are now in, does it?"

Timulty, rising, focused the picture and nodded. "I'll mind me manners."

"Hist! Here we are!" cried Riordan.

"Jesus, stop saying things like 'that's the place' and 'here we are,'" said Casey. "We see the damned house. Now what do we do next?"

"Destroy it?" suggested Murphy tentatively.

"Gah, you're so dumb you're hideous," said Casey. "Of course we destroy it, but first . . . blueprints and plans."

"It seemed simple enough back at Hickey's Pub," said Murphy. "We would just come tear the damn place down. Seeing as how my wife outweighs me, I need to tear *something* down."

"It seems to me," said Timulty, drinking from the bottle, "we go rap on the door and ask permission."

"Permission!" said Murphy. "I'd hate to have you running Hell; the lost souls would never get fried! We—"

But the front door swung wide suddenly, cutting him off.

A man peered out into the night.

"I say," said a gentle and reasonable voice, "would you mind keeping your voices down. The lady of the house is sleeping before we drive to Dublin for the evening, and—"

The men, revealed in the hearth-light glow of the door, blinked and stood back, lifting their caps.

"Is that you, Lord Kilgotten?"

"It is," said the man in the door.

"We will keep our voices down," said Timulty, smiling, all amiability.

"Beg pardon, Your Lordship," said Casey.

"Kind of you," said His Lordship. And the door closed gently.

All the men gasped.

" 'Beg pardon, Your Lordship,' 'We'll keep our voices down, Your Lordship.' " Casey slapped his head. "What were we saying? Why didn't someone catch the door while he was still there?"

"We was dumbfounded, that's why. He took us by surprise, just like them damned high and mighties. I mean, we weren't *doing* anything out here, were we?"

"Our voices *were* a bit high," admitted Timulty.

"Voices, hell," said Casey. "The damned lord's come and gone from our fell clutches!"

"*Shh*, not so loud," said Timulty.

Casey lowered his voice. "So let us sneak up on the door—and—"

"That strikes me as unnecessary," said Nolan. "He *knows* we're here now."

"Sneak up on the door," repeated Casey, grinding his teeth, "and batter it down—"

The door opened again.

The lord, a shadow, peered out at them, and the soft, patient, frail old voice inquired, "I say, what *are* you doing out there?"

"Well, it's this way, Your Lordship—" began Casey, and stopped, paling.

"We come," blurted Murphy, "we come . . . to *burn* the place!"

His Lordship stood for a moment looking out at the men, watching the snow, his hand on the doorknob. He shut his eyes for a moment, thought, conquered a tic in both eyelids after a silent struggle, and then said, "Hmm. Well, in that case, you had best come in."

The men said that was fine, great, good enough, and started off, when Casey cried, "Wait!" Then, to the old man in the doorway: "We'll come in when we are good and ready."

"Very well," said the old man. "I shall leave the door ajar, and when you have decided the time, enter. I shall be in the library."

Leaving the door a half-inch open, the old man started away, when Timulty cried out, "When we are *ready*? Jesus, God, when will we ever be readier? Out of the way, Casey!"

And they all ran up on the porch.

Hearing this, His Lordship turned to look at them with his bland and not-unfriendly face, the face of an old hound who has seen many foxes killed and just as many escape, who has run well and now, in late years, paced himself down to a soft, shuffling walk.

"Scrape your feet, please, gentlemen."

"Scraped they are." And everyone carefully got the snow and mud off his shoes.

"This way," said His Lordship, going off, his clear, pale eyes set in lines and bags and creases from too many years of drinking brandy, his cheeks bright as cherry wine. "I will get you all a drink, and we shall see what we can do about your ... how did you put it? Burning the place?"

"You're sweet reason itself," admitted Timulty, following as Lord Kilgotten led them into the library, where he poured whiskey all around.

"Gentlemen." He let his bones sink into a wing-backed chair. "Drink."

"We decline," said Casey.

"Decline?" gasped everyone, the drinks almost in their hands.

"This is a sober thing we are doing and we must be sober for it," said Casey, flinching from their gaze.

"Who do we listen to?" asked Riordan. "His Lordship or Casey?"

For answer, all the men downed their drinks and fell to coughing and gasping. Courage showed immediately in a red color through their faces, which they turned so that Casey could see the difference. Casey drank his, to catch up.

Meanwhile, the old man sipped his whiskey, and something about his calm and easy way of drinking put them far out in Dublin Bay and sank them again. Until Casey said, "Your Honor, you've heard of the Troubles? I mean, not just the Kaiser's war going on across the sea, but our own very great Troubles and the Rebellion that has reached even this far, to our town, our pub, and now your place?"

"An alarming amount of evidence convinces me this is an unhappy time." said His Lordship. "I suppose what must be must be. I know you all. You have worked for me. I think I have paid you rather well on occasion."

"There's no doubt of that, Your Lordship." Casey took a step forward. "It's just 'the old order changeth,' and we have heard of the great houses out near Tara and the great manors beyond Killashandra going up in flames to celebrate freedom and—"

"Whose freedom?" asked the old man mildly. "Mine? From the burden of caring for this house, which my wife and I rattle around in like dice in a cup, or . . . Well, get on. *When* would you like to burn the place?"

"If it isn't too much trouble, sir," said Timulty, "now."

The old man seemed to sink deeper into his chair.

"Oh, dear," he said.

"Of course," said Nolan quickly, "if it's inconvenient, we could come back later—"

"Later! What kind of talk is *that?*" asked Casey.

"I'm terribly sorry," said the old man. "Please allow me to explain. Lady Kilgotten is asleep now, we have guests coming to take us into Dublin for the opening of a play by Synge—"

"That's a damn fine writer," said Riordan.

"Saw one of his plays a year ago," said Nolan, "and—"

"Stand off!" said Casey.

The men stood back. His Lordship went on with his frail moth voice: "We have a dinner planned back here at midnight for ten people. I don't suppose ... you could give us until tomorrow night to get ready?"

"No," said Casey.

"Hold on," said everyone else.

"Burning," said Timulty, "is one thing, but tickets is another. I mean, the theater is *there*, and a dire waste not to see the play, and all that food set up, it might as well be eaten. And all the guests coming. It would be hard to notify them ahead."

"Exactly what I was thinking," said His Lordship.

"Yes, I know!" shouted Casey, shutting his eyes, running his hands over his cheeks and jaw and mouth and clenching his fists and turning around in frustration. "But you *don't* put off burnings, you *don't* reschedule them like tea parties, dammit, you *do* them!"

"You do if you remember to bring the matches," said Riordan under his breath.

Casey whirled and looked as if he might hit Riordan, but the impact of the truth slowed him down.

"On top of which," said Nolan, "the Missus above is a fine lady and needs a last night of entertainment and rest."

"Very kind of you." His Lordship refilled the man's glass.

"Let's take a vote," said Nolan.

"Hell." Casey scowled around. "I see the vote counted already. Tomorrow night will do, dammit."

"Bless you," said old Lord Kilgotten. "There will be cold cuts laid out in the kitchen, you might check in there first;

you shall probably be hungry, for it will be heavy work. Shall we say eight o'clock tomorrow night? By then I shall have Lady Kilgotten safely to a hotel in Dublin. I should not want her knowing until later that her home no longer exists."

"God, you're a Christian," muttered Riordan.

"Well, let us not brood on it," said the old man. "I consider it past already, and I never think of the past. Gentlemen."

He arose. And like a blind old sheepherder-saint, he wandered out into the hall, with the flock straying and ambling and softly colliding after.

Half down the hall, almost to the door, Lord Kilgotten saw something from the corner of his blear eye and stopped. He turned back and stood brooding before a large portrait of an Italian nobleman.

The more he looked, the more his eyes began to tic and his mouth to work over a nameless thing.

Finally Nolan said, "Your Lordship, what is it?"

"I was just thinking," said the lord at last. "You love Ireland, do you not?"

My God, yes! said everyone. Need he ask?

"Even as do I," said the old man gently. "And do you love all that is in it, in the land, in her heritage?"

That too, said all, went without saying!

"I worry, then," said the lord, "about things like this. This portrait is by Van Dyck. It is very old and very fine and very important and very expensive. It is, gentlemen, a National Art Treasure."

"Is *that* what it is!" said everyone, more or less, and crowded around for a sight.

"Ah, God, it's fine work," said Timulty.

"The flesh itself," said Nolan.

"Notice," said Riordan, "the way his little eyes seem to follow you?"

Uncanny, everyone said.

And they were about to move on, when His Lordship said, "Do you realize this Treasure, which does not truly belong to me, nor you, but to all the people as precious heritage, this picture will be lost forever tomorrow night?"

Everyone gasped. They had *not* realized.

"God save us," said Timulty, "we can't have that!"

"We'll move it out of the house first," said Riordan.

"Hold on!" cried Casey.

"Thank you," said His Lordship, "but where would you put it? Out in the weather it would soon be torn to shreds by wind, dampened by rain, flaked by hail. No, no, perhaps it is best it burns quickly—"

"None of that!" said Timulty. "I'll take it home myself."

"And when the great strife is over," said His Lordship, "you will then deliver into the hands of the new government this precious gift of Art and Beauty from the past?"

"Er... every single one of those things, I'll do," said Timulty.

But Casey was eyeing the immense canvas, and said, "How much does the monster weigh?"

"I would imagine," said the old man faintly, "seventy to one hundred pounds, within that range."

"Then how in hell do we get it to Timulty's house?" asked Casey.

"Me and Brannahan will carry the damn treasure," said Timulty, "and if need be, Nolan, *you* lend a hand."

"Posterity will thank you," said His Lordship.

They moved on along the hall, and again His Lordship stopped, before yet two more paintings.

"These are two nudes—"

They *are* that! said everyone.

"By Renoir," finished the old man.

"That's the French gent who made them?" asked Rooney. "If you'll excuse the expression?"

It looks French, all right, said everyone.

And a lot of ribs received a lot of knocking elbows.

"These are worth several thousand pounds," said the old man.

"You'll get no argument from me," said Nolan, putting out his finger, which was slapped down by Casey.

"I—" said Blinky Watts, whose fish eyes swam about continuously in tears behind his thick glasses. "I would like to volunteer a home for the two French ladies. I thought I might tuck those two Art Treasures one under each arm and hoist them to the wee cot."

"Accepted," said the lord with gratitude.

Along the hall they came to a vast landscape with all sorts of monster beast-men cavorting about, treading fruit and squeezing summer-melon women. Everyone craned forward to read the brass plate under it: *Twilight of the Gods*.

"Twilight, hell," said Rooney. "It looks more like the start of a great afternoon!"

"I believe," said the gentle old man, "there is irony intended in both title and subject. Note the glowering sky, the hideous figures hidden in the clouds. The gods are unaware, in the midst of their bacchanal, that Doom is about to descend."

"I do not see," said Blinky Watts, "the Church or any of her girly priests up in them clouds."

"It was a different kind of Doom in them days," said Nolan. "Everyone knows *that*."

"Me and Tuohy," said Flannery, "will carry the demon gods to my place. Right, Tuohy?"

"Right!"

And so it went now along the hall, the squad pausing here or there as on a grand tour of a museum, and each in turn volunteering to scurry home through the snowfall night with a Degas or a Rembrandt sketch or a large oil by one of the Dutch masters, until they came to a rather grisly oil of a man, hung in a dim alcove.

"Portrait of myself," muttered the old man, "done by Her Ladyship. Leave it there, please."

"You mean," gasped Nolan, "you want it to go up in the Conflagration?"

"Now, this next picture . . ." said the old man, moving on.

And finally the tour was at an end.

"Of course," said His Lordship, "if you really want to be saving, there are a dozen exquisite Ming vases in the house—"

"As good as collected," said Nolan.

"A Persian carpet on the landing—"

"We will roll it and deliver it to the Dublin Museum."

"And that exquisite chandelier in the main dining room."

"It shall be hidden away until the Troubles are over," sighed Casey, tired already.

"Well, then," said the old man, shaking each hand as he passed. "Perhaps you might start now, don't you imagine? I mean, you do indeed have a largish job preserving the National Treasures. Think I shall nap five minutes now before dressing."

And the old man wandered off upstairs.

Leaving the men stunned and isolated in a mob in the hall below, watching him go away out of sight.

"Casey," said Blinky Watts, "has it crossed your small mind, if you'd remembered to bring the matches there would be no such long night of work as this ahead?"

"Jesus, where's your taste for the ass-thetics?" cried Riordan.

"Shut up!" said Casey. "Okay, Flannery, you on one end

of the *Twilight of the Gods*, you, Tuohy, on the far end where the maid is being given what's good for her. Ha! *Lift!*"

And the gods, soaring crazily, took to the air.

By seven o'clock some of the paintings were out of the house and racked against each other in the snow, waiting to be taken off in various directions toward various huts. At seven-fifteen, Lord and Lady Kilgotten came out and drove away, and Casey quickly formed the mob in front of the stacked paintings so the nice old lady wouldn't see what they were up to. The boys cheered as the car went down the drive. Lady Kilgotten waved fraily back.

From seven-thirty until ten the rest of the Treasures walked out in ones and twos.

When all the pictures were gone save one, Kelly stood in the dim alcove worrying over Lady Kilgotten's Sunday painting of the old lord. He shuddered, decided on a supreme humanitarianism, and carried the portrait safely out into the night.

At midnight, Lord and Lady Kilgotten, returning with guests, found only great shuffling tracks in the snow where Flannery and Tuohy had set off one way with the dear bacchanal; where Casey, grumbling, had led a parade of Van Dycks, Rembrandts, Bouchers, and Piranesis another; and where, last of all, Blinky Watts, kicking his heels, had trotted happily into the woods with his nude Renoirs.

The dinner party was over by two. Lady Kilgotten went to bed satisfied that all the paintings had been sent out, en masse, to be cleaned.

At three in the morning, Lord Kilgotten still sat sleepless in his library, alone among empty walls, before a fireless hearth, a muffler about his thin neck, a glass of brandy in his faintly trembling hand.

About three-fifteen, there was a stealthy creaking of parquetry, a shift of shadows, and after a time, cap in hand, there stood Casey at the library door.

"Hist!" he called softly.

The lord, who had dozed somewhat, blinked his eyes wide. "Oh, dear me," he said, "is it time for us to go?"

"That's tomorrow night," said Casey. "And anyways, it's not you that's going, it's them is coming back."

"Them? Your friends?"

"No, *yours*." And Casey beckoned.

The old man let himself be led through the hall to look out the front door into a deep well of night.

There, like Napoleon's numbed dog army of foot-weary, undecided, and demoralized men, stood the shadowy but familiar mob, their hands full of pictures, pictures leaned against their legs, pictures on their backs, pictures stood upright and held by trembling, panic-whitened hands in the drifted snow. A terrible silence lay over and among the men. They seemed stranded, as if one enemy had gone off to fight far better wars while yet another enemy, as yet unnamed, nipped silent and trackless at their behinds. They kept glancing over their shoulders at the hills and the town as if at any moment Chaos herself might unleash her dogs from there. They alone, in the infiltering night, heard the far-off baying of dismays and despairs that cast a spell.

"Is that *you*, Riordan?" called Casey nervously.

"Ah, who the hell *would* it be!" cried a voice out beyond.

"What do they *want*?" asked the old party.

"It's not so much what *we* want as what *you* now want from *us*," called a voice.

"You see," said another, advancing until all could see it was Hannahan in the light, "considered in all its aspects, Your Honor, we've decided, you're such a fine gent, we—"

"We will *not* burn your house!" cried Blinky Watts.

"Shut up and let the man talk!" said several voices.

Hannahan nodded. "That's it. We will *not* burn your house."

"But see here," said the lord, "I'm quite prepared. Everything can easily be moved out."

"You're taking the whole thing too lightly, begging your pardon, Your Honor," said Kelly. "Easy for you is not easy for us."

"I see," said the old man, not seeing at all.

"It seems," said Tuohy, "we have all of us, in just the last few hours, developed problems. Some to do with the home and some to do with transport and cartage, if you get my drift. Who'll explain first? Kelly? No? Casey? Riordan?"

Nobody spoke.

At last, with a sigh, Flannery edged forward. "It's this way . . ." he said.

"Yes?" said the old man gently.

"Well," said Flannery, "me and Tuohy here got half through the woods, like damn fools, and was across two thirds of the bog with the large picture of the *Twilight of the Gods,* when we began to sink."

"Your strength failed?" inquired the lord kindly.

"Sink, Your Honor, just plain sink, into the *ground,*" Tuohy put in.

"Dear me," said the lord.

"You can say that again, Your Lordship," said Tuohy. "Why, together, me and Flannery and the demon gods must have weighed close onto six hundred pounds, and that bog out there is infirm if it's anything, and the more we walk the deeper we sink, and a cry strangled in me throat, for I'm thinking of those scenes in the old story where the Hound of the Baskervilles or some such fiend chases the heroine out in the moor, and down she goes in a watery pit, wishing she had kept at that diet, but it's too late, and bubbles rise, to pop on the surface. All of this athrottling in me mind, Your Honor."

"And so?" the lord put in, seeing he was expected to ask.

"And so," said Flannery, "we just walked off and left the damn gods there in their twilight."

"In the middle of the *bog?*" asked the elderly man, just a trifle upset.

"Ah, we covered them up; I mean, we put our mufflers over the scene. The gods will not die twice, Your Honor. Say, did you hear *that*, boys? The gods—"

"Ah, shut up," cried Kelly. "Ya dimwits. Why didn't you bring the damn portrait in off the bog?"

"We thought we would come get two more boys to help—"

"Two more!" cried Nolan. "That's four men, plus a parcel of gods. You'd all sink *twice* as fast, and the bubbles rising, ya nitwit!"

"Ah!" said Tuohy. "I never thought of that."

"It has been thought of now," said the old man. "And perhaps several of you will form a rescue team—"

"It's done, Your Honor," said Casey. "Bob, you and Tim dash off and save the pagan deities."

"You won't tell Father Leary?"

"Father Leary, my behind. Get!" And Tim and Bob panted off.

His Lordship turned now to Nolan and Kelly.

"I see that you, too, have brought your rather large picture back."

"At least we made it within a hundred yards of the door, sir," said Kelly. "I suppose you're wondering *why* we have returned it, Your Honor?"

"With the gathering in of coincidence upon coincidence," said the old man, going back in to get his overcoat and putting on his tweed cap so he could stand out in the cold and finish what looked to be a long converse, "yes, I was given to speculate."

"It's me back," said Kelly. "It gave out not five hundred yards down the main road. The back has been springing out and in for five years now, and me suffering the agonies of Christ. I sneeze and fall to my knees, Your Honor."

"I have suffered the selfsame delinquency," said the old man. "It is as if someone had driven a spike into one's spine." The old man touched his back, carefully, remembering, which brought a gasp from all, nodding.

"The agonies of Christ, as I said," said Kelly.

"Most understandable, then, that you could not finish your journey with that heavy frame," said the old man, "and most commendable that you were able to struggle back this far with the dreadful weight."

Kelly stood taller immediately, as he heard his plight described. He beamed. "It was nothing. And I'd do it again, save for the string of bones above me ass. Begging pardon, Your Honor."

But already His Lordship had passed his kind if tremulous gray-blue, unfocused gaze toward Blinky Watts, who had, under either arm, like a dartful prancer, the two Renoir peach ladies.

"Ah, God, there was no trouble with sinking into bogs or knocking my spine out of shape," said Watts, treading the earth to demonstrate his passage home. "I made it back to the house in ten minutes flat, dashed into the wee cot, and began hanging the pictures on the wall, when my wife came up behind me. Have ya ever had your wife come up behind ya, Your Honor, and just stand there mum's the word?"

"I seem to recall a similar circumstance," said the old man, trying to remember if he did, then nodding as indeed several memories flashed over his fitful baby mind.

"Well, Your Lordship, there is no silence like a woman's silence, do you agree? And no standing there like a woman's standing there like a monument out of Stonehenge. The mean temperature dropped in the room so quick I suffered from the polar concussions, as we call it in our house. I did not dare turn to confront the Beast, or the daughter of the Beast, as I call her in deference to her mom. But finally I heard her suck in a great breath and let it out very cool and calm like a Prussian general. 'That woman is naked as a jaybird' and 'That other woman is raw as the inside of a clam at low tide.'

" 'But,' said I, 'these are studies of natural physique by a famous French artist.'

" 'Jesus come after me French,' she cried. 'Skirts half up to your bum French. Dress half down to your navel French. And the gulping and smothering they do with their mouths in their dirty novels French. And now you come home and nail 'French' on the walls. Why don't you, while you're at it, put the crucifix down and nail one fat naked lady *there*?'

"Well, Your Honor, I just shut up my eyes and wished my ears would fall off. 'Is *this* what you want our boys to look at last thing at night as they go to sleep?' she says. Next thing I know, I'm on the path, and here I am and here's the raw-oyster nudes, Your Honor, beg your pardon, thanks, and much obliged."

"They do seem to be unclothed," said the old man, looking at the two pictures, one in either hand, as if he wished to find all that this man's wife said was in them. "I had always thought of summer, looking at them."

"From your seventieth birthday on, Your Lordship, perhaps. But *before* that?"

"Uh, yes, yes," said the old man, watching a speck of half-remembered lechery drift across one eye.

When his eye stopped drifting, it found Bannock and Toolery on the edge of the far rim of the uneasy sheepfold crowd. Behind each, dwarfing them, stood a giant painting.

Bannock had got his picture home, only to find he could not get the damn thing through the door, nor any window.

Toolery had actually got his picture *in* the door, when his wife said what a laughingstock they'd be, the only family in the village with a Rubens worth half a million pounds and not even a cow to milk!

So that was the sum, total, and substance of this long night. Each man had a similar chill, dread, and awful tale to tell, and all were told at last, and as they finished, a cold snow began to fall among these brave members of the local, hard-fighting IRA.

The old man said nothing, for there was nothing really to say that wouldn't be obvious as their pale breaths ghosting the wind. Then, very quietly, he opened wide the front door and had the decency not even to nod or point.

Slowly and silently they began to file by, as past a familiar teacher in an old school, and then faster they moved. So in flowed the river returned, the Ark emptied out before, not after, the Flood, and the tide of animals and angels, nudes that flamed and smoked in the hands, noble gods that pranced on wings and hoofs, went by, and the old man's eyes shifted gently, and his mouth silently named each, the Renoirs, the Van Dycks, the Lautrec, and so on, until Kelly, in passing, felt a touch at his arm.

Surprised, Kelly looked over.

And saw that the old man was staring at the small painting beneath Kelly's arm.

"My wife's portrait of me?"

"None other," said Kelly.

The old man stared at Kelly and at the painting beneath his arm and then out toward the snowing night.

Kelly smiled.

Walking soft as a burglar, he vanished out into the wilderness, carrying the picture. A moment later, you heard him laughing as he ran back, hands empty.

The old man shook Kelly's hand, once, tremblingly, and shut the door.

Then he turned away, as if the event was already lost to his wandering child mind, and toddled down the hall with his scarf like a gentle weariness over his thin shoulders, and the mob followed him inside, where they found drinks in their great paws and saw that Lord Kilgotten was blinking at the picture over the fireplace as if trying to remember, was the Sack of Rome there in the years past? or was it the Fall of Troy? Then he felt their gaze and looked full on the encircled army and said:

"Well now, what shall we *drink* to?"

The men shuffled their feet.

Then Flannery cried, "Why, to His Lordship, of course!"

"His Lordship!" cried all eagerly, and drank, and coughed and choked and sneezed, while the old man felt a peculiar glistening about his eyes, and did not drink at all till the commotion stilled, and then said, "To our Ireland," and drank, and all said Ah, God and amen to that, and the old man looked at the picture over the hearth and then at last shyly observed, "I do hate to mention it... that picture..."

"Sir?"

"It seems to me," said the old man apologetically, "to be a trifle off center, on the tilt. I wonder if you might..."

"*Mightn't* we, boys!" cried Casey.

And fourteen men rushed to put it right.

"....put it right," said Finn, at the end of his tale.

There was silence.

At almost the same moment, John and I leaned forward and said:

"Is all that true?"

"Well," said Finn, "it is the skin of the apple, if not the core."

13

"A fool," I said. "That's what I am."

"Why?" asked John. "What for?"

I brooded by my third-floor hotel window. On the Dublin street below, a man passed, his face to the lamplight.

"Him," I muttered. "Two days ago . . ."

Two days ago, as I was walking along, someone had hissed at me from the hotel alley. "Sir, it's important! Sir!"

I turned into the shadow. This little man, in the direst tones, said, "I've a job in Belfast if I just had a pound for the train fare!" I hesitated.

"A most important job!" he went on swiftly. "Pays well! I'll—I'll mail you back the loan! Just give me your name and hotel."

He knew me for a tourist. It was too late; his promise to pay had moved me. The pound note crackled in my hand, being worked free from several others.

The man's eye skimmed like a shadowing hawk.

"And if I had *two* pounds, why, I could eat on the way."

I uncrumpled two bills.

"And *three* pounds would bring the wife, not leave her here alone."

I unleafed a third.

"Ah, hell!" cried the man. "Five, just five poor pounds, would find us a hotel in that brutal city, and let me get to the job, for sure!"

What a dancing fighter he was, light on his toes, in and out, weaving, tapping with his hands, flicking with his eyes, smiling with his mouth, jabbing with his tongue.

"Lord thank you, bless you, sir!"

He ran, my five pounds with him.

I was halfway in the hotel before I realized that for all his vows, the man had not recorded my name.

"Gah!" I cried then.

"Gah!" I cried now, my director behind me, at the window.

For there, passing below, was the very fellow who should have been in Belfast two nights before.

"Oh, I know *him*," said John. "He stopped me this noon. Wanted train fare to Galway."

"Did you give it to him?"

"No," said John simply. "Well, a shilling maybe . . ."

Then the worst thing happened. The demon far down on the sidewalk glanced up, saw us, and damn if he didn't *wave*!

I had to stop myself from waving back. A sickly grin played on my lips.

"It's got so I hate to leave the hotel," I said.

"It's cold out, all right." John was putting on his coat.

"No," I said. "Not the cold. *Them*."

And we looked again from the window.

There was the cobbled Dublin street, with the night wind blowing in a fine soot along one way to Trinity College, another to St. Stephen's Green. Across by the sweet shop, two men stood mummified in the shadows. On the corner, a single man, hands deep in his pockets, felt for his entombed bones, a muzzle of ice for a beard. Farther up, in a doorway, was a bundle of old newspapers that would stir like a pack of mice and wish you the time of evening if you walked by. Below, by the hotel entrance, stood a feverish hothouse rose of a woman, a force of nature.

"Oh, the beggars," said John.

"No, not just 'oh, the beggars,' " I said, "but oh, the people in the streets, who somehow became beggars."

"It looks like a motion picture. I could direct the lot," said John. "All of them waiting down there in the dark for the hero to come out. Let's go to dinner."

"The hero," I said. "That's *me*. Damn."

John peered at me. "You're not afraid of them?"

"Yes, no. Hell. It's a big chess game for me now. All these months I've sat up here with my typewriter, studying their off hours and on. When they take a coffee break *I* take one, run for the sweet shop, the bookstore, the Olympia Theatre. If I time it right, there's no handout, no my wanting to trot them into the barbershop or the kitchen. I know every secret exit in the hotel."

"Jesus." John laughed. "You're driven."

"I am. But most of all by that beggar on O'Connell Bridge! He's a wonder, a terror. I hate him, I love him. Come on."

The elevator, which had haunted its untidy shaft for a hundred years, came wafting skyward, dragging its ungodly chains and dread intestines after. The door exhaled open. The lift groaned as if we had trod its stomach. In a great protestation of ennui, the ghost sank back toward earth.

On the way John said, "If you hold your face right, the beggars won't bother you."

"My face," I explained patiently, "is my face. It's from Apple Dumpling, Wisconsin; Sarsaparilla, Maine. 'Kind to Dogs' is writ on my brow. Let the street be empty, then let me step forth and a strikers' march of freeloaders leap from manholes for miles around."

"If you could just learn to look over, around, or through those people, stare them *down*." John mused. "I've lived here for two years. Shall I show you how to handle them?"

"Show me!"

John flung the elevator door wide, and we advanced

through the Royal Hibernian Hotel lobby to squint out at the sooty night.

"Jesus come and get me," I murmured. "There they are, their heads up, eyes on fire. They smell apple pie already."

"Meet me down by the bookstore," whispered John. "Watch."

"Wait!" I cried.

But he was out the door, down the steps and on the sidewalk.

I watched, nose pressed to the glass pane.

The beggars on one corner, the other, across from, in front of the hotel *leaned* toward my employer. Their eyes glowed.

John gazed calmly back at them.

The beggars hesitated, creaking, I was sure, in their shoes. Then their bones settled. Their mouths collapsed. Their eyes snuffed out. Huston stared hard. They looked away.

With a rap-rap like a drum, John's shoes marched briskly away. From behind me, in the Buttery, below, I heard music and laughter. I'll run down, I thought, slug in a quick one, and bravery resurgent...

Hell, I thought, and swung the door wide.

The effect was as if someone had struck a great Mongolian bronze gong.

I heard shoe leather flinting the cobbles in sparks. The men came running, fireflies sprinkling the bricks under their hobnailed shoes. I saw hands waving. Mouths opened on smiles like old pianos. Someone shouted, "There's only a few of us left!"

Far down the street, at the bookshop, my director waited, his back turned. But that third eye in the back of his head must have caught the scene: Columbus greeted by Indians, Saint Francis amidst his squirrel friends, with a bag of nuts. Or he saw me as the Pope on Saint Peter's balcony, with a tumult below.

I was not half off the hotel steps when a woman in a gray shawl charged up, thrusting a wrapped bundle at me.

"Ah, see the poor child!" she wailed.

I stared at her baby.

The baby stared back.

God in heaven, did or did not the thing *wink* at me?

No, the babe's eyes are shut, I thought. She's filled it with gin to keep it warm for display.

My hands, my coins, blurred reaching out to her and the rest of her team.

"God thanks you, sir!"

I broke through them, running. Defeated, I could have scuffed slowly the rest of the way, my resolve so much putty in my mouth, but no, on I rushed, hearing a babe's wail down the cold wind. Blast! I thought, she's pinched it to make it weep and crack my soul!

John, without turning, saw my reflection in the bookshop window and nodded.

I stood getting my breath, brooding at my own image: my summer eyes, my ebullient and defenseless mouth.

"Say it!" I sighed. "I hold my face wrong!"

"I like the way you hold your face." John held my arm. "I wish I could do it too."

We looked back as the beggars strolled off in the blowing dark with my shillings. The street was empty now. It was starting to rain.

"Well," I said at last, "let me show you the even bigger mystery: the man who provokes me to wild rages, then calms me to delight. Solve him and you solve all the beggars that ever were."

"On O'Connell Bridge?" John guessed.

"On O'Connell Bridge," I said.

And we walked on down in the gently misting rain.

Halfway to the bridge, as we were examining some fine

Irish crystal in a window, a woman with a shawl over her head plucked at my elbow.

"Destroyed!" The woman sobbed. "My poor sister. Cancer. Her dead next month! Ah, God, can you spare a penny!"

I felt John's arm tighten to mine. I looked at the woman, split, one half of me saying, "A penny is all she asks!" the other half doubting: "Gah, she knows that by *underasking* you'll over*pay!*"

I gasped. "You're..."

Why, I thought, you're the woman who was just back by the hotel with the babe!

"I'm sick!" She pulled back in shadow. "And asking for the half dead!"

You've stashed the babe somewhere, I thought, and put on a green instead of gray shawl and run the long way 'round to cut us off.

"Cancer..." One bell in her tower, but she knew how to toll it. "Cancer..."

John cut in crisply. "Pardon, but aren't you the same woman he just paid at the hotel?"

The woman and I were both shocked at this rank insubordination.

The woman's face crumpled. I peered closer. And God, it was a *different* face. How admirable! She knew what actors know, sense, learn: that by thrusting, yelling, all fiery-lipped arrogance, one moment you are one character; then by sinking away, crumpling the mouth and eyes, in pitiful collapse, you are another. The same woman, yes, but the same face and role? No, no!

"Cancer," she whispered.

John lost my arm, and the woman found my cash. As if on roller skates, she whisked around the corner, sobbing happily.

"Lord!" In awe, I watched her go. "She's studied Stanislavsky. In one book he says that squinting one eye and twitching one lip to the side will disguise you. And what if it was true? Everything she said? And she's lived with it so long she can't cry anymore, and so has to playact in order to survive? What if?"

"Not true," said John. "But by God, she gets a role in *Moby Dick*! Can't you see her down at the docks, in the fog, when the *Pequod* sails, wailing, mourning? Yes!"

Wailing, weeping, I thought, somewhere in the chimney-smoking dark.

"Now," said John, "on to O'Connell Bridge?"

The street corner was probably empty in the falling rain for a long time after we were gone.

There stood the gray-stone bridge bearing the great O'Connell's name, and there the River Liffey rolling cold gray waters under, and even from a block off I heard faint singing. My mind ran back to ten days before.

"Christmas," I murmured, "is the best time of all in Dublin."

For beggars, I meant, but left it unsaid.

For in the week before Christmas the Dublin streets had teemed with raven flocks of children herded by schoolmasters or nuns. They clustered in doorways, peered from theater lobbies, jostled in alleys, "God Rest Ye Merry, Gentlemen" on their lips, "It Came Upon a Midnight Clear" in their eyes, tambourines in hand, snowflakes shaping a collar of grace about their tender necks. It was singing everywhere and anywhere in Dublin on such nights, and there was no night I had not walked up Grafton Street to hear "Away in a Manger" being sung to the queue outside the cinema or "Deck the Halls" in front of The Four Provinces pub. In all, I counted in Christ's season one night half a hundred bands of convent girls or public-school boys lacing the cold air and weaving great treadles of song up, down, over, and across from end to end of Dublin. Like walking in snowfalls, you could not walk among them and not be touched. The sweet beggars, I called them, who gave in turn for what you gave as you went your way.

Given such examples, even the most dilapidated beggars of Dublin had washed their hands, mended their torn smiles, borrowed banjos or bought a fiddle and killed a cat. They had even gathered for four-part harmonics. How could they stay silent when half the world was singing and the other half, idled by the tuneful river, was paying dearly, gladly, for just another chorus?

So Christmas was best for all; the beggars *worked*—off key, it's true, but there they were, one time in the year, *busy*.

But Christmas was gone, the licorice-suited children back in their aviaries, and most of the beggars of the town, shut and glad for the silence, returned to their workless ways. All but the beggars on O'Connell Bridge, who, through the year, most of them, tried to give as good as they got.

"They have their self-respect," I said, walking with John. "I'm glad that first man up ahead strums a guitar, the next one a fiddle. And there, now, by God, in the very *center* of the bridge!"

"The man we're looking for?"

"That's him. Squeezing the concertina. It's all right to look. Or I *think* it is."

"What do you mean? He's blind, isn't he?"

The rain fell gently, softly upon gray-stoned Dublin, gray-stoned riverbank, gray lava-flowing river.

"That's the trouble," I said at last. "I don't know."

And we both, in passing, looked at the man standing there in the very middle of O'Connell Bridge.

He was a man of no great height, a bandy statue swiped

from some country garden perhaps, and his clothes, like the clothes of most in Ireland, too often laundered by the weather, and his hair too often grayed by the smoking air, and his cheeks sooted with beard, and a nest or two of witless hair in each cupped ear, and the blushing cheeks of a man who has stood too long in the cold and drunk too much in the pub so as to stand too long in the cold again. Dark glasses covered his eyes, and there was no telling what lurked behind. I had begun to wonder, weeks before, if his sight prowled me along, damning my guilty speed, or if only his ears caught the passing of a harried conscience. There was an awful fear he might seize, in passing, the glasses from his nose. But I feared much more the abyss I might find, into which his senses, in one terrible roar, might tumble. Best not to know if civet's orb or interstellar space gaped behind the smoked panes.

But even more, there was a special reason why I could not let the man be.

In the rain and the wind and snow, for many long cold weeks, I had seen him standing here with no cap or hat on his head.

He was the only man in all of Dublin I saw in the downpours and drizzles who stood by the hour alone with the drench mizzling his ears, threading his ash-red hair, plastering it over his skull, riveting his eyebrows, and washing over the coal-black insect lenses of the glasses on his rain-pearled nose.

Down through the greaves of his cheeks, the lines about his mouth, and off his lips, like a storm on a gargoyle's flint, the weather ran. His sharp chin shot the guzzle in a steady fauceting off in the air, down his tweed scarf and locomotive-colored coat.

"Why doesn't he wear a hat?" I demanded.

"Why," said John, "maybe he hasn't *got* one."

"He *must* have one," I cried.

"He's *got* to have one," I said, quieter.

"Maybe he can't afford one."

"Nobody's *that* poor, even in Dublin. *Everyone* has a cap at least!"

"Well, maybe he has bills to pay, someone sick."

"But to stand out for days, weeks in the rain and not so much as flinch or turn his head, ignore the rain—it's beyond understanding." I shook my head. "I can only think it's a trick. Like the others, this is his way of getting sympathy, of making you cold and miserable as you pass, so you'll give him more."

"I bet you're sorry you said that already," John said.

"I am. I am." For even under my cap the rain was running off my nose. "Sweet God in heaven, what's the answer?"

"Why don't you ask him?"

"No!"

Then the terrible happened.

For a moment, while we had been talking in the cold rain, the beggar had been silent. Now, as if the weather had freshened him to life, he gave his concertina a great mash. From the folding, unfolding snake box he squeezed a series of asthmatic notes which were no preparation for what followed.

He opened his mouth. He sang.

The sweet clear baritone voice which rang over O'Connell Bridge, steady and sure, was beautifully shaped and controlled, not a quiver, not a flaw, anywhere. The man just opened his mouth, which meant that all kinds of secret doors in his body gave way. He did not sing so much as let his soul free.

"Fine," said John, "lovely."

"Lovely," I said. "Oh, *yes.*"

We listened while he sang the full irony of Dublin's Fair City where it rains forty days a month the winter through, followed by the white-wine clarity of Kathleen Mavourneen, Macushla, and all the other tired lads, lasses, lakes, hills, past glories, present miseries, but all somehow revived and moving about young and freshly painted in the light spring, suddenly-not-winter rain. If he breathed at all, it must have been through his ears, so smooth the line, so steady the putting forth of word following round-belled word.

"Why," John murmured, "he should be on the stage. He's too good to be standing here."

"I've thought that often."

John fumbled with his wallet. I looked from him to the beggar singing, the rain washing his bare head, streaming through his shellacked hair, trembling on his earlobes.

And then, the strange perversity. Before John could move to pay, I took his elbow and pulled him to the other side of the bridge. John resisted, gave me a look, then came along, cursing.

As we walked off, the man started another song. Glancing back, I saw him, head proud, black glasses taking the pour, mouth open, and the fine voice clear:

> I'll be glad when you're dead
>   in your grave, old man,
> Be glad when you're dead
>   in your grave, old man.
> Be glad when you're dead,
> Flowers over your head,
> And then I'll marry the journeyman ...

"Why *won't* you give him, of *all* people, money!?" said John.

The beggars of Dublin, who bothers to wonder on them, look, see, know, understand?

I for one did not in the next days.

When I did, I was sure that that stone-gargoyle man taking his daily shower on O'Connell Bridge while he sang Irish opera was *not* blind. Then again, his head to me was a cup of darkness.

One afternoon I found myself lingering before a tweed shop near O'Connell Bridge, staring in at a stack of good thick burly caps. I did not need another head cover, I had a life's supply collected in a suitcase, yet in I went to pay out money for a fine warm brown-colored cap, which I turned round and round in my hands, in a trance.

"Sir," said the clerk. "That cap is a seven. I would guess your head, sir, at a seven and one half."

"This will fit me. This will fit me." I stuffed the cap into my pocket.

"Let me get you a sack, sir—"

"No!" Hot-cheeked, suddenly suspicious of what I was up to, I paid and fled.

And there waited the bridge in the soft rain. All I need do now was walk over and—

In the middle of the bridge, the capless blind beggar was gone.

In his place stood an old man and woman cranking a great piano-box hurdy-gurdy, which ratcheted and coughed like a coffee grinder eating glass and rocks, giving forth no melody but a grand and melancholy sort of iron indigestion.

I waited for the tune, if tune it was, to finish. I kneaded the new tweed cap in my sweaty fist while the hurdy-gurdy prickled, spanged, and thumped.

"Be damned to ya!" the old man and old woman, furious with their job, seemed to say, their faces thunderous pale, their eyes red hot in the rain. "Pay us! Listen, but we'll give you no tune! Make up your own!" their mute lips said.

And standing there on the spot where the beggar always

sang without his cap, I thought: Why don't they take one fiftieth of the money they make each month and have the thing tuned? If I were cranking the box, I'd want a song, at least for myself! If *you* were cranking the box! I answered. But you're *not*! And it's obvious they hate the begging job— who'd blame them—and want no part of giving back a familiar song as recompense.

How different from my capless friend.

My *friend*?

I blinked with surprise, then stepped forward and nodded.

"Beg pardon. The man with the concertina . . ."

The woman stopped cranking and glared at me.

"Ah?"

"The man with no cap in the rain."

"Ah, *him*!" snapped the woman.

"He's not here today?"

"Do you *see* him?" cried the woman.

She started cranking the infernal device.

I put a penny in the tin cup.

She peered at me as if I'd spit on her hand.

I added another penny.

"Do you know where he is?" I asked.

"Sick. In bed. The damn cold! We heard him go off, coughing."

"Do you know where he lives?"

"No!"

"Do you know his name?"

"Now, who would know *that*!"

I stood there, feeling directionless, thinking of the man somewhere off in the town, alone. I looked at the new cap foolishly.

The two old people watched me.

I put a last shilling in the cup.

"He'll be all right," I said to no one.

The woman heaved the crank. The bucketing machine let loose a fall of glass and junk in its hideous interior.

"The tune," I said. "What *is* it?"

"You're deaf!" snapped the woman. "It's the national anthem! Do you mind removing your cap?"

I showed her the new cap in my hand.

She glared up. "Your cap, man, *your* cap!"

"Oh!" Blushing, I seized the old cap from my head.

Now I had a cap in each hand.

The woman cranked. The "music" played. The rain pelted my head, my eyelids, my mouth.

On the far side of the bridge, I stopped for the hard, the slow decision: which cap to pull on my drenched skull?

During the next week I passed the bridge often, but there was always just the old couple there with their pandemonium device, or no one there at all.

And then on a Friday night John brought a bottle and a retyped script to my room. Our talk was long and constructive, the hour grew late, there was a fire like an orange lion on the hearth, big and lively, and brandy in our glasses, and silence for a moment in the room, perhaps because quite suddenly we found silence falling in great soft flakes past the high windows.

John, glass in hand, watched the continual lace, then looked down at the midnight stones and at last said, under his breath, " 'There's only a few of us left.' "

I waited a moment and said: "I heard one of those beggars say that. What does it *mean*?"

John watched all those figures down there standing in the shadows and sipped his whiskey.

"Once I thought it meant he fought in the Troubles and there's just a few of the IRA left. But no. Or maybe he means in a richer world the begging population is melting away. But no to that too. So maybe, perhaps, he means there aren't many 'human beings' left to look, see, and understand well enough for one to ask and one to give. Everyone busy, running, jumping, there's no time to study one another. But I guess that's bilge and hogwash, slop and sentiment."

John turned from the window, walked over and took the new tweed cap from where I had placed it off the mantel and said, "Did you see the paper today?"

"No."

John took a crumpled tear sheet out of his pocket.

"There's just the item, bottom half of page five, *Irish Times*. It seems that beggar on O'Connell Bridge just got tired. He threw his concertina into the River Liffey. And jumped after it."

He was back again, then, yesterday! I thought. And I didn't see!

"The poor bastard." John laughed with a hollow exhalation. "What a funny, horrid way to die. That damn silly concertina—I hate concertinas, don't you?—wheezing on its way down, like a sick cat, and the man falling after. I laugh and I'm ashamed of laughing. Well. They didn't find the body. They're still looking."

"Oh, God!" I cried, getting up. "Oh, damn!"

John watched me carefully now. "You couldn't help it."

"I could! I never gave him a penny, not one, ever! I've been around town, shoveling out *pennies*. But never to *him*! Hell!"

I was at the window now too, staring down through the falling snow. "I thought his bare head was a trick to make me feel sorry. Damn, after a while you think everything's a trick! I used to pass there winter nights with the rain thick and him there singing, and he made me feel so cold I hated his guts. I wonder how many other people felt cold and hated him because he did that to them? So instead of getting money, he got nothing in his cup. I lumped him with the rest. But maybe he was one of the legitimate ones, the new poor just starting out this winter, not a beggar ever before, so you hock your clothes to feed a stomach and wind up a man in the rain without a cap."

The snow was falling fast now, erasing the lamps and the statues in the shadows of the lamps below.

"How do you tell the difference between them?" I asked. "How can you judge which is honest, which isn't?"

"The fact is," said John quietly, "you can't. There's no difference between them. Some have been at it longer than others and have gone shrewd, forgotten how it all started a long time ago. On a Saturday they had food. On a Sunday they didn't. On a Monday they asked for credit. On a Tuesday they borrowed their first match. Thursday a cigarette. And a few Fridays later they found themselves, God knows how, in front of a place called the Royal Hibernian Hotel. They couldn't tell you what happened or why. One thing's sure, though: they're hanging to the cliff by their fingernails. Poor bastard, someone must've stomped on that man's hands on O'Connell Bridge, and he just gave up the ghost and went over. So what does it prove? It's hard to stare them down or look away from them. I'm good at it, most of the time, but you can't run and hide forever. You can only give to them all. If you start drawing lines, someone gets hurt. I'm sorry now I didn't give that blind singer a shilling. Well. Well. Let us console ourselves, hope it wasn't money but something at home or in his past did him in. No way to find out. The paper lists no name."

Snow fell silently across our sight. Below, the dark shapes of men waited. It was hard to tell whether snow was making sheep of the wolves or sheep of the sheep, gently mantling their shoulders, their backs, their hats and shawls.

John said good night and left.

Five minutes later, going down in the haunted night elevator, I carried the new tweed cap in my hand.

Coatless, in my shirtsleeves, I stepped out into the winter night.

I gave the cap to the first man who came. I never knew if it fit. What money I had in my pockets was soon gone.

Then, left alone, shivering, I glanced up. I froze, blinking up through the drift, the drift, the silent drift of blinding snow. I saw the high hotel windows, the lights, the shadows.

What's it like up there? I thought. *Are fires lit? Is it warm as breath? Who are all those people? Are they drinking? Are they happy?*

Do they even know I'm here?

14

"Well, have you solved the puzzle of the Irish as yet?" said Finn.

"They are a crossword puzzle with no numbers," I said, red-penciling a scene from my screenplay, laid out on the bar.

"We are that," said Finn proudly.

It was the hour before opening and Finn had let me in through the side door so I might have a quiet time flensing if not solving the Whale and his territories.

"There's not a one of us knows who he is, nor would we want to know," added Finn, wiping the bar as if his words were there temporarily and must now be erased. "We are a mystery inside a box inside a maze with no door and no key. We are a soup that's all flavor and little sustenance."

"I wouldn't say *that,* Finn."

"All right then, I take it back. If you have not solved the Irish, have you X-rayed the Whale and discovered the bones?"

"A rough equivalent." I underlined some words in my text. "He was all white, white as an ice floe at dawn, white as a panic dream that will not turn off. An illumination gone to sea. A terror behind your eyes that will not fade. Which, Finn?"

"Put 'em all in," said Finn. "They pass the time."

"You're not supposed to pass the time in screenplays, Finn."

"It's my way of speaking. But you must admit, most fillums pass time but do not serve."

"Why, you're a movie critic, Finn!"

"No, only one who when he finds the popcorn unsalted knows he's in for a bad night. When you finish that damned script, will you leave the day before or the week after? I mean, if you haven't figured Eire out, would you linger to read between the lines?"

"I am of two minds, Finn."

"Well, don't tear yourself in half. Lie easy in the ditch, as the hog farmers say."

"Let me write that down!"

"Lie easy . . ." Finn dictated it, leaning over the bar, pleased. " . . . in the ditch . . ."

15

The phone rang at three in the morning.

My wife, I thought, and then, no.

Nora, I thought. She's the only one in all the world, in all my life, would call and call at three a.m., of all ungodly hours.

I reached out from my bed in the dark, found the phone, put it to my ear, and declared:

"Nora!"

"My God," a woman's voice said, "how did you *guess*?!"

"Simple," I said, beginning to laugh. "It's the middle of

the night, halfway to sunrise. The only other one who bothers this late, this early, is God."

"Oh, William, Willy, Will!" cried Nora, off somewhere in snowstorms of static. "William!"

She had long ago dubbed me Shakespeare Second or was it Third, and never called me anything else except.

"Willie. Will! What's all this about White Whales and screenplays and famous directors? Are you fabulously rich at last? And do rich writers buy fabulous estates?"

"At five hours before dawn, if dawn ever comes in Ireland? Nora, Nora, don't you ever say hello?"

"Life's too short for hellos, and now there's no time for decent goodbyes. Could you buy Grynwood? Or might you take it as a gift if I gave it?"

"Nora, Nora, your family house, two hundred rich years old? What would happen to wild Irish social life, the parties, drinks, gossip? You can't throw it all away!"

"Can and shall. Oh, I've trunks of money waiting out in the rain this moment. But, Willie, William, I'm *alone* in the house. The servants have fled to help the Aga. Now, on this final night, Will, I need a writer man to see the Ghost. Does your skin prickle? Come. I've mysteries and a home to give away. Willie, oh, Will, oh, William!"

Click. Silence.

John was off in London to cast our film, so I was free. But it was too late Friday and too early Saturday for me to bother Mike to come from Kilcock to drive me to Bray, so I hired a chauffeur and car and we motored down the snake roads through the green hills toward the blue lake and the lush grass meadows of the hidden and fabulous house called Grynwood.

I laughed again, recalling our meeting so many years ago, a beggar writer taken in off the Dublin streets by this mad-woman driving by! Nora! Nora! For all her gab, a party was probably on the tracks this moment, lurched toward wondrous destruction. Actors might fly from London, designers from Paris, some of the Guinness girls might motor over from Galway.

You'll be beautifully mellow by eight o'clock, I thought, ricocheted to sleep, if you're not careful, by concussions of bodies before midnight, drowse till noon, then even more nicely potted by Sunday high tea. And somewhere in between, the rare game of musical beds with Irish and French countesses, ladies, and plain field-beast art majors crated in from the Sorbonne, some with chewable mustaches, some not, and Monday ten million years off. Tuesday, I would call Mike and motor oh so carefully back to Dublin, nursing my body like a great impacted wisdom tooth, gone much too wise and avoiding encounters with women, pain-flashing with memory and able, if my wife called, to plead innocence.

Traveling, I remembered the first time I had arrived at Nora's.

Nora had sent someone to pick me up. A mad old duchess with flour-talcumed cheeks and the teeth of a barracuda had wrestled me and a sports car down an Irish road that night, braying into the warm wind:

"You shall love Nora's menagerie zoo and horticultural garden! Her friends are beasts and keepers, tigers and pussies, rhododendrons and flytraps. Her streams run cold fish, hot trout. Hers is a great greenhouse where brutes grow outsize, force-fed by unnatural airs, enter Nora's on Friday with clean linen, sog out with the wet wash-soiled bedclothes Monday, feeling as if you had meantime inspired, painted, and lived through all Bosch's Temptations, Hells, Judgments, and Dooms! Live at Nora's and you reside in a great warm giant's cheek, deliciously gummed and morseled hourly. You will pass, like victuals, through her mansion. When it has crushed forth your last sweet-sour sauce and dismarrowed your youth-candied bones, you will be discarded in a cold iron-country train station lonely with rain."

"I'm *coated* with enzymes?" I cried above the engine roar. "No house can break down my elements or take nourishment from my Original Sin."

"Fool!" The duchess laughed. "We shall see most of your skeleton by sunrise Sunday!"

I came out of memory as we came out of the woods at a fine popping glide and slowed because the very friction of beauty stayed the heart, the mind, the blood, and therefore the foot of the driver upon the throttle.

There under a blue-lake sky by a blue-sky lake lay Nora's own dear place, the grand house called Grynwood. It nestled in the roundest hills by the tallest trees in the deepest forest in all Eire. It had towers built back in time by unremembered people and unsung architects for reasons never to be guessed. Its gardens had first flowered five hundred years ago, and there were outbuildings scattered from a creative explosion two hundred years gone amongst old tombyards and crypts. Here was a convent hall become a horse barn of the landed gentry, there were new wings built on in 1890. Out around the lake was a hunting-lodge ruin where wild horses might plunge through minted shadow to sink away in green-water grasses by yet further cold ponds and single graves of daughters whose sins were so rank they were driven forth even in death to the wilderness, sunk traceless in the gloom.

As if in bright welcome, the sun flashed vast tintinnabulations from scores of house windows. Blinded, the driver clenched the car to a halt.

Eyes shut, I licked my lips, remembering that long-ago first night at Grynwood.

Nora herself opening the front door. Standing stark naked, she announced:

"You're too late, Duchess! It's all over!"

"Nonsense. Hold this, boy, and this."

Whereupon the duchess, in three nimble moves, peeled herself raw as a blanched oyster in the summer doorway.

I stood aghast, gripping her clothes.

"Come in, boy, you'll die of the heat!" And the bare duchess walked serenely away among the well-dressed people.

"Beaten at my own game," cried Nora. "Now, to compete, I must put my clothes back on. And I was *so* hoping to shock you."

"Never fear," I said. "You have."

"Come help me dress."

In the alcove, we waded among her clothes, which lay in misshapen pools of musky scent upon a parqueted floor.

"Hold the panties while I slip into them."

I flushed, then burst into an uncontrollable fit of laughter. "Forgive me," I said at last, snapping her bra in back. "It's just here it is early evening, and I'm putting you *into* your clothes. I—"

A door slammed somewhere. I glanced around for the duchess.

"Gone," I murmured. "The house has devoured her already."

True. I didn't see the duchess again until the rainy Monday morn she had predicted. By then she had forgotten my name, my face, and the soul behind my face.

"My God," I said. "What's that, and *that*?"

Still dressing Nora, we had arrived at the library door. Inside, like a bright mirror-maze, the weekend guests turned.

"That"—Nora pointed—"is the Ballet Russe. Just arrived. To the left, the Viennese Dancers. Divine casting. Enemy ballet mobs unable, because of language, to express their scorn and vitriol. They must pantomime their catfight. Stand aside, Willie. What was Valkyrie must become Rhine Maiden. And those boys *are* Rhine Maidens. Guard your flank!"

Nora was right.

The battle was joined.

The tiger lilies leaped at each other, jabbering in tongues. Then, frustrated, they fell away, flushed. With a bombardment of slammed doors, the enemies plunged off to scores of rooms. What was horror became horrible friendship, and what was friendship became steam-room oven-bastings of unabashed and, thank God, hidden affection.

After that it was one grand crystal-chandelier avalanche of writer-artist-choreographer-poets down the swift-sloped weekend.

Somewhere I was caught and swept in the heaped pummel of flesh headed straight for a collision with the maiden-aunt reality of Monday noon.

Now, many lost parties, many lost years later, as my car drove away, here I stood.

And there stood Grynwood manse, very still.

No music played. No cars arrived.

Hello, I thought. A new statue down by the lake. Hello again. Not a statue . . . but Nora herself, seated alone, legs drawn under her dress, face pale, staring at Grynwood as if I had not arrived, was nowhere in sight.

"Nora . . . ?" But her gaze was so steadily fixed to the house wings, its mossy roofs and windows full of empty sky, I turned to stare at it myself.

Something *was* wrong. Had the house sunk two feet into the earth? Or had the earth sunk all about, leaving it stranded forlorn in the high chill air? Had earthquakes shaken the windows atilt so they mirrored intruders with distorted gleams and glares?

The front door of Grynwood stood wide open. From this door, the house breathed out upon me.

Subtle. Like waking by night to feel the push of warm air from your wife's nostrils, but suddenly terrified, for the scent of her breath has changed, the smells of someone else! You want to seize her awake, cry her name. Who *is* she, how, what? But heart thudding, you lie sleepless by some stranger in bed.

I walked. I sensed my image, caught in a thousand windows, moving across the grass to stand over a silent Nora.

A thousand of me sat quietly down.

Nora, I thought. Oh, dear God, here we are again.

That first visit to Grynwood . . .

And then here and there through the years we had met like people brushing in a crowd, like lovers across the aisle and strangers on a train, and, with the whistle crying the next quick stop, touched hands or allowed our bodies to be bruised together by the crowd cramming out as the doors flung wide, then, impelled, no more touch, no word, nothing for years.

Or it was as if at high noon midsummer every year or so we ran off up the vital strand, never dreaming we might come back and collide in mutual need. And then somehow another summer ended, a sun went down, and there came Nora dragging her empty sand pail and here I came with scabs on my knees, and the beach empty and a strange season gone, and just us left to say hello Nora, hello William, as the wind rose and the sea darkened as if a great herd of octopi suddenly swam by with their inks.

I had often wondered if a day might come when we would circle the long way round and stay. Somewhere back in time there had been one moment, balanced like a feather trembled by our breaths from either side, that held our love warmly and perfectly in poise.

But that was because I had bumped into Nora in Venice, with her roots packed, far from home, away from Grynwood. In Venice, free of her house, she might truly have belonged to someone else, perhaps even to me.

Somehow our mouths had been too busy with each other to ask permanence. Next day, healing our lips, puffed from mutual assaults, we had not the strength to say forever-as-of-now, more tomorrows this way, an apartment, a house anywhere! But not Grynwood, not Grynwood ever again. Stay! Perhaps the light of noon was cruel, perhaps it showed too many of our pores. Or perhaps, more accurately, the nasty children were bored again. Or terrified of a prison of two! Whatever the reason, the feather, once briefly lofted on champagne breath, fell. Neither of us knew which ceased breathing on it first. Nora pretended an urgent telegram and fled away to Grynwood.

We spoiled children never wrote. I did not know what sand castles she had smashed. She did not know what Indian Madras had bled color from passion's sweat on my back. Very simply, I married. Most incredibly, I was happy.

And now here we were again come from opposite directions late on a strange day by a familiar lake, calling to each other without calling, running to each other without moving, as if we had not been years apart.

"Nora." I took her hand. It was cold. "What's happened?"

"Happened!?" She laughed, grew silent, staring away. Suddenly she laughed again, that difficult laughter that might instantly flush with tears. "Oh, my dear Willie, think wild, think all, jump hoops, and come round to maniac dreams. Happened, Willie, happened?!"

She grew frightfully still.

"Where are the servants, the guests . . . ?"

"The party," she said, "was last night."

"Impossible! You've never had just a Friday-night bash. Sundays have always seen your lawn littered with demon wretches strewn and bandaged with bedclothes. Why . . . ?"

"Why did I invite you out today, you want to ask, Willie?"

Nora still looked only at the house. "To give you Grynwood. A gift, Will, if you can force it to let you stay, if it will put up with you—"

"I don't want the house!" I burst in.

"Oh, it's not if you want *it*, but if it wants *you*. It threw us *all* out, Willie."

"Last night . . . ?"

"Last night the last great party at Grynwood didn't come off. Mag flew from Paris. The Aga sent a fabulous girl from Nice. Roger, Percy, Evelyn, Vivian, Jon were here. That bull-fighter who almost killed the playwright over the ballerina was here. The Irish dramatist who falls off stages drunk was here. Ninety-seven guests teemed in that door between five and seven last night. By midnight they were gone."

I walked across the lawn. I looked down. Yes, still fresh in the grass: the tire marks of four dozen cars.

"It wouldn't let us have the party, William," Nora called faintly.

I turned blankly. "It? The house?"

"Oh, the music was splendid but went hollow upstairs. We heard our laughter ghost back from the topmost halls. The party clogged. The *petits fours* were clods in our throats. The wine ran sour down our chins. No one got to bed for even three minutes. Doesn't it sound a lie? But Limp Meringue Awards were given to all and they went away and I slept bereft on the lawn all night. Guess why? Come look, Willie."

We walked up to the open front door of Grynwood.

"What shall I look for?"

"Everything. All the rooms. The house itself. The mystery. Guess. And when you've guessed a thousand times I'll tell you why I can never live here again, must leave, why Grynwood is yours if you wish. Go in, alone."

And in I went, slowly, one step at a time.

I moved quietly on the lovely lion-yellow hardwood parquetry of the great hall. I gazed at the Aubusson wall tapestry. I examined the ancient white marble Greek medallions displayed on green velvet in a crystal case.

"Nothing," I called back to Nora out there in the late cooling day.

"No. Everything," she called. "Go on."

The library was a deep warm sea of leather smell where five thousand books gleamed their colors of hand-rubbed cherry, lime, and lemon bindings. Their gold eyes, bright titles, glittered. Above the fireplace, which could have kenneled two firedogs and ten great hounds, hung the exquisite Gainsborough *Maidens and Flowers* that had warmed the family for generations. It was a portal overlooking summer weather. One wanted to lean through and sniff wild seas of flowers, touch harvests of peach-maiden girls, hear the machinery of bees bright-stitching up the glamorous airs.

"Well?" called a far voice.

"Nora!" I cried. "Come in! There's nothing to fear! It's still daylight!"

"No," said the far voice sadly. "The sun is going down. What do you see, William?"

Out in the hall again, by the spiral stairs, I called, "The parlor. Not a dust speck on the air. I'm opening the cellar door. A million barrels and bottles. Now the kitchen. Nora, this is lunatic!"

"Yes, isn't it?" wailed the far voice. "Go back to the library. Stand in the middle of the room. See the Gainsborough *Maidens and Flowers* you always loved?"

"It's there."

"It's not. See the silver Florentine humidor?"

"I see it."

"You don't. See the great maroon leather chair where you drank sherry with Father?"

"Yes."

"No," sighed the voice.

"Yes, *no*? Do, *don't*? Nora, enough!"

"More than enough, Will. Can't you guess? Don't you *feel* what happened to Grynwood?"

I ached, turning. I sniffed the strange air.

"William," said Nora, far out by the open front door. "Four years ago," she said faintly, "four years ago . . . Grynwood burned completely to the ground."

I ran.

I found Nora pale at the door.

"It *what*!?" I shouted.

"Burned to the ground," she said. "Utterly. Four years ago."

I took three long steps outside and looked up at the walls and windows.

"Nora, it's standing, it's all here!"

"No, it isn't, Will. That's not Grynwood."

I touched the gray stone, the red brick, the green ivy. I ran my hand over the carved Spanish front door. I exhaled. "It *can't* be."

"*Is*," said Nora. "All new. Everything from the cellar stones up. New, Will. New, Willie. New."

"This *door*?"

"Sent up from Madrid last year."

"This pavement?"

"Quarried near Dublin fourteen months ago. The windows from Waterford last spring."

I stepped through the front door.

"The parqueting?"

"Finished in France and shipped over autumn last."

"But . . . but that *tapestry*!?"

"Woven near Paris, hung in April."

"But it's all the *same*, Nora!"

"Yes, isn't it? I traveled to Greece to duplicate the marble relics. The crystal case I had made too, in Rheims."

"The library!"

"Every book, all bound the same way, stamped in similar gold, put back on similar shelves. The library alone cost one hundred thousand pounds to reproduce."

"The same, the same, Nora," I cried, in wonder, "oh God, the same," and we were in the library and I pointed at the silver Florentine humidor. "That, of course, was saved out of the fire?"

"No, no, I'm an artist. I remembered. I sketched, I took the drawings to Florence. They finished the fraudulent fake in July."

"The Gainsborough *Maidens and Flowers*!?"

"Fritzi's work! Fritzi, that horrible drip-dry beatnik painter in Montmartre? Who threw paint on canvas and flew them as kites over Paris so the wind and rain patterned beauty for him, which he sold for exorbitant prices? Well, Fritzi, it turns out, is a secret Gainsborough fanatic. He'd kill me if he knew I told. He painted this *Maidens* from memory. Isn't it *fine*?"

"Fine, fine—oh God, Nora, are you telling the truth?"

"I wish I weren't. Do you think I've been mentally ill, William? Naturally you *might* think. Do you believe in good and evil, Willie? I didn't used. But now, quite suddenly, I have turned old and rain-dowdy. I have hit forty, forty has hit me, like a locomotive. Do you know what I think? The house destroyed *itself*."

"It *what*?"

She went to peer into the halls, where shadows gathered now, coming in from the gray day.

"When I first came into my money, at eighteen, when people said Guilt, I said Bosh. They cried Conscience. I cried

Crapulous Nonsense! But in those days the rain barrel was empty. A lot of strange rain has fallen since and gathered in me, and to my cold surprise I find me to the brim with old sin and know there *is* conscience and guilt.

"There are a thousand young men in me, William.

"They thrust and buried themselves there. When they withdrew, William, I thought they withdrew. But no, no, now I'm sure there is not a single one whose barb, whose lovely poisoned thorn, is not caught in my flesh, one place or another. God, God, how I loved their barbs, their thorns. God, how I loved to be pinned and bruised. I thought the medicines of time and travel might heal the grip marks. But now I know I am all fingerprints. There lives no inch of my flesh, Will, that is not FBI file systems of palm print and Egyptian whorl of finger stigmata. I have been stabbed by a thousand lovely boys and thought I did not bleed, but God, I do bleed now. I have bled all over this house. And my friends who denied guilt and conscience, in a great subway heave of flesh, have trammeled through here and jounced and mouthed each other and sweat upon floors and buckshot the walls with their agonies and descents, each from the other's crosses. The house has been stormed by assassins, Willie, each seeking to kill the other's loneliness with their short swords, no one finding surcease, only a momentary groaning out of release.

"I don't think there has ever been a happy person in this house, Will, I see that now.

"Oh, it all *looked* happy. When you hear so much laughter and see so much drink and find human sandwiches in every bed, pink and white morsels to munch on, you think: what joy! how happy-fine!

"But it is a lie, Willie, you and I know that, and the house drank the lie in my generation and Father's before me and Grandfather's beyond. It was always a happy house, which means a dreadful estate. The assassins have wounded each other here for long over two hundred years. The walls dripped. The doorknobs were gummy. Summer turned old in the Gainsborough frame. So the assassins came and went, Will, and left sins and memories of sins, which the house kept.

"And when you have caught up just so much darkness, Willie, you must vomit, *mustn't* you?

"My life is my emetic. I choke on my own past. So did this house.

"And finally, guilt-ridden, terribly sad, one night I heard the friction of old sins rubbing together in attic beds. And with this spontaneous combustion the house smoldered ablaze. I heard the fire first as it sat in the library, devouring books. Then I heard it in the cellar drinking wine. By that time I was out the window and down the ivy and on the lawn with the servants. We picnicked on the lakeshore at four in the morning with champagne and biscuits from the gatekeeper's lodge. The fire brigade arrived from town at five to see the roofs collapse and vast fire founts of spark fly over the clouds and the sinking moon. We gave them champagne also and watched Grynwood die finally, at last, so at dawn there was nothing.

"It had to destroy itself, didn't it, William, it was so evil from all my people and from me?"

We stood in the cold hall. At last I stirred myself and said, "I guess so, Nora."

We walked into the library where Nora drew forth blue-prints and a score of notebooks.

"It was then, William, I got my inspiration. Build Gryn-wood again. A gray jigsaw puzzle put back together! Phoenix reborn from the soot bin. So no one would know of its death through sickness. Not you, Willie, or any friends off in the world; let all remain ignorant. My guilt over its destruction was immense. How fortunate to be rich. You can buy a fire brigade with champagne and the village newspapers with four cases of gin. The news never got a mile out that Grynwood was strewn sackcloth and ashes. Time later to tell the world. Now to work! And off I raced to my Dublin solicitor's, where my father had filed architectural plans and interior details. I sat for months with a secretary, word-associating to summon up Grecian lamps, Roman tiles. I shut my eyes to recall every hairy inch of carpeting, every fringe, every rococo ceiling oddment, all brasswork decor, firedog, switchplates, log bucket, and doorknob. And when the list of thirty thousand items was compounded, I flew in carpenters from Edinburgh, tile setters from Sienna, stonecutters from Perugia, and they hammered, nailed, thrived, carved, and set for four years, Willie, and I loitered at the factory outside Paris to watch spiders weave my tapestry and floor the rugs. I rode to hounds at Waterford while watching them blow my glass.

"Oh, Will, I don't think it has ever happened, has it in history, that anyone ever put a destroyed thing back the way it was? Forget the past, let the bones cease! Well, not for me, I thought, no: Grynwood shall rise and be as ever it was. But while looking like the old Grynwood, it would have the advantage of being really new. A fresh start, I thought, and while building it I led such a *quiet* life, William. The work was adventure enough.

"As I did the house over, I thought I did myself over. While I favored it with rebirth, I favored myself with joy. At long last, I thought, a happy person comes and goes at Grynwood.

"And it was finished and done, the last stone cut, the last tile placed, two weeks ago.

"And I sent invitations across the world, Willie, and last night they all arrived, a pride of lion-men from New York, smelling of Saint John's bread, the staff of life. A team of light-foot Athens boys. A Negro corps de ballet from Johannesburg. Three Sicilian bandits, or were they actors? Seventeen lady violinists who might be ravished as they laid down their violins and picked up their skirts. Four champion polo players. One tennis pro to restring my guts. A darling French poet. Oh, God, Will, it was to be a swell grand fine reopening of the Phoenix from the Fire Estates, Nora Gryndon, proprietress. How did I know, or guess, the house would not want us here?"

"Can a house want or not want?"

"Yes, when it is very new and everyone else, no matter what age, is very old. It was freshly born. We were stale and dying. It was good. We were evil. It wished to stay innocent. So it turned us out."

"How?"

"Why, just by being itself. It made the air so quiet, Willie, you wouldn't believe. We all felt someone had died.

"After a while, with no one saying but everyone feeling it, people just got in their cars and drove away. The orchestra shut up its music and sped off in ten limousines. There went the entire party, around the lake drive, as if heading for a midnight outdoor picnic, but no, just going to the airport or the boats, or Galway, everyone cold, no one speaking, and the house empty, and the servants themselves pumping away on their bikes, and me alone in the house, the last party over, the party that never happened, that never could begin. As I said, I slept on the lawn all night, alone with my old thoughts, and I knew this was the end of all the years, for I was ashes, and ashes cannot build. It was the new grand lovely fine bird lying in the dark, to itself. It hated my breath in the dooryard. I was over. It had begun. There."

Nora was finished with her story.

We sat silently for a long while in the very late afternoon as dusk gathered to fill the rooms and put out the eyes of the windows. A wind rippled the lake.

I said, "It can't all be true. Surely you *can* stay here."

"A final test, so you'll not argue with me again. We shall try to spend the night here."

"Try?"

"We won't make it through till dawn. Let's fry a few eggs, drink some wine, sleep early. But lie on top of your covers with your clothes on. You shall want your clothes, swiftly, I imagine."

We ate almost in silence. We drank wine. We listened to the new hours striking from the new brass clocks everywhere in the new house.

At ten, Nora sent me up to my room.

"Don't be afraid," she called to me on the landing. "The house means us no harm. It simply fears *we* may hurt *it*. I shall sleep in a sleeping bag out on the front walk. When you are ready to leave, no matter what hour, come for me."

"I shall sleep snug as a bug," I said.

"*Shall* you?" said Nora.

And I went up to my new bed and lay in the dark, drinking cognac, feeling neither afraid nor smug, calmly waiting for any sort of happening at all.

I did not sleep at midnight.

I was awake at one.

At three, my eyes were still wide.

The house did not creak, sigh, or murmur. It waited, as I waited, timing its breath to mine.

At three-thirty in the morning the door to my room slowly opened.

There was simply a motion of dark upon dark. I felt the wind draft over my hands and face.

I sat up slowly in the dark.

Five minutes passed. My heart slowed its beating.

And then, far away below, I heard the front door open.

Again, not a creak or whisper. Just the click and the shadowing change of wind motioning the corridors.

I got up and went out into the hall.

From the top of the stairwell I saw what I expected: the front door open. Moonlight flooded the new parqueting and shone upon the new grandfather's clock which ticked with a fresh-oiled bright sound.

I went down and out the front door.

"*There* you are," said Nora, standing down by her car in the drive.

I went to her.

"You didn't hear a thing," she said, "and yet you heard something, right?"

"Right."

"Are you ready to leave now, Willie?"

I looked up at the house. "Almost."

"You know now, don't you, it is all over? You feel it, surely, that it is the dawn come up on a new morning? And feel my heart, my soul beating pale and mossy within my heart, my blood so black, Will, you have felt it often beating under your own body, you know how old I am. You know how full of dungeons and racks and late afternoons and blue hours of French twilight I am. Well..."

Nora looked at the house.

"The night I telephoned you, I lay in bed at two in the morning, I heard the front door drift open. I knew that the whole house had simply leaned itself ajar to let the latch free and glide the door wide. I went to the top of the stairs. And looking down, I saw the creek of moonlight laid out fresh in the hall. And the house so much as said, Here is the way you go, tread the cream, walk the milky new path out of this and away, go, old one, go with your darkness. You are with child. The sour-gum ghost is in your stomach. It will never be born. And because you cannot drop it, one day it will be your death. What are you waiting for?

"Well, Willie, I was afraid to go down and shut that door. And I knew it was true, I would never sleep again. So I went down and out.

"I have a dark old sinful place in Geneva. I'll go there to live. But you are younger and fresher, Will, so I want this place to be yours."

"Not so young."

"Younger than I."

"Not so fresh. It wants me to go too, Nora. The door to *my* room just now. It opened too."

"Oh, William," breathed Nora, and touched my cheek. "Oh, Willie," and then, softly, "I'm sorry."

"Don't be. We'll go together."

Nora opened her car door.

"I'll drive. I *must* drive now, very fast, all the way to Dublin. Do you mind?"

"No. But what about your luggage?"

"What's in there, the house can have. Where are you going?"

I stopped. "I must shut the front door."

"No," said Nora. "Leave it open."

"But . . . people will come in."

Nora laughed quietly. "Yes. But only *good* people. So that's all right, isn't it?"

I finally nodded. "Yes. That's all right."

I came back to stand by the car, reluctant to leave. Clouds were gathering. It was beginning to rain. Great gentle soft flurries fell down out of the moonlit sky as harmlessly soft as the gossip of angels.

We got in and slammed the car doors. Nora gunned the motor.

"Ready?" she said.

"Ready."

"William?" said Nora. "When we get to Dublin, will you sleep with me, I mean *sleep,* the next few days? I shall need someone for a few nights. Will you?"

"Of course."

"I wish," she said, and tears filled her eyes, "oh, God, how I wish I could burn myself down and start over. Burn myself down so I could go up to the house now and go in and live forever like a dairy maid full of berries and cream who might walk by tomorrow and see the open door and the house will let her in and let her stay. Oh, but hell. What's the use of talk like that?"

"Drive, Nora," I said gently.

And she drummed the motor and we ran out of the valley, along the lake, with gravel buckshotting out behind, and up the hills and through the deep forest, and by the time we reached the last rise, Nora's tears were shaken away, she did not look back, and we drove fast through the dense, falling and thicker night toward a darker horizon and a cold stone city, and all the way, never once letting go, in silence I held one of her hands.

The next morning I woke and the bed was a fall of snow with dents in it. I arose feeling, inside my mildewed suit, that I had just taken a four-day, four-night trip across country in a Greyhound bus.

There was a note pinned to the other pillow:

"Gone to Venice or Hell, whichever comes first. Thanks for the snugfest. If your wife ever leaves, come find: Nora of the long rains and the terrible fires."

"Nora," I said, looking out the window at the storm. "Goodbye."

16

Finn had an eye in the midst of the white hair over his medulla oblongata. The hair stirred. Finn's back stiffened.

"Do I hear a Yank's tread half in the door?" he said, peering into a goblet he was wiping dry, as if it were a crystal ball.

"Is my walk familiar?" I asked.

"Fingerprints and the way men walk; no two alike."

Finn turned to consider my face, hovering in gloom above the aforementioned tread.

"Are you fleeing himself?"

"Does it show?"

"He does not let up, does he?"

Finn looked around at his grand organ-console display of stouts and ales, but decided on a cognac and waited for me to come fetch.

"That will take the hinges off the hatch," he observed.

"They're gone." I wiped my mouth.

"Is it that you work seven days a week, seven to ten hours a day, with no time off? Does he let you go to the cinema?"

"Only by permission."

"To the Gents'?"

"I must beg to be excused."

"Forgive the intrusion, lad, but since you been here all this while, have you shadowed the path of any of our nice spring onion colleens, or the rutabaga and bag-of-potatoes mothers or aunts of the like? Excuse."

"I have a wife married to me at home," I said, "who may

soon be here. She'll find no lipstick on my collar or long hairs on my coat."

"Pity, and you look as if you had the strength of nine."

"Illusion," I said. "Women knock me down and carry me out."

"There's all sorts of ways to travel," admitted Finn. "But now, this day, you are in need of a brief rest before going back to hand-wrestle the two Beasts, one in the sea, one on a horse."

I sighed, and Finn replenished my brandy.

"Has he got you to take riding lessons yet?" guessed Finn. "He's great for that. A dozen pals have run through here, hired the horse, followed the hunt, and broken their selves, collarbone over ass, in the years before you limped in."

"It's these riding boots I bought."

"Which makes you halfway to the stable or the hospital or both, as of this hour. But here comes the boyos. Say not a word about himself. They would look down on you if they knew what you were hiding from here."

"Don't they look down on me already?"

"As a Yank? Sure. But as a fellow drinker? No. Hush."

And the young men and the old of Kilcock blundered in for the stuff that cleans mirrors and makes headlights shine.

I retreated to the philosopher's cubby to think.

17

I walked straight into the back workroom of Courtown House, where John was going over and answering some mail, and I did not hand him my usual six pages of screenplay. Instead, holding the pages in my hand, I took my tweed cap off my head, looked at it, looked down at my hacking coat and twill pants and jodhpur half boots and said, "John, I'm getting rid of at least half of these clothes."

John looked up and gave me that lazy, half-lidded iguana stare.

"Now, why would you do that, kid?" he said.

"No more riding lessons, John."

"Oh?"

"No more lessons and no more even trying around the edges to ride to hounds."

"Why do you say that, kid?"

"John." I took a deep breath. "What's more important, riding to hounds or killing the Whale?"

John mused it over behind his eyelids for a moment.

"What counts?" I said. "Me alive and the Whale dead or me six feet under and the screenplay not finished?"

"Let me get this clear—"

"No, John, let *me* get this clear. I almost fell three times this morning at the riding academy. It's a long way down from a horse, John, and I'm not going to go there."

"Jesus, kid, you sound upset."

"Do I?" I listened to myself. "Yeah, I am. Is it a deal, John? From here on, no black horses, just white whales?"

"Jesus Christ," said John, "if that's the way you *feel* about it—"

18

Someone's born, and it may take the best part a day for the news to ferment, percolate, or circumnavigate the Irish meadows to the nearest town, and the dearest pub, which is Heeber Finn's.

But let someone die, and a whole symphonic band lifts in the fields and hills. The grand ta-ta slams across country to ricochet off the pub slates and shake the drinkers to calamitous cries for More!

So it was this long day with suddenly no rain and—look there!—the sun returned in fraudulent simulation of some lost summer. The pub was no sooner opened, aired, and mobbed than Finn, at the door, saw a dust flurry up the road.

"That's Doone," muttered Finn. "Swift at bringing news. And the news is bad, it's *that* fast he's running!"

"Ha!" cried Doone, as he leapt across the sill. "It's done, and he's dead!"

The mob at the bar turned, as did I.

Doone enjoyed his moment of triumph, making us wait.

"Ah, God, here's a drink. Maybe that'll make you talk!"

Finn shoved a glass in Doone's waiting paw. Doone wet his whistle and arranged the facts.

"Himself," he gasped at last. "Lord Kilgotten. Dead. And not an hour past!"

"Ah, God," said one and all, quietly. "Bless the old man. A sweet nature. A dear chap."

For Lord Kilgotten had wandered their fields, pastures, barns, and this bar all the years of their lives, they agreed. His departure was like the Normans' rowing back to France or the damned Brits pulling out of Bombay.

"A fine man," said Finn, drinking to the memory, "even though he *did* spend two weeks a year in London."

"How old was he?" asked Brannigan. "Eighty-five? Eighty-eight? We thought we might have buried him long since."

"Men like that," said Doone, "God has to hit with an ax to scare them off. Paris, now, we thought *that* might have slain him, years past; but no. Drink, that should have drowned him, but he swam for the shore; no, no. It was that teeny bolt of lightning in the field's midst an hour ago, and him under the tree picking strawberries with his nineteen-year-old secretary lady."

"Jesus," said Finn. "There's no strawberries this time of year. It was *her* hit him with a bolt of fever. Burned to a crisp!"

They fired off a twenty-one-gun salute of laughs that hushed itself down when they considered the subject, and more townsfolk arrived to breathe the air and bless himself.

"I wonder," mused Heeber Finn at last, in a voice that would make the Valhalla gods sit still at table and not scratch. "I wonder. What's to become of all that wine? The wine, that is, which Lord Kilgotten has stashed in barrels and bins, by the quarts and the tons, by the scores and precious thousands, in his cellars and attics and, who knows, under his bed?"

"Aye," said everyone, stunned, suddenly remembering. "Aye. Sure. *What?*"

"It has been left, no doubt, to some damn Yank drift-about cousin or nephew, corrupted by Rome, driven mad by Paris, who'll jet in tomorrow, who'll seize and drink, grab and run, and Kilcock and us left beggared and buggered on the road behind!" said Doone, all in one breath. "Forgive my going on, Yank." He turned to see me exiting the cubby. "I meant only half what I said."

"Aye." Their voices, like muffled dark velvet drums, marched toward the night. "Aye."

"There *are* no relatives!" said Finn. "No dumb Yank nephews or dimwit nieces falling out of gondolas in Venice but swimming this way. I have made it my business to know."

Finn waited. It was his moment now. All stared. All leaned to hear his mighty proclamation.

"Why not, I been thinking, if Kilgotten, by God, left all ten thousand bottles of Burgundy and Bordeaux to the citizens of the loveliest town in Eire? To *us!*"

There was an antic uproar of comment on this, cut across

when the front doorflaps burst wide and Finn's wife, who rarely visited the sty, stepped in, glared around, and snapped:

"Funeral's in an hour!"

"An hour?" cried Finn. "Why, he's only just cold—"

"Noon's the time," said the wife, growing taller the more she looked at this dreadful tribe. "The Doc and the priest have just come from the place. Quick funeral was His Lordship's will. 'Uncivilized,' said Father Kelly, 'and no hole dug.' 'But there *is*!' said the Doc. 'Hanrahan was supposed to die yesterday but took on a fit of mean and survived the night. I treated and treated him, but the man persists! Meanwhile, there's his hole, unfilled. Kilgotten can have it, dirt and headstone.' All's invited. Move your bums!"

The double-wing doors whiffled shut. The mystic woman was gone.

"A funeral!" cried Doone, prepared to sprint.

"No!" Finn beamed. "Get out. Pub's closed. A *wake*!"

I followed them, glad to be silent myself.

"Even Christ," gasped Doone, mopping the sweat from his brow, "wouldn't climb down off the cross to walk on a day like this."

"The heat," said Mulligan, "*is* intolerable."

Coats off, they trudged up the hill, past the Kilgotten gatehouse, to encounter the town priest, Father Padraic Kelly, doing the same. He had all but his collar off, and was beet-faced in the bargain.

"It's hell's own day," he agreed. "*None* of us will keep!"

"Why all the rush?" said Finn, matching fiery stride for stride with the holy man. "I smell a rat. What's up?"

"Aye," said the priest. "There *was* a secret codicil in the will—"

"I *knew* it!" said Finn.

"What?" asked the crowd, fermenting close behind in the sun.

"It would have caused a riot if it got out," was all Father Kelly would say, his eyes on the graveyard gates. "You'll find out at the penultimate moment."

"Is that the moment before or the moment after the end, Father?" asked Doone innocently.

"Ah, you're so dumb you're pitiful." The priest sighed. "Get your ass through that gate. Don't fall in the hole!"

Doone did just that. The others followed, their faces assuming a darker tone as they passed through. The sun, as if to observe this, moved behind a cloud, and a sweet breeze came up for some moment of relief.

"There's the hole." The priest nodded. "Line up on both sides of the path, for God's sake, and fix your ties, if you have some, and check your flies, above all. Let's run a nice show for Kilgotten, and here he *comes!*"

And here, indeed, came Lord Kilgotten, in a box carried on the planks of one of his farm wagons, a simple good soul, to be sure, and behind that wagon, a procession of other vehicles, cars and trucks that stretched half down the hill in the now once more piercing light.

"What a parade," I said, but no one heard.

"I never seen the like!" cried Doone.

"Shut up," said the priest politely.

"My God," said Finn. "Do you see the *coffin?*"

"We see, Finn, we *see!*" gasped all.

For the coffin, trundling by, was beautifully wrought, finely nailed together with silver and gold nails, but the special strange wood of it . . . ?

Plankings from wine crates, staves from boxes that had sailed from France, only to collide and sink in Lord Kilgotten's cellars!

A storm of exhalations swept the men from Finn's pub. They toppled on their heels. They seized each other's elbows.

"*You* know the words, Yank," whispered Doone. "Tell us the *names*!"

I eyed the coffin made of vintage shipping crates and at last exhaled:

"Good lord! There's Châteauneuf-du-Pape, Château Lafite Rothschild! Upside down, *that* label, Le Corton! Downside up: La Lagune! What style, my God, what class! I wouldn't so much mind being buried in burned-stamp-labeled wood like that myself!"

"I wonder," mused Doone. "Can he *read* the labels from *inside?*"

"Put a sock in it," muttered the priest. "Here comes the *rest!*"

If the body in the box was not enough to pull clouds over the sun, this second arrival caused an even greater ripple of uneasiness to oil the sweating men.

"It reminds me of that wake," Doone murmured, "when someone slipped, fell in the grave, broke an ankle, and spoiled the *whole* afternoon!"

For the last part of the procession was a series of wagons and trucks ramshackle-loaded with French vineyard crates, and finally a great old brewery wagon from early Guinness days, drawn by a team of proud white horses, draped in black and sweating with the surprise they drew behind.

"I will be damned," said Finn. "Lord Kilgotten's brought his own wake *with* him!"

"Hurrah!" was the cry. "What a dear soul."

"He must've known the day would ignite a nun, or kindle a priest, and our tongues out on our chests!"

"Gangway! Let it pass!"

The men stood aside as all the vehicles, carrying strange

labels from southern France and northern Italy, making tidal sounds of bulked liquids, lumbered into the churchyard.

"Someday," whispered Doone, "we must raise a statue to Kilgotten, a philosopher of friends!"

"Pull up your socks," said the priest. "It's too soon to tell. For here comes something *worse* than an undertaker!"

"What could be worse?" I blurted, then stepped back.

With the last vehicle drawn up about the grave, a single man strode up the road, hat on, coat buttoned, cuffs properly shot, shoes polished against all reason, mustache waxed and cool, unmelted, a prim case like a lady's purse tucked under his clenched arm, and about him an air of the icehouse, a thing fresh born from a snowy vault, tongue like an icicle, stare like a frozen pond.

"Jesus," said Finn.

"It's a *lawyer*!" said Doone.

All stood aside.

The lawyer, for that is what it was, strode past like Moses as the Red Sea obeyed, or King Louis on a stroll, or the haughtiest tart on Piccadilly: choose *one*.

"It's Kilgotten's law," hissed Muldoon. "I seen him stalking Dublin like the Apocalypse. With a lie for a name: Clement! Half-ass Irish, full-ass Briton. The *worst*!"

"What can be worse than death?" I wondered.

"We," murmured the priest, "shall soon see."

"Gentlemen!"

A voice called. The mob turned.

Lawyer Clement, at the rim of the grave, took the prim briefcase from under his arm, opened it, and drew forth a symboled and ribboned document, the beauty of which bugged the eye and rammed and sank the heart.

"Before the obsequies," he said, "before Father Kelly orates, I have a message, this codicil in Lord Kilgotten's will, which I shall read aloud."

"I bet it's the Eleventh Commandment," murmured the priest, eyes down.

"What would the Eleventh Commandment *be?*" asked Doone, scowling.

"Why not: 'Thou shalt shut up and listen,' " said the priest. *"Shh."*

For the lawyer was reading from his ribboned document, and his voice floated on the hot summer wind, like this:

" 'And whereas my wines are the finest—' "

"They are *that!*" I whispered.

" '—and whereas the greatest labels from across the world fill my cellars, and whereas the people of this town, Kilcock, do not appreciate such things, but prefer the—er—hard stuff—' "

"Who *says?!*" cried Doone.

"Back in your ditch," warned the priest, *sotto voce.*

" 'I do hereby proclaim and pronounce,' " read the lawyer, with a great smarmy smirk of satisfaction, " 'that contrary to the old adage, a man can *indeed* take it with him. And I so order, write, and sign this codicil to my last will and testament in what might well be the final month of my life.' Signed, William, Lord Kilgotten."

The lawyer stopped, folded the paper, and stood, eyes shut, waiting for the thunderclap that would follow the lightning bolt.

"Does that mean," asked Doone, wincing, "that the lord intends to . . . ?"

Someone pulled a cork out of a bottle.

It was like a fusillade that shot all the men in their tracks.

It was only, of course, the good lawyer Clement, at the rim of the damned grave, corkscrewing and yanking open the plug from a bottle of La Vieille Ferme '49!

"Is this the *wake*, then?" Doone laughed nervously.

"It is *not*," mourned the priest.

With a smile of summer satisfaction, Clement, the lawyer, poured the wine, glug by glug, down into the grave, over the wine-carton box in which Lord Kilgotten's thirsty bones were hid.

"Hold on! He's gone mad! Grab the bottle! No!"

There was a vast explosion, like that from the crowd's throat that has just seen its soccer champion slain midfield!

"Wait! My God!"

"Quick. Run get the lord!"

"Dumb," muttered Finn. "His Lordship's *in* that box, and his wine is *in* the grave!"

Stunned by this unbelievable calamity, the mob and I could only stare as the last of the first bottle cascaded down into the holy earth.

Clement handed the bottle to Doone and uncorked a second.

"Now wait just one moment!" cried the voice of the Day of Judgment.

And it was, of course, Father Kelly, who stepped forth, bringing his higher law with him.

"Do you mean to say," cried the priest, his cheeks blazing, his eyes smoldering with bright sun, "you are going to dispense all that stuff in Kilgotten's pit?"

"That," said the lawyer, "is my intent."

He began to pour the second bottle. But the priest stiff-armed him, to tilt the wine back.

"And do you mean for us to just stand and *watch* your blasphemy?!"

"At a wake, yes, that would be the polite thing to do." The lawyer moved to pour again.

"Just hold it, right there!" The priest stared around, up, down, at his friends from the pub, at Finn their spiritual leader, at the sky where God hid, at the earth where Kilgotten lay playing Mum's the Word, and at last at lawyer Clement and his damned ribboned codicil. "Beware, man. You are provoking civil strife!"

"Yah!" cried everyone, atilt on the air, fists at their sides, grinding and ungrinding invisible rocks.

"Yah!" I heard myself echo.

"What year is this wine?" Ignoring them, Clement calmly eyed the label in his hands. "Le Corton, 1938. The best wine in the finest year. Excellent." He stepped free of the priest and let the wine spill.

"*Do* something!" shouted Doone. "Have you no curse handy?"

"Priests do not curse," said Father Kelly. "But Finn, Doone, Hannahan, Burke. Jump! Knock heads."

The priest marched off, and the men and I rushed after to knock our heads in a bent-down ring and a great whisper with the father. In the midst of the conference the priest stood up to see what Clement was doing. The lawyer was on his third bottle.

"Quick!" cried Doone. "He'll waste the *lot!*"

A fourth cork popped, to another outcry from Finn's team, the Thirsty Warriors, as we would later dub ourselves.

"Finn!" the priest was heard to say, deep in the heads-together. "You're a genius!"

"I am!" agreed Finn, and the huddle broke and the priest hustled back to the grave.

"Would you mind, sir," he said, grabbing the bottle out of the lawyer's grip, "reading, one *last* time, that damned codicil?"

"Pleasure." And it was. The lawyer's smile flashed as he fluttered the ribbons and snapped the will.

" '. . . that contrary to the old adage, a man can indeed take it with him . . .' "

He finished and folded the paper, and tried another smile, which worked to his own satisfaction, at least. He reached for the bottle confiscated by the priest.

"Hold on." Father Kelly stepped back. He gave a look to the crowd who waited on each fine word. "Let me ask you a question, Mr. Lawyer, sir. Does it anywhere say there just *how* the wine is to get into the grave?"

"Into the grave is into the grave," said the lawyer.

"As long as it finally *gets* there, *that's* the important thing, do we agree?" asked the priest, with a strange smile.

"I can pour it over my shoulder, or toss it in the air," said the lawyer. "As long as it lights to either side or atop the coffin when it comes down, all's well."

"Good!" exclaimed the priest. "Men! One squad here. One battalion over there. Line up! Doone!"

"Sir?"

"Spread the rations. Jump!"

"Sir!" Doone jumped.

To a great uproar of men bustling and lining up.

"I," said the lawyer, "am going to find the police!"

"Which is *me*," said a man at the far side of the mob. "Officer Bannion. Your complaint?"

Stunned, lawyer Clement could only blink and at last, in a squashed voice, bleat: "I'm leaving."

"You'll not make it past the gate alive," said Doone cheerily.

"I," said the lawyer, "am staying. But—"

"But?" inquired Father Kelly, as the corks were pulled and the corkscrew flashed brightly along the line.

"You go against the letter of the law!"

"No," explained the priest calmly. "We but shift the punctuation, cross new T's, dot new I's."

"Tenshun!" cried Finn, for all was in readiness.

On both sides of the grave, the men and I waited, each

with a full bottle of vintage Château Lafite Rothschild or Le Corton or Chianti.

"Do we drink it *all?*" asked Doone.

"Shut your gab," observed the priest. He eyed the sky. "O, Lord." The men bowed their heads and grabbed off their caps. "Lord, for what we are about to receive, make us truly thankful. And thank you, Lord, for the genius of Heeber Finn, who thought of this."

"Aye," said all, gently.

" 'Twas nothin'," said Finn, blushing.

"And bless this wine, which may circumnavigate along the way, but finally wind up where it should be going. And if today and tonight won't do, and all the stuff not drunk, bless us as we return each night until the deed is done and the soul of the wine's at rest."

"Ah, you *do* speak dear," murmured Doone.

"Shh!" hissed all.

"And in the spirit of this time, Lord, should we not ask our good lawyer friend Clement, in the fullness of his heart, to join *with* us?"

Someone slipped a bottle of the best into the lawyer's hands. He seized it, lest it should break.

"And finally, Lord, bless the old Lord Kilgotten, whose years of saving up now help us in this hour of putting away. *Amen.*"

"Amen," said all.

"Amen," said I.

"Tenshun!" cried Finn.

The men stiffened and lifted their bottles. I did the same.

"One for His Lordship," said the priest.

"And," added Finn, "one for the road!"

There was a dear sound of drinking and, Doone claimed, a glad sound of laughter from the box in the grave.

19

It was twilight in Heeber Finn's pub, with only Finn and myself and Doone and Timulty there to listen to the spigots and nurse the suds.

"There is no figuring us," said Finn. "We Irish are as deep as the sea and as broad. Quicksilver one moment. Clubfooted the next."

"To what do you refer, Finn?" I asked.

"Take the case of the AMA invited to Dublin in the final part of last year, for instance," said Finn.

"The American Medical Association?"

"That one, yes."

"*They* were invited to Dublin?"

"They were, and did."

"To what purpose?"

"To enlighten us." Finn turned to gaze in the mirror and comb his soul straight. "For we *need* enlightenment. The great unwashed is what we are. Have you stood in line at the pustoffice . . . ?"

"*Post* office? Yes." I wrinkled my nose.

"Is it not like trudging about a sheep-sty pigpen?"

"Well . . ."

"Admit it! By midwinter, the average Dubliner, for months not out of his clothes or into the tub, walks higher than his shoes by Christmas. You could plant bulbs in his armpits by New Year's. Pick penicillin off his shins Easter morn."

"What a poet," said Doone admiringly.

"Get to the point, Mr. Finn," I said, and stopped.

For you must never ask an Irishman to get to the point. The long way around and half again is more like it. Getting to the point could spoil the drink and ruin the day.

"Ahem." Finn waited for the apology.

"Sorry."

"Where was I? Oh. The AMA! Invited to Dublin they was, to teach us the cleanliness that lives skintight to godliness."

"How many medics were invited?"

"A team of surgeon-rascals, and a platoon of pill-prescribing learned physicians. There was a big ta-ta about it in the *Irish Times*. Headlines, by God. 'American Doctors Arrive to Educate the Irish and Preserve Lives!'"

"Sounds wonderful."

"It was, as long as the good feelings lasted."

"They *didn't?*"

"The College of Surgeons, Dublin branch, invited their American cousins across. It seemed a grand idea in the pub, along the bar and over the drinks. Someone must have sent a telegram late at night, when all was awash and no one recalled. Next thing you know the New York surgeons respond: 'Yes, by God. Stand back! Here we *are!*'"

"And no sooner the cable read when at Shannon a planeload of menthol-smelling docs step off and smile 'round, full of brains and lacking the wisdom to use same carefully."

"But they were given the grand tour, nevertheless?"

"Embarrassed, because they could not remember having sent the drunken telegram, the College of Surgeons, Dublin branch, put on a brave face and gave them the free rein to peer in this ward, then that, for a full week. A terrible mistake. The surgeons pared every fingernail, checked laundries for unwashed frocks, tested scalpels to see if they could split hairs or cut cheese, took snorts of oxygen, tried the anesthetics on for size, and at last—can you think it?—unmasked the Irish surgeons, college and all. A devastation."

"What happened then?"

"Why, hell man, we threw them *out* of the country!"

"They *let* themselves be thrown out?"

"It was that or be served fresh for the postmortem. They was hustled to Shannon!"

"They flew back *home?*"

"With their tails between their legs!"

"But they were invited . . ."

"None of that! They should have known, by reading the tacked-together way of the telegram, it was insufficient wits that sent the words."

"I suppose they should've . . ."

"But no, they *came!* They looked. Looking was bad enough. It was *remembering* what they saw 'twas bad. And worse, *commenting* on it! It got in the papers. The *Irish Times* rioted. Drive them from the country! the headlines said. Down AMA! Goodbye, surgeons, so long American docs. Farewell and to hell with you, Yanks!"

"And off they went?"

"Never to return."

"Yes, well, if I were *them*—"

"But you *aren't,* thank God." Finn refilled my glass.

"Will Dublin *ever* reform its hospitals, do you think?"

"No need, when there's the pustoffice at hand."

"And penicillin *in* the post office."

"On every sheepfold man and winter-moldy girl. We lug our own cures *with* us."

"I'll drink to that," I said.

"I'll join you!" said Finn.

20

"Have you ever thought, Finn—"

"I try *not* to."

"Have you ever noticed life is like those masks seen in theaters—comedy here, tragedy there?" I said.

"Before the curtain and during intermissions at the Gate, I *have* seen those masks. And?"

"Doesn't it strike you that the events of each day, or the expressions on the faces of all of us, resemble those masks, every hour changing and changing back?" I said.

"You run deep. It's simple."

"Is it?"

"On the good days, when a laugh is splitting your face like you been hit with an ax, you use the *front* door of Finn's."

"And on the bad?"

"Sneak in the *back* so no one sees you. Hide in the philosopher's cubby, where doubles and triples line up."

"I'll remember your back door, Finn."

"Do that. And stop thinking. It'll increase your ruins. My uncle in Rome once, died of the ruins. He saw so many spoiled buildings he took a fit of melancholy, sailed home, ran in my front door, and sank before he could reach the bar. If he'd only thought to use the *back*, he might have lived to drink again."

"Which uncle was that, Finn?"

"It will come. Meanwhile, take your sweaty hands off your mind. Have you ever thought, all the college professors who've wandered in here with migraines?"

"I never—"

"It's from trying for answers that brain damage occurs. Do you agree?"

"I'd like to, Finn."

"Shall I tell you what those professors need? To attend a funeral. Like the one we just had. Yes! After a great long sermon and longer drinks, they'd be glad they're alive and get the hell out and promise not to read another book for a month, or if read, don't believe it. Are you heading back to Dublin early this night?"

"I am."

"Then take this card. It's a pub on upper Grafton Street with a fine back door, where the cure is quicker and the results longer."

I looked at the card. "The Four Provinces. Is there another pub as good as Finn's in Dublin? Why didn't you tell me!"

"I like your palaver and feared the competition. Go. It's not the best, but 'twill do when Sunday stays on a full week from noon to sundown."

"Provinces," I said, reading the card aloud. "Four."

21

It was Sunday noon and the fog touching at the hotel windows when the mist did not and rain rinsing the fog and then leaving off to let the mist return and coffee after lunch was prolonging itself into tea with the promise of high tea ahead and beyond that the Buttery pub opening belowstairs, or the Second Coming and the only sound was porcelain cups against porcelain teeth and the whisper of silk or the creak of shoes until at last a swinging door leading from the small library–writing room squealed softly open and an old man, holding on to the air should he fall, shuffled out, stopped, looked around at everyone, slowly, and said in a calm drear voice:

"Getting through Sunday some*how*?"

Then he turned, shuffled back through, and let the door creak-whisper shut.

Sunday in Dublin.

The words are Doom itself.

Sunday in Dublin.

Drop such words and they never strike bottom. They just fall through emptiness toward five in the gray afternoon.

Sunday in Dublin. How to get through it somehow.

Sound the funeral bells. Yank the covers up over your ears. Hear the hiss of the black-feathered wreath as it rustles, hung on your silent door. Listen to those empty streets below your hotel room waiting to gulp you if you venture forth before noon. Feel the mist sliding its wet flannel tongue under the window ledges, licking hotel roofs, its great bulk dripping of ennui.

Sunday, I thought. Dublin. The pubs shut tight until late afternoon. The cinemas sold out two or three weeks in advance. Nothing to do but perhaps go stare at the uriny lions at the Phoenix Park Zoo, at the vultures looking as though they'd fallen, covered with glue, into the ragpickers' bin. Wander by the River Liffey, see the fog-colored waters. Wander in the alleys, see the Liffey-colored skies.

No, I thought wildly, go back to bed, wake me at sunset, feed me high tea, tuck me in again, good night, all!

But I staggered out, a hero, and in a faint panic at noon considered the day outside from the corners of my eyes. There it lay, a deserted corridor of hours, colored like the upper side of my tongue on a dim morn. Even God must be bored with days like this in northern lands. I could not resist thinking of Sicily, where any Sunday is a fete in regalia, a celebratory fireworks parade as springtime flocks of chickens and humans strut and pringle the warm pancake-batter alleys, waving their combs, their hands, their feet, tilting their sun-blazed eyes, while music in free gifts leaps or is thrown from each never-shut window.

But Dublin! Dublin! Ah, you great dead brute of a city! I thought, peering from the hotel lobby window at the rained-on, sooted-over corpse. Here are two coins for your eyes!

Then I opened the door and stepped out into all of that criminal Sunday which awaited only me.

I shut another door in The Four Provinces. I stood in the deep silence of this Sabbath pub. I moved noiselessly to whisper for the best drink and stood a long while nursing my soul. Nearby, an old man was similarly engaged in finding the pattern of his life in the depths of his glass. Ten minutes must have passed when, very slowly, the old man raised his head to stare deep beyond the fly specks on the mirror, beyond me, beyond himself.

"What have I done," he mourned, "for a single mortal soul this day? Nothing! And that's why I feel so terrible destroyed."

I waited.

"The older I get," said the man, "the less I do for people. The less I do, the more I feel a prisoner at the bar. Smash and grab, that's me!"

"Well—" I said.

"No!" cried the old man. "It's an awesome responsibility when the world runs to hand you things. For an instance: sunsets. Everything pink and gold, looking like those melons they ship up from Spain. That's a gift, ain't it?"

"It is."

"Well, who do you thank for sunsets? And don't drag the Lord in the bar, now! Any remarks to Him are too quiet. I mean someone to grab and slap their back and say thanks for the fine early light this morn, boyo, or much obliged for the look of them damn wee flowers by the road this day, and the grass laying about in the wind. Those are gifts too, who'll deny it?"

"Not me," I said.

"Have you ever waked middle of the night and felt summer

coming on for the first time, through the window, after the long cold? Did you shake your wife and tell her your gratitude? No, you lay there, a clod, chortling to yourself alone, you and the new weather! Do you see the pattern I'm at, now?"

"Clearly," I said.

"Then ain't you horribly guilty yourself? Don't the burden make you hunchback? All the lovely things you got from life, and no penny down? Ain't they hid in your dark flesh somewhere, lighting up your soul, them fine summers and easy falls, or maybe just the clean taste of stout here, all gifts, and you feeling the fool to go thank any mortal man for your fortune. What befalls chaps like us, I ask, who coin up all their gratitude for a lifetime and spend none of it, misers that we be? One day, don't we crack down the beam and show the dry rot?"

"I never thought—"

"Think, man!" he cried. "You're American, ain't you, and young? Got the same natural gifts as me? But for lack of humbly thanking someone somewhere somehow, you're getting round in the shoulder and short in the breath. Act, man, before you're the walking dead!"

With this he lapsed quietly into the final half of his reverie, with the Guinness lapping a soft lace mustache slowly along his upper lip.

I stepped from the pub into the Sunday weather.

I stood looking at the gray-stone streets and the gray-stone clouds, watching the frozen people trudge by exhaling gray funeral plumes from their wintry mouths.

Days like this, I thought, all the things you never did catch up with you, unravel your laces, itch your beard. God help any man who hasn't paid his debts this day.

Drearily, I turned like a weathercock in a slow wind. I stood very still. I listened.

For it seemed the wind had shifted and now blew from the west country and brought with it a prickling and tingling: the strum of a harp.

"Well," I whispered.

As if a cork had been pulled, all the heavy gray sea waters vanished roaring down a hole in my shoe; I felt my sadness go.

And around the corner I went.

And there sat a little woman, not half as big as her harp, her hands held out in the shivering strings like a child feeling a fine clear rain.

The harp threads flurried; the sounds dissolved like shudders of disturbed water nudging a shore. "Danny Boy" leapt out of the harp. "Wearin' of the Green" sprang after, full-clothed. Then "Limerick Is My Town, Sean Liam Is My Name" and "The Loudest Wake That Ever Was." The harp sound was the kind of thing you feel when champagne, poured in a full big glass, prickles your eyelids, sprays soft on your brow.

Spanish oranges bloomed in my cheeks. My breath fifed my nostrils. My feet minced, hidden, a secret dancing in my motionless shoes.

The harp played "Yankee Doodle."

And then I turned sad again.

For look, I thought, she doesn't see her harp. She doesn't hear her music!

True. Her hands, all alone, jumped and frolicked on the air, picked and pringled the strings, two ancient spiders busy at webs quickly built, then, torn by wind, rebuilt. She let her fingers play abandoned, to themselves, while her face turned this way and that, as if she lived in a nearby house and need only glance out on occasion to see her hands had come to no harm.

"Ah . . ." My soul sighed in me.

Here's your chance! I almost shouted. Good God, of course!

But I held to myself and let her reap out the last full falling sheaves of "Yankee Doodle."

Then, heartbeat in throat, I said:

"You play beautifully."

Thirty pounds melted from my body.

The woman nodded and began "Summer on the Shore," her fingers waving mantillas from mere breath.

"You play very beautifully indeed," I said.

Another twenty pounds fell from my limbs.

"When you play forty years," she said, "you don't notice."

"You play well enough to be in a theater."

"Be off with you!" Two sparrows pecked in the shuttling loom. "Why should I think of orchestras and bands?"

"It's indoors work," I said.

"My father," she said, while her hands went away and returned, "made this harp, played it fine, taught me how. God's sake, he said, keep out from under roofs!"

The old woman blinked, remembering. "Play out back, in front, around the sides of theaters, Da said, but don't play in where the music gets snuffed. Might as well harp in a coffin!"

"Doesn't this rain hurt your instrument?"

"It's inside places hurt harps with heat and steam, Da said. Keep it out, let it breathe, take on fine tones and timbres from the air. Besides, Da said, when people buy tickets, each thinks it's in him to yell if you don't play up, down, sideways, for him alone. Shy off from that, Da said; they'll call you handsome one year, brute the next. Get where they'll pass on by; if they like your song—hurrah! Those that don't will run from your life. That way, girl, you'll meet just those who lean from natural bent in your direction. Why closet yourself with demon fiends when you can live in the streets' fresh wind with abiding angels? But I do go on. Ah, now, why?"

She peered at me for the first time, like someone come from a dark room, squinting.

"Who are you?" she asked. "You set my tongue loose! What're you up to?"

"Up to no good until a minute ago when I came around this corner," I said. "Ready to knock over Nelson's pillar. Ready to pick a theater queue and brawl along it, half weeping and half blasphemous . . ."

"I don't see you doing it." Her hands wove out another yard of song. "What changed your mind?"

"You," I said.

I might have fired a cannon in her face.

"Me?" she said.

"You picked the day up off the stones, gave it a whack, set it running with a yell again."

"*I* did that?"

For the first time, I heard a few notes missing from the tune.

"Or, if you like, those hands of yours that go about their work without your knowing."

"The clothes must be washed, so you wash them."

I felt the iron weights gather in my limbs.

"Don't!" I said. "Why should we, coming by, be happy with this thing, and not you?"

She cocked her head; her hands moved slower still.

"And why should you bother with the likes of *me*?"

I stood before her, and could I tell what the man told me in the lulling quiet of The Four Provinces. Could I mention the hill of beauty that had risen to fill my soul through a lifetime, and myself with a toy sand-shovel doling it back to the world in dribs and drabs? Should I list all my debts to

people on stages and silver screens who made me laugh or
cry or just come alive, but no one in the dark theater to turn
to and dare shout, "If you ever need help, I'm your friend!"
Should I recall for her the man on a bus ten years before who
chuckled so easy and light from the last seat that the sound
of him melted everyone else to laughing warm and rollicking
off out the doors, but with no one brave enough to pause and
touch the man's arm and say, "Oh, man, you've favored us
this night; Lord bless you!" Could I tell how she was just one
part of a great account long owed and due? No, none of this
could I tell.

"Imagine something."

"I'm ready," she said.

"Imagine you're an American writer, looking for material,
far from home, wife, children, friends, in a cheerless hotel,
on a bad gray day with naught but broken glass, chewed
tobacco, and sooty snow in your soul. Imagine you're walking
in the damned cold streets and turn a corner, and there's this
little woman with a golden harp and everything she plays is
another season—autumn, spring, summer—coming, going
in a free-for-all. And the ice melts, the fog lifts, the wind
burns with June, and ten years shuck off your life. Imagine,
if you please."

She stopped her tune.

She was shocked at the sudden silence.

"You *are* daft," she said.

"Imagine you're me," I said. "Going back to my hotel now.
And on my way I'd like to hear anything, anything at all.
Play. And when you play, walk off around the corner and
listen."

She put her hands to the strings and paused, working her
mouth. I waited. At last she sighed, she moaned. Then suddenly she cried:

"Go on!"

"What . . . ?"

"You've made me all thumbs! Look! You've spoilt it!"

"I just wanted to thank—"

"Me behind!" she cried. "What a clod, what a brute! Mind your business! Do your work! Let be, man! Ah, these poor fingers, ruint, ruint!"

She stared at them and at me with a terrible glaring fixity.

"Get!" she shouted.

I ran around the corner in despair.

There! I thought, you've done it! By thanks destroyed, that's her story. Fool, why didn't you keep your mouth shut?

I sank, I leaned, against a building. A minute must have ticked by.

Please, woman, I thought, come on. Play. Not for me. Play for yourself. Forget what I said! *Please*.

I heard a few faint, tentative harp whispers.

Another pause.

Then, when the wind blew again, it brought the sound of her very slow playing.

The song itself was an old one, and I knew the words. I said them to myself.

> Tread lightly to the music,
> Nor bruise the tender grass,
> Life passes in the weather
> As the sand storms down the glass.

Yes, I thought, go on.

> Drift easy in the shadows,
> Bask lazy in the sun,
> Give thanks for thirsts and quenches,
> For dines and wines and wenches.

Give thought to life soon over,
Tread softly on the clover,
So bruise not any lover.

So exit from the living,
Salute and make thanksgiving,
Then sleep when all is done,
That sleep so dearly won.

Why, I thought, how wise the old woman is.
Tread lightly to the music.
And I'd almost squashed her with praise.
So bruise not any lover.
And she was covered with bruises from my kind thought-lessness.

But now, with a song that taught more than I could say, she was soothing herself.

I waited until she was well into the third chorus before I walked by again, tipping my hat.

But her eyes were shut and she was listening to what her hands were up to, moving in the strings like the fresh hands of a very young girl who has first known rain and washes her palms in its clear waterfalls.

She had gone through caring not at all, and then caring too much, and was now busy caring just the right way.

The corners of her mouth were pinned up, gently.

A close call, I thought. Very close.

I left them like two friends met in the street, the harp and herself.

I ran for the hotel to thank her the only way I knew how: to do my own work and do it well.

But on the way I stopped at The Four Provinces.

The music was still being treaded lightly and the clover was still being treaded softly, and no lover at all was being bruised as I let the pub door hush and looked all around for the man whose hand I most wanted to shake.

22

And on and on it went as day after day I struck and flensed the Whale, and read Marcus Aurelius and admired his suicide, and had myself taxied out each night to discuss my eight pages of daily script with the man who arose from women to ride with hounds. Then, each midnight, when I was ready to turn back to the tidal rains and the Royal Hibernian Hotel, John would wake the operator in the Kilcock village exchange and have her put me through to the warmest, if totally un-heated, spot in town.

"Heeber Finn's pub?" I'd shout, once connected. "Is Mike there? Could you send him along, please?"

My mind's eye saw them, the local boys, lined up, peering over the barricade at that freckled mirror-frozen winter pond and themselves all drowned and deep in that lovely ice. I heard Heeber Finn sing out from the phone and Mike's quick shout:

"Just look! I'm headin' for the door!"

Early on, I learned that "headin' for the door" was no nerve-shattering process that might affront dignity or destroy the fine filigree of any argument being woven with great and breathless beauty at Finn's. It was, rather, a gradual disengagement, a leaning of the bulk so one's gravity was diplomatically shifted toward that far empty side of the public room where the door, shunned by all, stood neglected.

Timing it, I figured the long part of Mike's midnight journey—the length of Finn's—took half an hour. The short part—from Finn's to the house where I waited—but five minutes.

So it was on a night late in February when I called and waited.

And at last, down through the night forest thrashed the 1928 Nash, peat-turf-colored on top, like Mike. Car and driver gasped, sighed, wheezed softly, easily, gently, as they nudged into the courtyard and I stepped down under a moonless and for a change rainless brightly starred sky.

I peered through the car window at unstirred dark; the dashboard lights had been dead these many years.

"Mike . . . ?"

"None other," he whispered secretly. "And ain't it a fine warm evenin'?"

The temperature was forty. But Mike'd been no nearer Rome than the Tipperary shoreline; so weather was relative.

"A fine warm evening." I climbed up front and gave the squealing door its absolutely compulsory, rust-splintering slam. "Mike, how've you been since?"

"Ah." He let the car bulk and grind itself down the forest path. "I got me health. Ain't that all-and-everything with Lent comin' on tomorra?"

"Lent," I mused. "What will *you* give up for Lent, Mike?"

"I been turnin' it over." Mike sucked his cigarette suddenly; the pink, lined mask of his face blinked off the smoke. "And why not these terrible things ya see in me mouth? Dear as gold fillin's, and a dread congestor of the lungs they be. Put it all down, add 'em up, and ya got a sick loss by the year's turnin', ya know. So ya'll not find these filthy creatures in me face again the whole time of Lent, and, who knows, after!"

"Bravo!" said I, a nonsmoker.

"Bravo, says I to meself," wheezed Mike, one eye flinched with smoke.

"Good luck."

"I'll need it," whispered Mike, "with the sin's own habit to be broke."

And we moved with firm control and thoughtful shift of weight, down and around a turfy hollow and through a mist and into Dublin at thirty-one easy miles an hour.

Bear with me while I stress it: Mike was the most careful driver in all God's world, including any sane, small, quiet, butter-and-milk producing country you name.

Above all, Mike stood innocent and sainted when compared to those motorists who key that small switch marked paranoia each time they fuse themselves to their bucket seats in Los Angeles, Mexico City, or Paris. Also, to those blind men who, forsaking tin cups and canes but still wearing their Hollywood dark glasses, laugh insanely through the Via Veneto, shaking brake-drum linings like carnival serpentine out their race-car windows. Consider the Roman ruins; surely they are the wreckage strewn by motorbiking otters who, all night beneath your hotel shriek down dark Roman alleys, Christians hell-bent for the Colosseum lion pits.

Mike, now. See his easy hands loving the wheel in a slow clocklike turning as soft and silent as winter constellations snow down the sky. Listen to his mist-breathing voice all night-quiet as he charms the road, his foot a tenderly benevolent pat on the whispering accelerator, never a mile under thirty, never two miles over. Mike, Mike, and his steady boat gentling a mild sweet lake where all Time slumbers. Look, compare. And bind such a man to you with summer grasses, gift him with silver, shake his hand warmly at each journey's end.

"Good night, Mike," I said at the hotel. "See you tomorrow."

"God willing," he murmured.

And he drove softly away.

Let twenty-three hours of sleep, breakfast, lunch, supper, late nightcap pass. Let hours of writing bad script into fair script fade to peat mist and rain, and here this young writer comes again, another midnight, out of that Georgian mansion, its door throwing a warm hearth of color before me as I tread down the steps to feel Braille-wise in fog for the car I knew hulked there. I heard its enlarged and asthmatic heart gasping in the blind air, and Mike coughing his "gold by the ounce is not more precious" cough.

"Ah, there you are, sir!" said Mike.

And I climbed in the sociable front seat and gave the door its slam. "Mike," I said, smiling.

And then the impossible! The car jerked as if shot from the blazing mouth of a furnace, roared, bounced, skidded, then cast itself in full, stoning ricochet down the path among shattered bushes and writhing shadows. I snatched my knees as my head hit the roof in staccato.

Mike! I almost shouted. Mike!

Visions of Los Angeles, Mexico City, Paris, jumped through my mind. I gazed in frank dismay at the speedometer. Eighty, ninety, one hundred miles; we shot out a great blast of gravel to hit the main road, rocked over a bridge, and slid down in the midnight streets of Kilcock. No sooner in than out of town at one hundred ten miles, I felt all Ireland's grass put down its ears when we, with a yell, soared over a rise.

Mike! I thought, and turned.

There he sat, only one thing the same. On his lips a cigarette burned, smoking first one eye, then the other.

But the rest of Mike, above the cigarette, was changed as if the Adversary himself had squeezed, molded, and fired him with dark hands. There he was, whirling the wheel round about, over around; here we frenzied under trestles, out of tunnels, here knocked crossroad signs spinning like weathercocks in whirlwinds.

Mike's face: the wisdom was drained from it, the eyes neither gentle nor philosophical, the mouth neither tolerant nor at peace. It was a face washed raw, a scalded, peeled potato, a face more like a blinding searchlight raking its steady and meaningless glare ahead while his quick hands snaked and bit and bit the wheel again to lean us round curves and jump us off cliff after cliff of night.

It's not Mike, I thought, it's his brother. No, a dire thing's hit his life, some affliction or blow, a family sorrow or sickness, yes, that's it.

And then Mike spoke, and his voice, it was changed too. Gone was the mellow peat bog, the moist sod, the warm fire in out of the cold rain, gone the gentle grass. Now the voice cracked at me, a clarion, a trumpet, all iron and tin.

"Well, how ya been since! How is it with ya!" he cried.

And the car, it too had suffered violence. It protested the change, yes, for it was an old and much-beaten thing that had done its time and now only wished to stroll along, like a crusty beggar, toward sea and sky, careful of its breath and bones. But Mike would have none of that, and cadged the wreck on as if thundering toward Hell, there to warm his cold hands at some special blaze. Mike leaned, the car leaned; great livid gases blew out in fireworks from the exhaust. Mike's frame, my frame, the car's frame, racked all together, shuddered and ticked wildly.

My sanity was saved from being torn clean off the bone by a simple act. My eyes, seeking the cause of their plaguing flight, ran over the man blazing there like a sheet of ignited vapor from the Abyss, and laid hold to the answering clue.

"Mike," I gasped, "it's the first night of *Lent*!"

"So?"

"So," I said, "remembering your Lenten promise, why's that cigarette in your *mouth*?"

Mike cast his eyes down, saw the jiggling smoke, and shrugged.

"Ah," he said, "I gave up the *ither*."

"The *ither*?" I cried.

"The *other*!" He corrected the word.

And suddenly it was all clear.

For what seemed like a thousand nights, at the door of the old Georgian house, I had accepted from Odd John a fiery douse of Irish "against the chill." Then, breathing hot summer charcoal from my scorched mouth, I had walked out to a cab where sat a man who, during all the long evenings' waiting for me to phone for his services, had *lived* in Heeber Finn's pub.

Fool! I thought. How could you have forgotten!

And there in Heeber Finn's, during the long hours of lazy talk that was like planting and bringing to crop a garden among busy men, each contributing his seed or flower, and wielding the implements, their tongues, and the raised, foam-hived glasses, their own hands softly curled about the dear drinks, there Mike had taken into himself a mellowness.

And that mellowness had distilled itself down in a slow rain that damped his smoldering nerves and put the wilderness fires in every limb of him out. Those same showers laved his face to leave the tidal marks of wisdom, the lines of Plato and Aeschylus, there. The harvest mellowness colored his cheeks, warmed his eyes soft, lowered his voice to a husking mist, and spread in his chest to slow his heart to a gentle trot. It rained out his arms to loosen his hard-mouthed hands on the shuddering wheel and sit him with grace and ease in his horsehair saddle as he gentled through the fogs that kept us and Dublin apart.

And with the malt on my own tongue, fluming up my sinus with burning vapors, I had never detected the scent of any spirits on my old friend here.

"Ah," said Mike again, "yes; I give up the *other*."

The last bit of jigsaw fell in place.

Tonight, the first night of Lent.

Tonight, for the first time in all the nights I had driven with him, Mike was sober.

All those other one hundred and forty–odd nights, Mike hadn't been driving careful and easy just for my safety, no, but because of the gentle weight of mellowness sloping now on this side, now on that side of him as we took the long, scything curves.

Oh, who really knows the Irish, and which half of them is which? Mike? Who is Mike—and what in the world is he? Which Mike's the real Mike, the one that *everyone* knows?

I will not think on it! I thought.

There is only *one* Mike for me. The one that Ireland shaped herself with her weathers and waters, her seedings and har-vestings, her brans and mashes, her brews, bottlings, and ladlings-out, her summer-grain-colored pubs astir and adance with the wind in the wheat and barley by night: you may hear the good whisper way out in forest, on bog, as you roll by. That's Mike to the teeth, eye, and heart, to his easygoing hands. If you ask what makes the Irish what they are, I'd point on down the road and tell where you turn to Heeber Finn's.

The first night of Lent, and before you could count nine, we were in Dublin!

The next night I was at Kilcock and coming out of the great himself's house, and there was my taxi waiting and puttering its motor. I leaned in to put a special bottle in the hands of dear Mike.

Earnestly, pleadingly, warmly, with all the friendly urging in the world, I looked into that fine man's raw, strange, torchlike face.

"Mike," I said.

"Sir!" he shouted.

"Do me a favor," I said.

"Anything!" he shouted.

"Take this," I said. "It's the best bottle of Irish moss I could find. And just before we leave now, Mike, drink it down, drink all or some. Will you do that, Mike? Will you promise me, cross your heart and hope to die, to do that?"

He thought on it, and the very thought damped the ruinous blaze in his face.

"Ya make it terrible hard on me," he said.

I forced his fingers shut on the bottle.

"Give up something *else* for Lent, Mike," I said.

"There's nothing else to give up, in all of Ireland. Wait a minute! I'll give up women!"

"Have you ever *had* any?"

"No," said Mike, "but I'll give them up anyway!"

He drank.

And as he drank, a great calm, a great peace, a great serenity came over his mouth, his eyes, his face; his bones quietly slumped in his clothes.

I looked into that face.

"Ah, Mike, Mike," I said, "you're *back*!"

"I was long away," he said.

We drove to Dublin, slowly.

23

It was when I was going into the Royal Hibernian Hotel that a beggar woman shoved her filthy baby in my face and cried:

"Ah, God, pity! It's pity we're in need of! Have you *some*?!"

I had some somewhere on my person, and slapped my pockets and fetched it out, and was on the point of handing it over when I gave a small cry, or exclamation. The coins spilled from my hand.

In that instant, the babe was eyeing me, and I the babe.

Then it was snatched away. The woman bent to paw after the coins, glancing up at me in some sort of panic.

"What on earth?" I guided myself up into the lobby, where, stunned, I all but forgot my name. "What's wrong? What *happened* out there?"

It was the baby, the beggar's child. It was the same, same nose and mouth, but the eyes, the same eyes seen years ago, when I traveled Ireland and saw the poor. Far back in 1939, yes, but—my God!—the same!

I walked slowly back to the hotel door and opened it to look out.

The street was empty. The beggar woman and her bundle had run off to some other alley, some other hotel, some other arrival or departure.

I shut the door and wandered to the elevator.

"No!" I said. "It can't be."

And suddenly remembering to move, got in.

The child would not go away.

The memory, that is.

The recollection of other years and days in rains and fogs,

the mother and her small creature, and the soot on that tiny face, and the cry of the woman herself, which was like a shrieking of brakes put on to fend off damnation.

Sometimes, late at night, I heard her wailing as she went off the cliff of Ireland's weather and down upon rocks where the sea never stopped coming or going but stayed forever in tumult.

But the child stayed too.

I caught myself brooding at tea or after supper over the Irish coffee and saying, "*That* again? Silly! Silly!"

I've always made fun of metaphysics, astrology, palmistry. But this is genetics, I thought. That *is* the same woman begged my gaze and displayed an unlovely unwashed child fourteen years ago! And what of that child; did she have a new one, or borrow one to display, as the seasons passed?

Not quite, I thought. She's a solved puzzle to me. But the babe? There was the true and incredible mystery! It, like her, had *not* changed! Incredible! Impossible! Madness!

And so it was I found myself, whenever I fled encounters with the two destroyers, film director and Whale, searching the Dublin streets for the beggar woman and her changeless babe.

From Trinity College on up O'Connell Street and way around back to St. Stephen's Green, I pretended a vast interest in fine architecture but secretly watched for her and her dire burden.

I bumped into the usual haggle of banjo pluckers and shuffle dancers and hymn singers and tenors gargling in their sinuses and baritones remembering a buried love or fitting a stone on their mother's grave, but nowhere did I surprise my quarry.

At last I approached the doorman at the Royal Hibernian Hotel.

"Nick," I said.

"Sir," said he.

"That woman who often lurks about at the foot of the steps . . ."

"Ah, the one with the *babe?*"

"Do you know her!?"

"Know her! Sweet Jesus, she's been the plague of my years since I was thirty, and look at the gray in my hair now!"

"She's been begging *that* long?"

"And forever beyond."

"Her name . . . ?"

"Molly's as good as any. McGillahee, I think. Beg pardon, sir, why do you ask?"

"Have you *looked* at her child, Nick?"

His nose winced at a sour smell. "Years back, I quit. These beggar women keep their kids in a dread style, sir, a condition roughly equivalent to the bubonic. They neither wipe nor bathe nor mend. Neatness would work against beggary, do you see? The fouler the better, that's the motto, eh?"

"Right. Nick, so you've never *really* examined that infant?"

"Aesthetics being a secret part of my life, I'm a great one for averting the gaze. It's blind I am to help you, sir. Forgive."

"Forgiven, Nick." I passed him two shillings. "Oh . . . have you seen those two lately?"

"Strange. Come to think, sir. They have not come here in"—he counted on his fingers and showed surprise—"why, it must be a couple of weeks! They never done *that* before."

"Never? Thanks, Nick."

And I wandered down the steps, back to the search.

It was obvious she was hiding out.

I did not for a moment believe she or the child was sick. Our collision in front of the hotel, the baby's eyes and mine striking flint, had startled her like a fox and shunted her off God-knows-where, to some other alley, some other road, some other town.

I smelled her evasion. She was a vixen, yes, but I felt myself, day by day, a better hound.

I took to walking earlier, later, in the strangest locales. I would leap off buses in Ballsbridge and prowl the fog, or taxi halfway out to Kilcock and hide in pubs. I even knelt in Dean Swift's church to hear the echoes of his Houyhnhnm voice, but stiffened alert as the merest whimper of a child carried through.

It was all madness, to pursue such a brute idea. Yet on I went, scratching where the damned thing itched.

And then by sheer and wondrous accident, while I took my nightly swim in a dousing downpour that smoked the gutters and fringed my cap with a thousand drops, I turned a corner . . .

And this woman shoved a bundle in my face and cried a familiar cry:

"If there's mercy in your soul—"

She stopped, riven. She spun about. She ran.

For in the instant, she *knew*. And the babe in her arms, with the shocked small face and the swift bright eyes, he knew *too*! Both let out some kind of fearful cry.

God, how that woman could race.

She put a block between her backside and me while I gathered breath to yell: "Stop, thief!"

It seemed an appropriate yell. The baby was a mystery I wished to solve. And there she vaulted off with it, a wild thief.

So I dashed after, crying. "Stop! Help! *You* there!"

She kept a hundred yards between us for the first half mile, up over bridges across the Liffey and finally up Grafton Street, where I jogged into St. Stephen's Green, to find it . . . empty.

She had absolutely vanished.

Unless, of course, I thought, turning in all directions, letting my gaze idle, it's into The Four Provinces pub she's gone ...

That's where I went.

It was a good guess.

I shut the door quietly.

There, at the bar, was the beggar woman, putting a pint of Guinness to her own face and giving a shot of gin to the babe for happy sucking.

I let my heart pound down to a slower pace, then took my place at the bar and said, "Bombay gin, please."

At my voice, the baby gave one kick. The gin sprayed from his mouth. He fell into a spasm of choked coughing.

The woman turned him over and thumped his back to stop the convulsion. As she did so, the red face of the child faced me, eyes squeezed shut, mouth wide, and at last the seizure stopped, the cheeks grew less red, and I said:

"You there, baby."

There was a hush. Everyone in the bar waited.

I finished:

"You need a shave."

The babe flailed about in his mother's arms with a loud strange wounded cry, which I cut off with a simple:

"It's all right. I'm not the police."

The woman relaxed as if all her bones had gone to porridge.

"Put me down," said the babe.

She put him down on the floor.

"Give me my gin."

She handed him his little glass of gin.

"Let's go in the saloon bar, where we can talk."

The babe led the way with some sort of small dignity, holding his swaddling clothes about him with one hand and the gin glass in the other.

The saloon bar was empty, as I had guessed. The babe,

without my help, climbed up into a chair at a table and finished his gin.

"Ah, Christ, I need another," he said in a tiny voice.

While his mother went to fetch a refill, I sat down, and the babe and I eyed each other for a long moment.

"Well," he said at last, "what do ya think?"

"I don't know. I'm waiting and watching my own reactions," I said. "I may explode into laughter or tears at any moment."

"Let it be laughter. I couldn't stand the other."

On impulse, he stuck out his hand. I took it.

"The name is McGillahee. Better known as McGillahee's Brat. Brat, for short."

"Brat," I said, and gave him my name.

He gripped my hand hard with his tiny fingers.

"Your name fits nothing. But Brat, well, don't a name like that go ten thousand leagues under? And what, you may ask, am I doing down here? And you up there so tall and fine and breathing the high air? Ah, but here's your drink, the same as mine. Put it in you, and listen."

The woman was back with shots for both. I drank, watched her, and said, "Are you the mother . . . ?"

"It's me sister she is," said the babe. "Our mother's long since gone to her reward: a ha'penny a day for the next thousand years, nuppence dole from there on, and cold summers for a million years."

"Your sister?!" I must have sounded my disbelief, for she turned away to nibble her ale.

"You'd never guess, would you? She looks ten times my age. But if winter don't age you, poor will. And winter and poor is the whole tale. Porcelain cracks in this weather. And once she was the loveliest porcelain out of the summer oven." He gave her a gentle nudge. "But mother she is now, for thirty years—"

"Thirty years you've been . . . !"

"Out front of the Royal Hibernian Hotel? And more! And our mother before that, and our father too, and *his* father, the whole tribe! The day I was born, no sooner sacked in diapers than I was on the street and my mother crying Pity and the world deaf, stone dumb blind and deaf. Thirty years with my sister, ten years with my mother, McGillahee's Brat has been on display!"

"Forty?" I cried, and drank my gin to straighten my logic. "You're really forty? And all those years . . . how?"

"How did I get into this line of work?" said the babe. "You do not get; you are, as we say, *born* in. It's been nine hours a night, no Sundays off, no time clocks, no paychecks, and mostly dust and lint fresh paid out of the pockets of the rambling rich."

"But I still don't understand," I said, gesturing to his size, his shape, his complexion.

"Nor will I, ever," said McGillahee's Brat. "Am I a midget born to the blight? Some kind of dwarf shaped by glands? Or did someone warn me to play it safe, stay small?"

"That could hardly—"

"Couldn't it!? It could! Listen. A thousand times I heard it, and a thousand times more my father came home from his beggary route and I remember him jabbing his finger in my crib, pointing at me, and saying, 'Brat, whatever you do, don't grow, not a muscle, not a hair! The Real Thing's out there; the World. You *hear* me, Brat? Dublin's beyond, and Ireland on top of that, and England hard-assed above us all. It's not worth the consideration, the bother, the planning, the growing up to try and make do, so listen here. Brat, we'll stunt your growth with stories, with truth, with warnings and predictions, we'll wean you on gin and smoke you with Spanish cigarettes until you're a cured Irish ham, pink, sweet, and small—small, do you hear, Brat? I did not want you in this world. But now you're in it, lie low, don't walk, creep; don't talk, wail; don't work, loll; and when the world is too much for you, Brat, give it back your opinion: *wet* yourself! Here, Brat, here's your evening poteen; fire it down. The Four Horsemen of the Apocalypse wait by the Liffey. Would you see their like? Hang on. Here we go!'

"And out we'd duck for the evening round, my dad banging a banjo, with me at his feet holding the cup, or him doing a tap dance, me under one arm, the musical instrument under the other, both making discord.

"Then, home late, we'd lie four in a bed, a crop of failed potatoes, discards of an ancient famine.

"And sometimes in the midst of the night, for lack of something to do, my father would jump out of bed in the cold and run outdoors and fist his knuckles at the sky—I remember, I remember, I heard, I saw—daring God to lay hands on him, for so help him, Jesus, if *he* could lay hands on God, there would be torn feathers, ripped beards, lights put out, and the grand theater of Creation shut tight for Eternity! Do ya hear, God, ya dumb clod with your perpetual rainclouds turning their black behinds on me, do ya *care*!?

"For answer the sky wept, and my mother did the same all night, all night.

"And the next morn out I'd go again, this time in *her* arms, and back and forth between the two, day on day, and her grieving for the million dead from the famine of '51 and him saying goodbye to the four million who sailed off to Boston . . .

"Then one night Dad vanished too. Perhaps he sailed off on some mad boat like the rest, to forget us all. I forgive him. The poor beast was wild with hunger and nutty for want of something to give us and no giving.

"So then my mother simply washed away in her own tears, dissolved, you might say, like a sugar-crystal saint, and was gone before the morning fog rolled back, and the grass took her, and my sister, aged twelve, overnight grew tall, but I, me, oh, me? I grew small. Each decided, you see, long before that, of course, on going his or her way.

"But then part of my decision happened early on. I knew— I swear I did!—the quality of my own thespian performance!

"I heard it from every decent beggar in Dublin when I was nine days old. 'What a beggar's babe *that* is!' they cried.

"And my mother, standing outside the Abbey Theatre in the rain when I was twenty and thirty days old, and the actors and directors coming out tuning their ears to my Gaelic laments, *they* said I should be signed up and trained! So the stage would have been mine with size, but size never came. And there's no brat's roles in Shakespeare. Puck, maybe; what else? So meanwhile at forty days and fifty nights after being born my performance made hackles rise and beggars yammer to borrow my hide, flesh, soul, and voice for an hour here, an hour there. The old lady rented me out by the half day when she was sick abed. And not a one bought and bundled me off did not return with praise. 'My God,' they cried, 'his yell would suck money from the Pope's poor box!'

"And outside the cathedral one Sunday morn, an American cardinal was riven to the spot by the yowl I gave when I saw his fancy skirt and bright cloth. Said he: 'That cry is the first cry of Christ at his birth, mixed with the dire yell of Lucifer churned out of Heaven and spilled in fiery muck down the landslide slops of Hell!'

"That's what the dear cardinal said. Me, eh? Christ and the devil in one lump, the gabble screaming out my mouth half lost, half found—can you *top* that?"

"I cannot," I said.

"Then, later on, many years further, there was this old wise church bishop. The first time, he spied me, took a quick look, and . . . winked! Then grabbed my scabby fist and tucked the pound note in and gave it a squeeze and another wink, and him gone. I always figured, whenever we passed, he had my number, but I never winked back. I played it dumb. And there was always a good pound in it for me, and him proud of my not giving in and letting him know that I knew that he knew.

"Of all the thousands who've gone by in the grand ta-ta, he was the only one ever looked me right in the eye, save you! The rest were all too embarrassed by life to so much as gaze as they paid out the dole.

"Well, I mean now, what with that bishop, and the Abbey Players, and the other beggars advising me to go with my own natural self and talent and the genius busy in my baby fat, all *that* must have turned my head.

"Added to which, my having the famines tolled in my ears, and not a day passed we did not see a funeral go by or watch the unemployed march up and down in strikes . . . well, don't you see? Battered by rains and storms of people and knowing so much, I *must* have been driven down, driven back, don't you think?

"You cannot starve a babe and have a man; or do miracles run different than of old?

"My mind, with all the drear stuff dripped in my ears, was it likely to want to run around free in all that guile and sin and being put upon by natural nature and unnatural man? No. No! I just wanted my little cubby, and since I was long out of that, and no squeezing back, I just squinched myself small against the rains. I flaunted the torments.

"And do you know? I won."

You did, Brat, I thought. You did.

"Well, I guess that's my story," said the small creature there perched on a chair in the empty saloon bar.

He looked at me for the first time since he had begun his tale.

The woman who was his sister, but seemed his gray mother, now dared to lift her gaze also.

"Do," I said, "do the people of Dublin know about you?"

"Some," the babe said. "And envy me. And hate me, I guess, for getting off easy from God and his plagues and fates."

"Do the police know?"

"Who would tell them?"

There was a long pause.

Rain beat on the windows.

Somewhere a door hinge shrieked like a soul in torment as someone went out and someone else came in.

Silence.

"Not me," I said.

"Ah, Christ, Christ . . ."

And tears rolled down the sister's cheeks.

And tears rolled down the sooty strange face of the babe.

Both of them let the tears go, did not try to wipe them off, and at last they stopped, and they drank up the rest of their gin and sat a moment, and then I said: "The best hotel in town is the Royal Hibernian—the best for beggars, that is."

"True," they said.

"And for fear of meeting me, you've kept away from the richest territory?"

"We have."

"The night's young," I said. "There's a flight of rich ones coming in from Shannon just before midnight."

I stood up. "If you'll let . . . I'll be happy to walk you there now."

"The saints' calendar is full," said the woman, "but somehow we'll find room for you."

Then I walked the woman McGillahee and her brat back through the rain toward the Royal Hibernian Hotel, and we talked along the way of the mobs of people coming in from the airport just before twelve, drinking and registering at that late hour, that fine hour for begging and, with the cold rain and all, not to be missed.

I carried the babe for some part of the way because she looked tired, and when we got in sight of the hotel, I handed him back, saying:

"Is this the first time, ever?"

"We was found out by a tourist? Aye," said the babe. "You have an otter's eye."

"I'm a writer."

"Nail me to the Cross," said he. "I might have known! You won't..."

"No," I said. "I won't write a single word about this, about you, for another thirty years or more."

"Mum's the word?"

"Mum."

We were a hundred feet from the hotel steps.

"I must shut up here," said Brat, lying there in his old sister's arms, fresh as peppermint candy from the gin, round-eyed, wild-haired, swathed in dirty linens and wools, small fists gently gesticulant. "We've a rule, Molly and me, no chat while at work. Grab ahold."

I grabbed the small fist, the little fingers. It was like holding a sea anemone.

"God bless you," he said.

"And God," I said, "take care of you."

"Ah," said the babe, "in another year we'll have enough saved for the New York boat."

"We will," she said.

"And no more begging, and no more being the dirty babe crying by night in the storms, but some decent work in the open, do you know, do you see, will you light a candle to that?"

"It's lit." I squeezed his hand.

"Go on ahead."

"I'm gone," I said.

And walked quickly to the front of the hotel, where airport taxis were starting to arrive.

Behind, I heard the woman trot forward, I saw her arms lift, with the Holy Child held out in the rain.

"If there's mercy in you!" she cried. "Pity ... !"

And heard the coins ring in the cup and heard the sour babe wailing, and more cars coming and the woman crying Mercy and Thanks and Pity and God Bless and Praise Him, and wiping tears from my own eyes, feeling eighteen inches tall, somehow made it up the high steps and into the hotel and to bed, where rains fell cold on the rattled windows all the night and where, in the dawn, when I woke and looked out, the street was empty save for the steady-falling storm ...

24

The incredible news came by cable.

The National Institute of Arts and Letters was proud to award me a special prize in literature and a cash stipend of five thousand dollars. Would I please appear in New York City on May 24 to receive the Award, the plaudits, and the check?

Would I?!

My God, I thought. At last! God! For years people have called me Buck Rogers or Flash Gordon. People have said no rockets would ever be built. People have claimed we won't go to Mars or the Moon. But now, maybe someone will call me by my right name.

I took the news with me out to a late breakfast at Courtown. Late breakfast, hell, all of the breakfasts were late. It was ten thirty by the time I got there with the cable folded in my pocket. I walked in on Ricki and John and Jake Vickers over their eggs, bacon, and biscuits. Jake was over visiting, helping John figure out Kipling's *The Man Who Would be King* for a film up ahead. John must have smelled the cable in my shirt, for he studied my face as I regrouped my omelette on my plate and made faces on the eggs with ketchup.

"Well, if that doesn't look like the cougar that ate the boa constrictor, head and tail. Cough it up, kid."

"Naw," I said, pleased.

"Come on, son, tell!"

I took the cable from my shirt and tossed it across the table. John read it thoughtfully and then handed it over to Jake.

"Well, now, if I won't be damned. We've got a bloody genius under the roof."

"I wouldn't say that."

"Nor would I, kid. A figure of speech. Did you *read* that, Jake?"

"Sure did." Jake passed the cable to Ricki, with a look of stunned surprise. "God! You write literature, do you?"

"For *Dime Detective* and *Weird Tales*," I said, to take the edge off everyone's attention.

"Read that out loud, *Ricki*," said John.

"You already *read* it." Ricki laughed and ran around the table to give me a hug. "Congratulations!"

She stood by my side and read the cable out loud. That was a mistake. John hadn't really intended for her to do so. He went back to cutting his ham and buttering his toast. "Now, now, kid," he said, gazing at his food, "you made up your mind, just what you're going to *do* with all that money?"

"Do?"

"Yes. *Do. Spend*. How do you figure to get rid of that astounding sum, O Son of Jules Verne?"

"I don't know," I said, flushed with joy, glad for their attention. "I've only had the cable for about three hours. I'll talk it over with Maggie. We've been in our new tract house three years. Some of the rooms still don't have furniture. And I work out in the garage where we don't have a car, so I have an old Sears Roebuck sixty-dollar desk. Maybe I'll buy me more bookcase space. Maybe a set of golf clubs for my dad, who's never had a decent set in his life—"

"Jesus, God, what a list!" shouted Huston.

I glanced up, thinking he was praising me. Instead, I saw that he had collapsed back in his chair in a misery of concern for my future.

"Jake, did you just *hear*?"

"Yep," said Jake.

Hold on, I thought. Wait—

"Isn't that the damndest dumbest list you ever heard? My God," cried John, "you are a great writer of science fiction, are you not? And a fine and superb writer of fantasy and the imagination?"

"I try," I said.

"*Try!* My God," said John, "use your head! All of a sudden you've got moola, money, cash! You're not going to put that stuff in the bank and let it *rot* there, are you?"

"I had imagined—"

"Hell, you didn't imagine *anything*!"

Ricki had been standing beside me during all this. Now I felt her fingers clutch the back of my neck, urging will power and strength. Then, sure that her act had been unseen, she marched back to her place at the head of the table, to douse her bacon with ketchup.

"Well, it sure looks like you're going to have to leave the investment of your Grand Prize Award to people who know how to live, which means Jake and me. Don't you agree, Vickers?" said John.

Jake nodded and gave me a big wink.

"Son, we'll put our minds to it," said John. "We really will. Okay, Jake? And by sunset today, we'll have found a way for you to invest . . . how much *was* it—?"

"Five thousand dollars," I said, weakly.

"Five thousand smackeroos! How much would you figure, Jake, we could earn for Flash Gordon's bastard brother here?"

"Twenty thousand, maybe . . ." said Jake, his mouth full.

"Let's figure fifteen to be fair. Let's not get greedy." John lay back like a scarecrow in his chair. "The main thing is, you can't let money sit. It rots. Right after breakfast, kid, first thing we do, the three of us, is find a way for you to get *really* rich this week, no waiting, no delays!"

"I—"

"Shut up and eat your mush," smiled John.

We ate in silence for a time, everyone casting glances at everyone else. John watching me, Jake watching John, me watching both of them, and Ricki, in the odd moment, giving me a brave nod to hold fast and fight fair in the midst of foul.

John watched me stir my food into a slow maelstrom and push it back. Then he changed the subject completely.

"What sort of reading do you do, kid?"

"Shaw. Shakespeare. Poe. Hawthorne. The Song of Songs which is Solomon's, the Old Testament. Faulkner. Steinbeck—"

"Uh, *huh*," said John, lighting a cigarillo. He sipped his coffee. "I see."

And at last, he dropped the other riding boot.

"Havelock Ellis?" he said.

"Sex?" I said.

"Well, now, he's not all sex and ten yards wide," said John, casually. "You got any opinions on same?"

"What has this to do with the prize I just got?"

"Patience, son. Not a thing. It's just, Jake and I, well,

we've read up. There's this Kinsey report a few years back. Read it?"

"My wife sold copies in the bookstore where I met her."

"Do tell! Well, what about all that homosexual stuff in there, kid? I find that rather interesting, don't you?"

"Well," I said.

"I mean," said John, gesturing for more coffee and waiting for Ricki to refill the cups, "there's not a man or boy or old man on earth hasn't at one time hankered for another man. Right, Jake?"

"That's common knowledge," said Jake.

Ricki was staring at us all and twitching her mouth and sliding her eyes at me to run, get away.

"I mean isn't it just plain human nature, with all the love in us," said Huston, "that we fall in love with the football coach or the track star or the best debater in the class? Girls fall in love with their badminton lady instructors or some dance teacher. Right, Ricki?"

Ricki refused to reply and looked ready to bound up and leap out of the room.

"Sometimes confession is good for the soul. I don't mind telling you," said John, stirring his coffee and looking deep into the cup, "when I was sixteen, there was this runner in my high school—my God, he could do anything, high jump, pole vault, hundred yards, four forty, cross-country, you name it. Beautiful boy. How could I not just think he was the greatest set of cat's pajamas in the world? And, Jake, fess up, now. Same thing happen to *you*?"

"Not to me," said Jake. "But to friends. A ski instructor took a pal of mine down the slopes, and if he had said, 'Marry me,' my friend would have. Maybe not stayed, but . . . sure."

"There, you *see*?" John nodded from Jake to Ricki to me. "All perfectly normal. Now it's your turn, kid."

"*My* turn?"

"Why—" he seemed a trifle astonished, "to fess up. I mean, if Jake here is a gut wonder of strength to share with us his pal's ski instructor—"

"Yeah," said Jake.

"And *I* am big enough to tell you about that all-American, cross-country, beefsteak-eating son-of-a-bitch, well, then," he sucked his cigarillo, "it's time," he sucked his coffee, "for . . . *you.*"

I took a deep breath and let it out.

"I got nothing to confess."

"Now hold on!" said John.

"Nope," I said. "I wish I could, but nothing ever happened to me, age fifteen or sixteen or seventeen. From eighteen on, nothing. Nineteen? Twenty?—zero. Twenty-one to twenty-six, only my writing. A few girls, but like my friend, Ray Harryhausen, who put all his libido in dinosaurs, I put all my libido in rockets, Mars, alien creatures, and one or two unlucky girls who, when I brought my stories over to the house, ran off whining with boredom after the first hour—"

"You don't mean to say?" said Jake.

"Nothing at *all?*" accused John.

"Wish there had been a gym coach, wish there had been a ski instructor," I admitted. "Wish I had been as lucky as both of you with a little off-trail smittance. But, no strange ones, no oddballs, no kumquats, no queens. Pretty boring, eh?"

I looked over at Ricki. She was dying with admiration for me, but said nothing.

"But *surely?*" said John.

"Come off it," said Jake. "We all have these foibles, these little dirty yearnings."

"Not me," I blinked. "No boy David. Only Aphrodite and the Venus de Milo. Girls' bums, not boys' behinds. I realize that makes me unusual. I tried. I really tried. But I just couldn't fall in love with Hugo Dinwiddy, my hygiene coach at L.A. High."

"I don't believe it!" said Huston.

"Neither do I," said Vickers.

"Now, *you*, John," I said. "I'm in love with you. But that's *different*, yes?"

He backed off. "Sure. I mean, yeah, of course."

"And, Jake," I said. "I'll be knocking at your door tonight. Leave it unlocked."

I saw the air going out of his Montgolfier balloon. "Sure," he said.

"Hooray!" Ricki rushed around the table, kissed me on the cheek, and fled the room. "Bravo."

Bloody Marys were served in silence.

During the silence I thought, Watch it. I served myself more eggs and sat down, waiting for John to try again.

"About that money of yours," said John, at last.

"I don't have any money."

"The money you're going to get, kid, in May from those sweet people in New York City?"

"Oh, *that* money." I scarfed my toast, ignored their stares.

"Well, you listening? Jake, don't you agree? We go to Phoenix Park tomorrow and pick the best horse in eight races and you lay it, the whole amount, on one horse, win or lose! How does that sound?"

"Nope," I said, at last.

"What kind of answer is that? That's not even accepted grammatical English."

"Nope? Sounds good to me. Nope."

"Holy shit," cried John, "what have I got on my hands here? A yellow belly? A coward? A gutless wonder?"

"That about describes it, and proud to be," I admitted.

"Moby Dick would spit on you."

"Most likely."

"Melville throw up on you."

"Don't doubt it."

"Hemingway wouldn't sit a two-hole outhouse crapper with you for shared male experience."

"No. *I* wouldn't share any outhouse with *him*."

"Look at him, Jake."

"I'm looking," said Jake.

"He's *refusing*!"

"Pretty yellow," said Jake.

"That's it," I said, and arose.

By then I was sick to my stomach. I took the cable out of my pocket. It was empty. There were no words on it. They had managed to burn, ravage, erase, and destroy the words, the message, the joy, during one long terrible hour.

I would have to go to a quiet room in Dublin with the empty paper and touch it with lit matches to scorch forth the gift: You have been awarded. You count. You are okay, or whatever in hell it had said at nine this morning. Whatever it was, I could not read it now.

I might have thrown the cable down, but I saw John was waiting for that pleasure. I wadded the cable and shoved it in my pocket.

"For your information," I said, "I have thought it over. Carefully. And at the last race in Primrose Park, I'm betting my found money, everything I've got—on—Oscar Wilde!!"

Then I picked up my Bloody Mary and very slowly strolled, did not stride angrily but strolled at leisure, waving my drink at John and Jake.

I went out the door.

Ricki found me on the back stone porch of Courtown House ten minutes later. Tears were dripping off the end of my nose.

"God," she said, "you're a wonderful son of a bitch."

"I wish I *felt* wonderful," I murmured.

I handed her the wadded cablegram. "Has it come back yet?"

"What?"

"The words. The prize. The announcement."

She held it up to the dim light.

"Yes." And then, quietly, seeing my face, "Yes!"

And the words were back because she read them to me. And I believed.

I telegraphed New York and I said I would be there, May 24, to get the award from John Hersey and Robert Sherwood and Norman Cousins and Lillian Hellman and all the rest.

I never mentioned the cable again.

Nor did John or Jake.

25

In a dream, I heard a wild knocking on my hotel door. I blundered up and staggered over to throw the door wide and find John himself standing astride my sill, grinning, dressed in a black wetsuit-and-snorkel outfit, holding a mask, a bright yellow bottle of oxygen, and an airgun harpoon.

"C'mon, kid!" he cried. "I'll teach you to snorkel!"

"At three in the *morning*?" I yelled.

"C'mon, kid, don't be chicken, don't be yellow!" he cried.

And like a damned fool, I went with him.

To be drowned.

And wake up from the nightmare in a blizzard sweat.

26

Finn shook my elbow.

"Lad," he said gently, "you'd best be off."

"What?" I said.

"It's the philosopher's cubby you been in all the while. That last drink did it. I had no heart to disturb, so I let you grind your teeth and fret in your sleep."

"Fret? Teeth?" I shrugged back from the enclosure of the private cubby.

"How do you feel?" asked Finn anxiously.

"Mad."

"Because you woke or because the dream wasn't true after all?"

"Both."

"I was beating the wife once and awoke. Seeing as I'd never laid hands on the woman in me life, it was a dread awakening. You need, once in a while, to even scores..."

"In your dream, did your wife scream?"

"She took her punishment quietly, which ruined my endeavor. It's just as well. I could not look at her by day if she complained to God in my nightmare."

"What time is it?"

"Late. Himself called, asking for your body if not your soul. I told him you were not here, which is a kind of truth, seeing as you looked not so much mad as sad when you came in. Was it a sadness that drove you mad?"

"It was."

"Is there something beyond drink I could hand to you?"

"Like what, Finn!?"

"A great lie based on a small truth. Another collision of

genius: a grand old man in his automobile years ago, and myself, a young soak."

Finn paused.

"Go on, Finn. I admit you're a genius. Who was the other?"

"The greatest playwright since Shakespeare!"

I perked up.

"And *that* would be ... ?"

"First things first ..."

"Tell it *all,* Finn."

"Do you *mean* that?" Finn shaped me with one eye and conjured memory with the other.

"I do. I'm in need of cheer, Finn. My head is full of beggars and rain!"

"Do you have the time?"

"I do, I *do*!"

Finn refilled my glass, then leaned forward with both elbows on the bar and fixed his gaze to some other bright, and distant year.

"Well, then," he said. "Hear this ..."

God, they say, works in mysterious ways (said Finn). He may not always note the sparrow fallen, but he has a sharp eye for the incongruities.

Which is to say, given half a chance, on certain days, God seems to lean toward borrowing a flint from Lucifer and a stone from Beelzebub, the better to light a path and ensure a collision.

On this particular day, bored out of mind, as any Irish God would be half through Sunday, the Lord bent a road and prepared the way for the arrival of a touring car lost from Dublin and aching with genius.

The particular car, having taken a wrong turn because God said so, and the driver drunk on top of that, arrived in the vicinity at about half past two this particular Sunday when the sun promised but the rain delivered. There was a parting of the storm long enough for the touring car to explode a tire and sink to its knees like a rifled elephant.

The sound of the explosion was such that the mob inside the pub soon became the mob outside, looking for the gunshot victim but finding instead the drunken chauffeur wandering about the chopfallen car, kicking the good tires as if that might reinvigorate the flat without having to pump.

Then like the devil's head popping into view on a small Punch and Judy stage, an old man's face suddenly rose in the car's rear window. His bright mean eyes flashed as he pointed his reddish beard and fired off his mouth:

"Sir, the tire, do not *kick* it to death. Where *are* we?"

"At the center of the universe!" I cried, wiping my hands on a barcloth, standing in the door.

"Finn's!" echoed each and all.

The old man's face vanished from the window but to reappear as he leaped out of the car door and stood with his hands on his hips. What a sport he was to behold, dressed in a fine woven hunting-walking suit with a Norfolk jacket. His eyes blazed with admiration. "A man is best known by his pride. *You* must be Finn!" he cried.

"Well said." I laughed. "And will you come in from the rain, your honor?"

"It's not raining!"

It began to rain.

"Thanks and done." The old man marched with the brisk stride of one forty years younger. The rain parted to let him pass.

"Gangway!" I said, and the mob parted, likewise to run for drinks. "And now, sir, before the world ends, your name?"

"Shaw!" cried the old man. "George Bernard Shaw!"

"And ..." The tall man with the blazing beard made a path through the pub that caused the air to rush, in a clap of thunder, behind. "And," he announced somewhat joyfully, "I am a teetotaler!"

The mob veered off as if he had pronounced a plague.

"And are you happy with that half-state of being?" I responded.

"If being busy instead of inebriated is happy, I am happy," said Shaw. "But since my car is ill in the road, I am sorely tempted to order a small drink. Something incredibly weak, if you please."

"Like the one son in each family is handed over to the Church, your honor?"

Shaw's beard liked that and beamed.

"You are *all* writers, it seems."

"If being poor and waiting in line for drinks and shooting off your mouth is writers, we're writers." I shoved a brandy at him. "Sink your teeth in *this*, sir!"

"No, no," he cried. "By weak I meant a simple glass of water."

"Ah, God," I said. "The last time we saw something that simple it was the priest's sister from Cork, Mr. Shaw!"

"Shaw?" said Timulty suddenly, bugging his eyes. "Hold on! I seen your picture in the *Irish Times*. It was you lit the fire beneath Saint Joan!"

"I wrote the play, yes!" said Shaw.

"Also," Doone piped in, "was it not you claimed the definition of an Irishman was a man who would climb over six naked women to reach his mother?"

"That's *near* the truth," said Shaw.

"If there's to be a plague of truth here," said Murphy, "we'd best not be sober for it."

I measured Shaw's shadow in the light.

"If you'll pardon, sir, I think it's time, once in a life, for a brandy offered in friendship."

Looking exasperated by the day and put upon by the attention, Shaw winced, looked left and right, and swigged the drink.

He worked his mouth over some unexpressed words, debated with himself and an invisible opponent, shrugged, opened his eyes, and said, quietly, "There." For his hand had crawled, under the influence of the drink, to a carpetbag he had placed on the bar.

"What's that?" I said.

"It could be a bomb," said Shaw. The men gasped. "Or it could be decorations for your honorable pub. Open it."

"I will," I said, and did.

I lifted out and placed on the bar four half largish pieces of painted porcelain.

"That's no bomb," I said.

"It's too early to tell," said Shaw.

There were words on the porcelain.

"STOP," I said, reading one.

"THINK," said Kelly, reading the next.

"CONSIDER," said Timulty.

"Do," Doone said.

"Strange," said Shaw. "I do not quite know what moved me, but I spied these in a tinker's roadside tray this morning. The very banality of their advice amused me. I spent four shillings for what now seems nothing."

"Well," said Doone, "whoever made these out of clay had reasons unaccountable. They're sort of toys, don't you see, to be played with. If you laid them about here, on the shelves, or on the bar, would they not open the trapdoors on our half-blind minds, Mr. Shaw?"

"I had no intention of starting a class in philosophy," said Shaw.

"But college it is. And each of these bits, these toys," said Doone, "the names of courses to be taken and wisdoms to be learned. Mr. Shaw, advise us. If these trinkets were yours to decorate Finn's as if it were hearth and home, would such decorations increase the IQ of all those who stand before you?"

"If I said no, you would think I perceive your intelligence as not capable of perfection," said Shaw. "If I say yes, you'll think I flatter you under the influence of drink."

"Ah, hell, flatter us!" said Timulty.

"Place the mottoes and make more brilliant your already brilliant minds," said Shaw.

"Done!" cried Doone, grabbing a porcelain word and hustling about the pub. "We put STOP by the door. That way it nails the gobs coming in and warns them to leave the world behind whilst here. And also STOP going out, so you run back to the bar for one last Guinness against the wife!"

"Go it, Doone!" said all.

I, being the pub's owner, grabbed the last two as Doone placed CONSIDER at the far end of the bar for consideration of all.

"What," I then asked, "do we do with THINK?"

Mr. Shaw, having watched the behavior of Doone, all but dancing about the place, cleared his throat, which cleared the noise.

"May I suggest," he said tartly, "that since there is one place in your honorable pub where the gaze is constantly and irrevocably fixed that you place THINK there? The mirror beyond your shoulder. That lake of ice beneath which all Ireland is sunk and where it sees itself yesterday midnight and tomorrow at twilight."

"God love us all," I said. "With forty years of glances and

glares, its a wonder the ice has not flaked from that mirror's backside. Here's THINK!"

And I hung the strange advice in the midst of the glass.

"Everyone," I cried. "Are you *thinking*?"

"We are!" said the mob.

"And Do," I added, handing it to Doone, "also by the exit, so you'll see STOP again and pause for a moment before you Do something stupid. *Now* what?"

"Do not take this as advice." Shaw stood ramrod straight at the bar, drinking plain water, which I had now served. "We simply . . . wait."

"For what?"

"Ah, well," said Shaw, and looked around mysterously.

As did we all, fastening our eyes first to STOP and then CONSIDER and then along to THINK and ending the tour with Do.

The men sipped their drinks and the clock ticked and the wind blew ever so gently through the swinging doors.

I could hear the men's eyes slide now to this corner, now to that, and the breath bending the hair in their nostrils and the suds popping in the glasses.

I held my breath.

My pub was still as the tomb.

Silence.

The men stood along the bar like a forest of Sleeping Beauties. It was like the night before Creation or the day after Annihilation.

"Free drinks!" I cried.

"Double rounds for all!" I went on, but no one stirred.

"Mr. Finn," said Shaw in his best stage whisper. "What," he wondered, "has," he went on, and finished, "happened?"

"Jaisus," I muttered. "This is the first hour and the first damned minute in twenty years there has been Silence in Finn's. *Listen!*"

Shaw listened and moved quietly among the men as if they were worn statues in an old museum.

"Send for the priest," I whispered.

"No!" said a voice. "The priest is *here*!"

Shaw wheeled to point his beard at the far end of the bar, where Father O'Malley, hidden till now in the private cubby, lifted his gray head, like Lazarus summoned.

"You." The priest fixed the old playwright with a gaze like Job accusing God. "Look what you've done!"

"I?" Shaw flushed with guilt whilst protesting innocence. "I?"

"You," said Father O'Malley, honing his razor to shave the beard, "and your devil's signs, your self-conscious blathering and annunciations. The Luciferean mottoes. *Those.*"

Shaw turned to glance at the places where STOP, CONSIDER, THINK, and Do were lodged.

The priest came in a slow dead march along the bar, amidst the dead buried alive in their own fell silences.

His hand snaked out with his empty glass. "Refill the *élan vital*, Finn."

"One *élan vital*, whatever in hell *that* is!" I hurried the life force into the clenched grip of the still gliding priest.

"Now, then," the priest breathed confessional spearmint breath on Shaw's beard, "Mr. Smarter than Punch and wiser than Ecclesiastes. Mr. Irish shipped to London and spoiled en route ... what have you to say for yourself and these enfeebling signs that have numbed and beaten us deaf and mute?"

"If this be the Inquisition," said Shaw, "fire away."

"You're dead!" Father O'Malley paced Shaw, like a beast circling his prey. "What does the *first* sign mean?!"

Only the frozen eyes of the stricken men at the bar twitched to find that sign: STOP!

"It means," said Shaw, "we do not stop often enough in life to cogitate, be still, let things *happen* to us."

"If it's a woman in your path, best not," said the priest.

"Yet," interrupted Shaw, "life runs us so fast our thoughts are lost."

"The bicycle," murmured Doone, "and other devices have done us in."

"Doone!" The priest dug his grave.

Doone lay down in it.

"You've come to Ireland to preach dismay and teach chaos. You have pretended at intelligence, but the sum is silence! No advice, please, from Lucifer!" said the priest.

"Slowly," cried Shaw. "I must note this!" said Shaw, scribbling on his pad.

Slowly, slowly, as if roused from a great hibernation, Doone leaned to watch Shaw's adroit pen skip, trace, and glide.

"Jeez," whispered Doone. "That ain't half bad."

"You're damn tootin' it ain't," said the priest, reading Shaw's scribble. "Well, now. I think that's the gist. The world is not ready for the likes of you and Gilbert Keith Chesterton! Them blasphemous *signs*! STOP! CONSIDER! THINK! DO! What the hell do they *mean* that has shut the gab here?"

Shaw underlined the words as he spoke. "It must be obvious that before you can THINK you must STOP for enough time to CONSIDER *what* to THINK, and then, with no delay, DO! DO!"

"Sure, that's how women and other things get done!" said Doone, eyes shut.

"Doone!"

Doone fell back.

"Continue," said Father O'Malley, with deadly sweetness.

"I am halfway there." Shaw added vinegar to the above. "I may in a moment of blind intuition have bought this ragbag mix to teach the A.C. as against the D.C. Creative Current."

"A.C.? D.C.?"

"Alternating current, which means STOP to CONSIDER. CON-SIDER what to THINK. THINK. And then DO. Or direct current: DO and *then* THINK and CONSIDER and STOP for a rest."

"*Again*," said the priest.

"Gladly," said Shaw. "Alternating current gives you varieties of creativity in art, dramatics, painting. But the one I recommend most is DO. The deed is father to the thought. DOING leads the mind into discovery."

"It sure as hell *does!*" The priest glowered.

"Time to THINK *after* the creative act," said Shaw.

"By then it's too late," said Doone. "For the woman, that is. Sorry, Father."

"You are not forgiven, Doone. Shaw, I am waiting for your *summation*."

"I have perforated the piano roll; you need but run the tune!" Shaw raised his thin fingers as if each were a spigot from which caprice might flow. "Do and DO *again* to *discover* what in blazes you're THINKING. Hide three signs and keep only DO at hand. *Direct current!* Or, alternating current, play scales amongst the four. Now *pause, chew the cud, maunder,* then *dive deep* then *hop, skip, run, leap, rise, create!*"

"Shaw!" mourned Father O'Malley, having lost the way.

"Why, Father," said Shaw, "I was inspired on the road this fine rainy morn to DO. Buy these bits of Rorschach test and further DO by having Finn place them in sight lines all about."

"Why?" droaned the priest. "Why, why?!"

"Why, Dublin and all of its streets and pubs are a stage and all of its souls cast into the world as actor-playwrights. I am one, shipped to London to write my vaudevilles and charm the sheep. I thought that if every Irish soul hid a dancing bear, how brilliant if I held the hoop! One brandy pushed me to act."

"And," said Father O'Malley, "See what it's done."

Shaw and Doone and the priest looked along the mortuary

statues of the dear men frozen for eternity in a blizzard self-made.

"It's enough," whispered Doone, "to make your socks crawl up and down your ankles. Listen!"

"The devil's job of confusion." said Father O'Malley.

"Angels confuse, also," said Shaw. "Witness the kind wives who, out of the fineness of their hearts, cause these chaps to run here, biting their fists and hard at drink, trying to understand that unfathomable sex!"

"Women," whispered Doone, "is the *fourth* Ghost, the next one over from the Holy Trinity!"

"Doone!" said the priest. Spluttering, he shifted gears.

"And look at your *shoes*!"

All, waking slowly, looked.

"That," Shaw said, "is the latest boot from the London last."

"That," said the priest, "is the latest cloven hoof from Dante's infirmary!"

"Splendid!"

"I want no praise from the playwright who helped the poor French maid out of her armor and into the flames!" said Father O'Malley.

Shaw bent to his pen, scribbling fast.

"And your *face*, sir," said the priest. "Is there not something of Mephistopheles in your waxed beard and mustache in tines, while you part your hair in *horns*!"

"Horns." Shaw wrote it down. "As a young critic weighing *Faust* and *Mephistopheles*, I found in the operatic Satans admirable roles. I deviled folks impiously. Continue, Father. What next?"

"Here goes!"

And there ensued a rain of fiery hailstones that wakened the last of the sleeping men.

The voice of the priest, once down, now rose to those peaks which Berlioz scaled, a symphony of outrage later known as the "Defilement of Shaw." The good father, atop his mania, planted the Church's beehive banner and lapsed into silence.

The faggots having been gathered to burn the Maid and take Shaw with, the playwright with the beard of Lucifer waited for the charcoals to die.

"Now," said Shaw.

Striding with a musical critic's quickstep, he moved to the dart-game board, seized the darts, spun about, paced off the proper paces, turned, and, with one eye shut, flung a dart.

"Sssst..." The breath leaked from all.

Pok! It was Freya's dart, striking Baldur the Beautiful and killing him, bull's-eye on.

All the hands moved to applaud if the priest gave permission. He gave none.

Shaw tossed the other darts slowly.

"My father drank," he said. "Nights dragging him out of pubs, I practiced darts. Bull's-eye! So! Your cries of blasphemy?" said Shaw. "Twattle!"

Shaw snatched up the brandy glass.

"I suppose I might do a temperance lecture...."

The men leaned toward him, making hidden fists.

"I could say that the hard stuff plus the soft plus these signs have melted their brainpans into their shoes."

More leaning, more fists.

"But," said Shaw, "I will *not.*"

The men's fists, out of their pockets, were mere hands again.

Now, tossing dart after dart, Shaw pointed his beard and fired the volleys:

"No, Father, it is not the machinery of ideas, as caught in these plaques, that has slowed the wits and stopped the *glotti* of these Irish bog warriors and conquerors of their spiteful, neglected wives. No, no. If that were true, then all of Ireland could have been conquered from my car, with a packet of plaques delivered here, and a toss of concepts and dire ideas planted there, seeding all Eire's pubs with darkness and stilling the air as if a final death had come upon the world."

"Ah, Jaisus," someone whispered, in awe, "say that *again*."

"Shh," said all, and Shaw went on.

"No, the wits here are not frail, and I have not reaped them, junked the chaff, to save the seed to use in Hell. It is you, sir, who roil the baptismal-font water, who has caused this calamity at Finn's."

"I?" cried Father O'Malley.

"You, sir, who down the years told these men *not* to THINK on certain things—"

"Women's underwear," Doone whispered.

"You told them never to STOP, never CONSIDER, but especially never DO," said Shaw. "So, between the storms of old-maid aunts, crazed mothers-in-law, and turnip wives telling them to THINK about DOING things around the yard, and your telling them *not* to THINK or DO yet others, the fell confusion you speak of, Father, arrived here today. Over the years it was only the alcohol that gave them a false sense of freedom and let their tongues wag in escape from the high dudgeons of the Church or the coal-scuttle raillery of the hearth. Then I let loose my abominable signs in a moment of one-brandy meanness and the *Fifth* Horseman of the Irish Apocalypse arrived."

"*Silence?*" I asked.

"Yes, Finn," said Shaw.

"So there's enough blame to go around, is there?" inquired Father O'Malley over his ale.

"Home, church, pub, booze, signs," said Shaw. "The sum of it would poison an elephant and kill a herd. I will confess my guilt, Father, here today if you will do the same with a nod. You need not speak it aloud. And you will surely not get the women at home to admit their guilt as sharp as the elbows they hide like knives in their shawls. And as for Mr. Finn and his pub . . ."

"Ah, hell." I pulled the lever. "*Guilty.*"

"The Irish," said Shaw quietly. "Here they come out of fog, here they stand lost in mist, there they go off in rain. The Irish."

"Yes . . . ?" was the whisper through all the pub.

Shaw paused, nodded, and went on. "Do they stand in Dublin midstage and act fresh lines each day? Who's the Prompter and where's the Book? Forty years on, I'll know your faces as you talked forever. I've caught your sound. What do you have in this island place? Poor on poor and the ships off to Boston and the young away, leaving the old to stare in pub mirrors at their Arctic souls, asides of philosophy beneath their tongues.

"The Irish. From so little they glean so much: squeeze the last ounce of joy from a flower with no petals, a night with no stars, a day with no sun. One seed and you lift a beanstalk forest to shake down giants of converse. The Irish? You step off a cliff and . . . fall *up*!"

Shaw was done.

He shoved his skinny hands into his jacket pockets and stood astride the astonished silence.

"Napoleon," said Father O'Malley quietly, "out of Moscow, made not such a gentlemanly retreat. Have the Irish ever been better punctured or painted?"

"I humbly think not," said Shaw. "But then I am no longer Irish."

"To hell you're not," said the priest, and looked all about at the porcelain signs.

"I think," mused Shaw, "I will not STOP anymore to CONSIDER or THINK. For now it's DO, which means *go*."

"But what will you be DOING up the road ten miles? Ruining logic and wrecking souls?" asked Father O'Malley.

Shaw nodded to the signs. We trotted swiftly to fetch them one by one, into the carpetbag. There went STOP, CONSIDER, and DO. But Shaw saved out THINK.

Then, as if it were a hard-boiled egg, he cracked it on wood, then moved swiftly to place the broken bits of THINK in the priest's hands and close his fingers on the biblical tablet shattered, no more to plague Egypt, or Finn's.

Shaw said, "To the deliverer out of darkness, these sinful shards. I bare my neck to receive the ax of the conqueror. May he be merciful."

That perplexed the priest, caught in this downpour without a bumbershoot.

"Go on, Father," said Doone, "be merciful!"

"Ah, what the hell," said the priest at last, pale but willing, "Shaw, you did not *know* what you were *doing*."

Shaw dropped the bag.

There was a nice explosion, muffled within the sack, not unlike a chandelier crashed in the dark.

"There goes a whole factory of philosophy," I said.

"Drinks all around!" said Father O'Malley.

"Father, that's the first you've *ever* bought!" I cried.

"Shut your lip and pull the levers."

I laid out a last brandy for the playwright.

"Ah, no." Shaw shook his head, which made his beard ignite. "It was that first shot, an hour ago, that grew my hooves and ran me to pandemonium. Time!"

Which alarmed the men.

"No, not *closing*." Shaw turned. "Time for me to leave."

"It is," cried Shaw's chauffeur from the door, dirty of hands and drawn of face. "The damn beast is fixed!"

Shaw was halfway to the door, practical shoes striking invisible sparks, when Father O'Malley said, "Wait!"

Shaw waited.

"You're not a bad sort," said the priest lamely. "And my temper is fierce. Your shoes do *not* resemble hooves. It was just a way of speaking. Have you written us *down*?"

"You," Shaw held up a full page of shorthand, "are *immortal*! Goodbye, goodbye."

Then his Punch and Judy face popped away from the doors and sailed off to the car. I followed to hear the chauffeur say: "Where *to*?"

"Hell," said Shaw smartly. "That will do nicely. Yes, Hell, I think."

The chauffeur tossed a map into the back seat. "Will you find it, sir, and shout *directions*?"

"Yes!" Shaw laughed. "So long, Mr. Finn, so long, so long!"

And they drove away.

Heeber Finn finished and was silent.

There was a similar silence in the men lined up as audience along the bar.

Then someone lifted a gnarled hand and a callused palm, to beat it slowly against another of the same. And then one more enthusiast moved his paws and banged the air, followed by some other atheists turned believers, leastwise in Finn if nothing else, until the pub let down dust from the chandeliers and hung its pictures askew.

Finn poured and I said:

"Did all that *truly* happen?"

Finn froze as if he had put wet fingers to a frosted winter pipe and could not free his hand.

"I meant to say," I mumbled, "your facts are right, but were they *rearranged*?"

"Rearrange," wondered Finn. "Is that a course they teach at Berlitz?"

I lifted my glass. "Here's to Finn's. And the inhabitants thereof. And to that devil's advocate—"

"Shaw!"

"Who wandered far," I said, "but to come home to truth."

"God," said Finn. "You sound like *us*!"

"Drinks," I said, "all around!"

27

It was at lunch after a long morning of the *Pequod* becalmed.

We were in a Dublin restaurant with two newspaper reporters from London.

Soup had just been served and I had taken up my spoon, when John, looking deep into his broth, made this remark:

"You know, it makes me very sad to say this, but I really don't think that our young screenwriter here has his heart in the writing of the screenplay of *Moby Dick*."

I froze in place.

The two reporters looked at John and then at me and waited. John did not look up from his soup but went on:

"No, I just don't think that our friend here has his heart and his soul in this important film work."

My spoon fell from my fingers and lay on the tablecloth. I could not lift my eyes. My heart pounded, and I felt that at any moment I might leap up and run from the table. Instead I stayed with my gaze on my food, as the soup was taken away and the meat served and the meat taken away and the wine poured, which I did not drink, while John talked with the reporters and did not once look at me.

When it was over I walked like a blind man out of the restaurant and accompanied John up to my room in the Royal Hibernian Hotel. When we got inside I stood, swaying, looking at John, afraid that I might faint.

John looked at me for a long while, questioningly and at last said:

"What's wrong, kid?"

"Wrong, John? Wrong!" I cried at last. "Did you *hear* yourself at lunch today?"

"What, kid?"

"My God," I said. "Of all the people in the world I wanted to work for, it was you. Of all the novels in the world I would most want to adapt, it was Melville's. I have put my heart, soul, and guts in this day after day, with all my sweat and all my love, and now *you*, at *lunch*! Jesus! Don't you ever *listen* to yourself!?"

John widened his eyes and gaped. "Why, hell, kid, it was a joke. That's all. A joke, sure, only a joke!"

"A joke!" I yelled, and shut my eyes and burst into tears.

John stepped forward swiftly and took my shoulders and shook me gently and then put my head on his shoulder and let me cry. "Christ, kid," he kept saying. "It was all in fun. Don't you see? Fun."

It took a full minute for me to stop crying. We talked for a while and John left, telling me to head out to Kilcock that night with my latest pages for dinner, chat, and late-night whiskey.

When he was gone, I sat at the typewriter for a long while, swaying, not able to see the paper. And then at last, instead of writing "*Moby Dick*, page 79, scene 30, shot 2," I wrote something else.

Very slowly, I typed these words:
                    BANSHEE
                    A story
And then I wrote steadily for the next two hours.

It was one of those nights, crossing Ireland, motoring through the sleeping towns from Dublin, where you came upon mist and encountered fog that blew away in rain to become a blowing silence. All the country was still and cold and waiting. It was a night for strange encounters at empty crossroads with great filaments of ghost spiderweb and no spider in a hundred miles. Gates creaked far across meadows, where windows rattled with brittle moonlight.

It was, as they said, banshee weather. I sensed, I knew this as my taxi hummed through a final gate and I arrived at Courtown House, so far from Dublin that if that city died in the night, no one would know.

I paid my driver and watched the taxi turn to go back to the living city, leaving me alone with twenty pages of screenplay in my pocket, and my employer waiting inside. I stood in the midnight silence, breathing in Ireland and breathing out the damp coal mines in my soul.

Then I knocked.

The door flew wide almost instantly. John was there, shoving a glass of sherry into my hand and hauling me in.

"Good God, kid. Get that coat off. Give me the script. Almost finished, eh? So *you* say. You got me curious. The house is empty. The family's in Paris. We'll have a good read, knock the hell out of your scenes, drink a bottle, you can stay over, be in bed by two and—what's *that?*"

The door still stood open. John took a step, tilted his head, closed his eyes, listened.

The wind rustled beyond in the meadows. It made a sound

in the clouds like someone turning back the covers of a vast bed.

I listened.

There was the softest moan and sob from somewhere off in the dark fields.

Eyes still shut, John whispered, "You know what that is, kid?"

"What?"

"Tell you later. Jump."

With the door slammed, he turned about and, the grand lord of the empty manor, strode ahead of me in his hacking coat, drill slacks, polished half-boots, his hair, as always, wind-blown from swimming upstream or down with strange women in unfamiliar beds.

Planting himself on the library hearth, he gave me one of those beacon flashes of laughter, the teeth that beckoned like a lighthouse beam swift and gone, as he traded me a second sherry for the screenplay, which he had to seize from my hand.

"Let's see what my genius, my left ventricle, my right arm, has birthed. Sit. Drink. Watch." He stood astride the hearthstones, warming his backside, leafing the manuscript pages, conscious of me drinking my sherry much too fast, shutting my eyes each time he let a page drop and flutter to the carpet. When he finished he let the last page sail, lit a small cigarillo and puffed it, staring at the ceiling, making me wait.

"You son of a bitch," he said at last, exhaling. "It's good. Damn you to hell, kid. It's good!"

My skeleton collapsed within me. I had not expected such a midriff blow of praise.

"It needs a little cutting, of course!"

My skeleton reassembled itself.

"Of course," I said.

He bent to gather the pages like a great loping chimpanzee and turned. I felt he wanted to hurl them into the fire. He watched the flames and gripped the pages.

"Someday, kid," he said quietly, "you must teach me to write."

I was relaxing now, accepting the inevitable, full of true admiration.

"Someday," I said, laughing, "you must teach me to direct."

"*The Beast* will be *our* film, son. Quite a team."

I arose and came to clink glasses with him.

"Quite a team we are!" He changed gears. "How are the wife and kids?"

"They've arrived and are waiting for me in Sicily, where it's warm."

"We'll get you to them, and sun, straight off! I—"

John froze dramatically, cocked his head, and listened.

"Hey, what goes on . . ." he whispered.

I turned and waited.

This time, outside the great old house, there was the merest thread of sound, like someone running a fingernail over the paint, or someone sliding down out of the dry reach of a tree. Then there was the softest exhalation of a moan, followed by something like a sob.

John leaned in a starkly dramatic pose, like a statue in a stage pantomime, his mouth wide, as if to allow sounds entry to the inner ear. His eyes now unlocked to become as huge as hens' eggs with pretended alarm.

"Shall I tell you what that sound is, kid? A banshee!"

"A what?" I cried.

"Banshee!" he intoned. "The ghosts of old women who haunt the roads an hour before someone dies. *That's* what that sound was!" He stepped to the window, raised the shade, and peered out. "Shh! Maybe it means . . . *us!*"

"Cut it out, John!" I laughed quietly.

"No, kid, no." He fixed his gaze far into the darkness, savoring his melodrama. "I've lived here two years. Death's out there. The banshee always *knows*! Where were we?"

John broke the spell as simply as that, strode back to the hearth and blinked at the script as if it were a brand-new puzzle.

"You ever figure, kid, how much the Beast is like me? The hero plowing the seas, plowing women left and right, off round the world and no stops? Maybe that's why I'm doing it. You ever wonder how many women I've had? Hundreds! I—"

He stopped, for my lines on the page had shut him again. His face took fire as the words sank in.

"Brilliant!"

I waited, uncertainly.

"No, not that!" He threw the manuscript aside to seize a copy of the London *Times* off the mantel. "*This!* A brilliant review of your new book of stories!"

"What?" I jumped.

"Easy, kid. I'll *read* this grand review to you! You'll love it. Terrific!"

My heart took water and sank. I could see another joke coming on or, worse, the truth disguised as a joke.

"Listen!"

John lifted the *Times* and read, like Ahab, from the holy text.

" 'These stories may well be the huge success of American literature—' " John stopped and gave me an innocent blink. "How you like it so far, kid?"

"Continue, John," I mourned. I slugged my sherry back. It was a toss of doom that slid down to meet a collapse of will.

" '—but here in London,' " John intoned, " 'we ask more from our tellers of tales. Attempting to emulate the ideas of

Kipling, the style of Maugham, the wit of Waugh, he drowns somewhere in mid-Atlantic. This is ramshackle stuff, mostly bad shades of superior scribes. Young man, go home!' "

I leaped up and ran, but John, with a lazy flip of his underhand, tossed the *Times* into the fire, where it flapped like a dying bird and swiftly died in flame and roaring sparks.

Imbalanced, staring down, I was wild to grab that damned paper out but finally glad the thing was lost.

John studied my face happily. My face boiled, my teeth ground shut. My hand, struck to the mantel, was a cold rock fist.

Tears burst from my eyes, since words could not burst from my aching mouth.

"What's wrong, kid?" John peered up at me with true curiosity, like a monkey edging up to another sick beast in its cage. "You feeling poorly?"

"John, for Christ's sake!" I burst out. "Did you have to do *that*!"

I kicked at the fire, making the logs tumble and a great firefly wheel of sparks gush up the flue.

"Why, kid, I didn't think—"

"Like hell you didn't!" I blazed, turning to glare at him with tear-splintered eyes. "What's *wrong* with you?"

"Hell, nothing, kid. It was a fine review, great! I just added a few lines, to get your goat!"

"I'll never know now!" I cried. "Look!"

I gave the ashes a final, scattering kick.

"You can buy a copy in Dublin tomorrow, kid. You'll see. They love you. God, I just didn't want you to get a big head, right? The joke's over. Isn't it enough, dear son, that you have just written the finest scenes you ever wrote in your life for your truly great screenplay?" John put his arm around my shoulder.

That was John: kick you in the tripes, then pour on the wild sweet honey by the larder ton.

"Know what your problem is, son?" He shoved yet another sherry in my trembling fingers. "Eh?"

"What?" I gasped, like a sniveling kid, revived and wanting to laugh again. "What?"

"The thing is, kid . . ." John made his face radiant. His eyes fastened to mine like Svengali's. "You don't love me half as much as I love you!"

"Come on, John . . ."

"No, kid, I *mean* it. God, son, I'd kill for you. You're the greatest living writer in the world, and I love you, heart and soul. Because of that, I thought you could take a little leg-pull. I see that I was wrong—"

"No, John," I protested, hating myself, for now John was making *me* apologize. "It's all right."

"I'm sorry, kid, truly sorry—"

"Shut up!" I gasped a laugh. "I still love you. I—"

"That's a boy! Now—" John spun about, brisked his palms together, and shuffled and reshuffled the script pages like a cardsharp. "Let's spend an hour cutting this brilliant, superb scene of yours and—"

For the third time that night, the tone and color of his mood changed.

"Hist!" he cried. Eyes squinted, he swayed in the middle of the room, like a dead man under water. "Kid, you hear?"

The wind trembled the house. A long fingernail scraped an attic pane. A mourning whisper of cloud washed the moon.

"Banshees." John nodded, head bent, waiting. He glanced up, abruptly. "Kid? Run out and *see*."

"Like hell I will."

"No, go on out," John urged. "This has been a night of

misconceptions, kid. You doubt *me,* you doubt *it.* Get my overcoat, in the hall. Jump!"

He jerked the hall closet door wide and yanked out his great tweed overcoat, which smelled of tobacco and fine whiskey. Clutching it in his two monkey hands, he beckoned it like a bullfighter's cape. "Huh, *toro!* Hah!"

"John," I sighed, warily.

"Or are you a coward, kid, are you yellow? You—"

For this, the fourth time, we both heard a moan, a cry, a fading murmur beyond the wintry front door.

"It's waiting, kid!" said John triumphantly. "Get out there. Run for the *team!*"

I was in the coat, anointed by tobacco scent and booze, as John buttoned me up with royal dignity, grabbed my ears, kissed my brow.

"I'll be in the stands, kid, cheering you on. I'd go with you, but banshees are shy. Bless you, and if you don't come back . . . I loved you like a son!"

"Jesus," I exhaled, and flung the door wide.

But suddenly John leaped between me and the cold blowing moonlight.

"Don't go out there, kid. I've changed my mind! If you got killed . . ."

"John," I shook his hands away. "You *want* me out there. You've probably got your stable girl out there now, making noises for your big laugh—"

"No!" he cried in that mock-insult serious way he had, eyes wide, as he grasped my shoulders. "I swear to God!"

"John," I said, half angry, half amused, "so long."

I ran out the door, to immediate regrets. John slammed and locked the portal. Was he laughing? Seconds later, I saw John's silhouette at the library window, sherry glass in hand, peering out at this night theater of which he was both director and hilarious audience.

I spun with a quiet curse, hunched my shoulders in Caesar's cloak, ignored two dozen stab wounds given me by the wind, and stomped down along the gravel drive.

I'll give it a fast ten minutes, I thought, worry John, turn his joke inside out, stagger back in, shirt torn and bloody, with some fake tale of my own. Yes, by God, *that* was the trick—

I stopped.

For in a small grove of trees below, I thought I saw something like a large paper kite blossom and blow away among the hedges.

Clouds sailed over an almost full moon and ran islands of dark to cover me.

Then there it was again, farther on, as if a whole cluster of flowers were suddenly torn free to snow away along the colorless path. At the same moment, there was the merest catch of a sob, the merest door hinge of a moan.

I flinched, pulled back, then glanced up at the house.

There was John's face, of course, grinning like a pumpkin in the window, sipping sherry, toast-warm and at ease.

"Ohh..." a voice wailed somewhere. "God..."

It was then that I saw the woman.

She stood leaning against a tree, dressed in a long, moon-colored dress over which she wore a hip-length heavy woolen shawl that had a life of its own, rippling and winging out and hovering with the weather.

She seemed not to see me or, if she did, did not care; I could not frighten her, nothing in the world would ever frighten her again. Everything poured out of her steady and unflinching gaze toward the house, that window, the library, and the silhouette of the man in the window.

She had a face of snow, cut from that white cool marble that makes the finest Irish women; a long swan neck, a generous if quivering mouth, and eyes a soft and luminous green. So beautiful were those eyes, and her profile against the blown tree branches, that something in me turned, agonized, and died. I felt that killing wrench men feel when beauty passes and will not pass again. You want to cry out: Stay. I love you. But you do not speak. And the summer walks away in her flesh, never to return.

But now the beautiful woman, staring only at that window in the far house, spoke.

"Is he in there?" she said.

"What?" I heard myself say.

"Is that him?" she wondered. "The beast," she said, with quiet fury. "The monster. Himself."

"I don't—"

"The great animal," she went on, "that walks on two legs. He stays. All others go. He wipes his hands on flesh; girls are his napkins, women his midnight lunch. He keeps them stashed in cellar vintages and knows their years but not their names. Sweet Jesus, and is that *him*?"

I looked where she looked, at the shadow in the window, far off across the croquet lawn.

And I thought of my director in Paris, in Rome, in New York, in Hollywood, and the millraces of women I had seen John tread, feet printing their skins, a dark Christ on a warm sea. A picnic of women, dancing on tables, eager for applause, and John, on his way out, saying, "Dear, lend me a fiver. That beggar by the door kills my heart."

I watched this young woman, her dark hair stirred by the night wind, and asked:

"Who *should* he be?"

"Him," she said. "Him that lives there and loved me and now does not." She shut her eyes to let the tears fall.

"He doesn't live there anymore," I said.

"He does!" She whirled, as if she might strike or spit. "Why do you lie?"

"Listen." I looked at the new but somehow old snow in her face. "That was another time."

"No, there's only *now*!" She made as if to rush for the house. "And I love him still, so much I'd kill for it, and myself lost at the end!"

"What's his name?" I stood in her way. "His *name*?"

"Why, Joe, of course. Joey. Joseph!"

She moved. I raised my arms and shook my head.

"There's only a Johnny there now. A John."

"You lie! I feel him there. His name's changed, but it's *him*. Look! Feel!"

She put her hands up to touch on the wind toward the house, and I turned and sensed with her, and it was another year, it was a time between. The wind said so, as did the night and the glow in that great window where the shadow stayed.

"That's him!"

"A friend of mine," I said gently.

"No friend of anyone, ever!"

I tried to look through her eyes and thought: My God, has it always been this way, forever some man in that house, forty, eighty, a hundred years ago! Not the same man, no, but all dark twins, and this lost girl on the road, with snow in her arms for love, and frost in her heart for comfort, and nothing to do but whisper and croon and mourn and sob until the sound of her weeping stilled at sunrise, but to start again with the rising of the moon.

"That's my friend in there," I said again.

"If that be true," she whispered fiercely, "then you are my enemy!"

I looked down the road where the wind blew dust through the graveyard gates.

"Go back where you came from," I said.

She looked at the same road and the same dust, and her

voice faded. "Is there to be no peace, then?" she mourned. "Must I walk here, year on year, and no comeuppance?"

"If the man in there," I said, "was really your Joe, your Joseph, what would you have me do?"

"Send him out to me," she said quietly.

"What would you do with him?"

"Lie down with him," she murmured, "and ne'er get up again. He would be kept like a stone in a cold river."

"Ah," I said, and nodded.

"Will you ask him, then, to be sent?"

"No. For he's not yours. Much like. Near similar. And breakfasts on girls and wipes his mouth on their silks, one century called this, another that."

"And no love in him, ever?"

"He says the word as fishermen toss their nets in the sea," I said.

"Ah, Christ, and I'm caught!" And here she gave such a cry that the shadow came to the window in the great house across the lawn. "I'll stay here the rest of the night," she said. "Surely he will feel me here, his heart will melt, no matter what his name or how deviled his soul. What year is this? How long have I been waiting?"

"I won't tell you," I said. "The news would crack your heart."

She turned and truly looked at me. "Are you one of the good ones, then, the gentle men who never lie and never hurt and never have to hide? Sweet God, I wish I'd known you first!"

The wind rose, the sound of it rose in her throat. A clock struck somewhere far across the country in the sleeping town.

"I must go in," I said. I took a breath. "Is there no way for me to give you rest?"

"No," she said, "for it was not you that cut the nerve."

"I see," I said.

"You don't. But you try. Much thanks for that. Get in. You'll catch your death."

"And you . . . ?"

"Ha!" she cried. "I've long since caught mine. It will not catch again. Get!"

I gladly went. For I was full of the cold night and the white moon, old time, and her. The wind blew me up the grassy knoll. At the door, I turned. She was still there on the milky road, her shawl straight out on the weather, one hand up-raised.

"Hurry," I thought I heard her whisper. "Tell him he's needed!"

I rammed the door, slammed into the house, fell across the hall, my heart a bombardment, my image in the great hall mirror a shock of colorless lightning.

John was in the library, drinking yet another sherry, and poured me some. "Someday," he said, "you'll learn to take anything I say with more than a grain of salt. Jesus, look at you! Ice cold. Drink that down. Here's another to go after it!"

I drank, John poured, I drank. "Was it all a joke, then?"

"What *else?*" John laughed, then stopped.

The croon was outside the house again, the merest finger-nail of mourn, as the moon scraped down the roof.

"There's your banshee," I said, looking at my drink, unable to move.

"Sure, kid, sure, uh-huh," said John. "Drink your drink, kid, and I'll read you that great review of your book from the London *Times* again."

"You burned it, John."

"Sure, kid, but I recall it as if it were this morn. Drink up."

"John," I said, staring into the fire, looking at the hearth where the ashes of the burned paper blew in a great breath. "Does . . . did that review really exist?"

"My God, of course, sure, yes. Actually . . ." Here he paused and gave it great imaginative concern. "The *Times* knew my love for you, kid, and asked me to review your book." John reached his long arm over to refill the glass. "I did it. Under an assumed name, of course—now ain't that swell of me? But I had to be fair, kid, had to be fair. So I wrote what I truly felt were the good things, the not-so-good things in your book. Criticized it just that way I would when you hand in a lousy screenplay scene and I make you do it over. Now ain't that A-one double absolutely square of me? Eh?"

He leaned at me. He put his hand on my chin and lifted it and gazed long and sweetly into my eyes.

"You're not upset?"

"No," I said, but my voice broke.

"By God, now, if you aren't. Sorry. A joke, kid, only a joke." And here he gave me a friendly punch on the arm.

Slight as it was, it was a sledgehammer striking home.

"I wish you hadn't made it up, the joke, I wish the article was real," I said.

"So do I, kid. You look bad. I—"

The wind moved around the house. The windows stirred and whispered.

Quite suddenly I said, for no reason that I knew:

"The banshee. It's out there."

"That was a joke, kid. You got to watch out for me."

"No," I said, looking at the window. "It's there."

John laughed. "You saw it, did you?"

"It's a young and lovely woman with a shawl on a cold night. A young woman with long black hair and great green eyes and a complexion like snow and a proud Phoenician prow of a nose. Sound like anyone you ever in your life knew, John?"

"Thousands." John laughed more quietly now, looking to see the weight of his joke. "Hell—"

"She's waiting for you," I said. "Down at the bottom of the drive."

John glanced, uncertainly, at the window.

"That was the sound we heard," I said. "She described you or someone like you. Called you Joey, Joe, Joseph. But I *knew* it was you."

John mused. "Young, you say, and beautiful, and out there right this moment . . . ?"

"The most beautiful woman I've ever seen."

"Not carrying a knife . . . ?"

"Unarmed."

John exhaled. "Well, then, I think I should just go out there and have a chat with her, eh, don't you think?"

"She's waiting."

He moved toward the front door.

"Put on your coat; it's a cold night," I said.

He was putting on his coat when we heard the sound from outside, very clear this time. The wail and then the sob and then the wail.

"God," said John, his hand on the doorknob, not wanting to show the white feather in front of me. "She's *really* there."

He forced himself to turn the knob and open the door. The wind sighed in, bringing another faint wail with it.

John stood in the cold weather, peering down that long walk into the dark.

"Wait!" I cried, at the last moment.

John waited.

"There's one thing I haven't told you," I said. "She's out there, all right. And she's walking. But . . . she's dead."

"I'm not afraid," said John.

"No," I said, "but I am. You'll never come back. Much as I hate you right now, I can't let you go. Shut the door, John."

The sob again, and then the wail.

"Shut the door."

I reached over to knock his hand off the brass doorknob, but he held tight, cocked his head, looked at me, and sighed.

"You're really good, kid. Almost as good as me. I'm putting you in my next film. You'll be a star."

Then he turned, stepped out into the cold night, and shut the door quietly.

I waited until I heard his steps on the gravel path, then locked the door and hurried through the house, putting out the lights. As I passed through the library, the wind mourned down the chimney and scattered the dark ashes of the London *Times* across the hearth.

I stood blinking at the ashes for a long moment, then shook myself, ran upstairs two at a time, banged open my tower room door, slammed it, undressed, and was in bed with the covers over my head when a town clock, far away, sounded one in the deep morning.

And my room was so high, so lost in the house and the sky, that no matter who or what tapped or knocked or banged at the door below, whispering and then begging and then screaming . . .

Who could possibly hear?

I arrived at Courtown House late.

When John answered the door, I shoved the short story in but did not follow.

"What's wrong, kid?" John asked.

"Read that."

"It looks like a story. Where's the script?"

"Later. The story first. And listen, don't throw it page by page on the floor as you walk through the house reading it."

John cocked his head to one side. "Now, why in hell would I do a thing like that, son?"

"God. Just don't."

He walked away, leaving me to shut the door. Down the hall, I saw him turning the pages, nodding. In the library, I heard him mutter:

"Well, now. Looks like no more practical jokes at lunchtime. No more jokes."

28

"Good God in heaven, what's that?" I said.

"What's what?"

"Are you blind, man? Look!" I said.

And Garrity, the elevator operator, looked out to see what I was staring at.

And in out of the Dublin morn, sweeping through the front doors of the Royal Hibernian Hotel, along the entryway, and to the registry was a tall willowy man of some forty years, followed by five short willowy youths of some twenty years, a burst of bird song, their hands clapping all about on the air as they passed, their eyes squinching, batting, and flickering, their mouths pursed, their brows enlightened and then dark, their color flushed and then pale—or was it both?—their voices now flawless piccolo, now flute, now melodious oboe, but always tuneful. Carrying six monologues, all sprayed forth upon each other at once, in a veritable cloud of self-commiseration, peeping and twitting the discouragements of travel and the ardors of weather, the *corps de ballet* as it were flew, cascaded, flowed eloquently in a greater bloom of cologne by me and the transfixed elevator man. They collided deliciously to a halt at the desk, where the manager glanced up, to be swarmed over by their music. His eyes made nice round O's with no centers in them.

"What," whispered Garrity, "was that?"

"You may well ask," I said.

At which point the elevator lights flashed and the buzzer buzzed. Garrity had to tear his eyes off the summery crowd and heft himself skyward.

I whipped out my notepad and pen, sensing a new book of Revelations was about to be born.

"We," said the tall slender man with a touch of gray at the temples, "should like a room, please."

The manager remembered where he was and heard himself say, "Do you have reservations, sir?"

"Dear me, no," said the older man, as the others giggled. "We flew in unexpectedly from Taormina," the tall man with the chiseled features and the moist flower mouth continued. "We were getting so awfully bored, after following summer around the world, and someone said, Let's have a complete change, let's do something wild. What? I said. Well, where's the most improbable place in the world? Let's name it and go there. Somebody said the North Pole, but that was silly. Then I cried, Ireland! Everyone fell down. When the pandemonium ceased we just scrambled for the airport. Now sunshine and Sicilian shorelines are like yesterday's lime sherbet to us, all melted to nothing. And here we are to do . . . something *mysterious*!"

"Mysterious?" asked the manager.

"We don't know what it is," said the tall man. "But we shall know it when we see it, or it happens, or perhaps we shall have to make it happen—right, cohorts?"

The cohorts responded with something vaguely like Tee-hee.

"Perhaps," said the manager, with good grace, "if you gave me some idea what you're looking for in Ireland, I could point out—"

"Goodness, no," said the tall man. "We shall just plummet forth with our intuitions scarved about our necks, taking the wind as 'twere, and see what we shall tune in on. When we solve the mystery and find what we came to find, you will know of our discovery by the ululations and cries of awe and wonder emanating from our small tourist group."

"You can say *that* again," said the manager, under his breath.

"Well, comrades, let us sign in."

The leader of the encampment reached for a scratchy hotel pen, found it filthy, and flourished forth his own absolutely pure fourteen-karat solid-gold pen, with which in an obscure but rather pretty cerise calligraphy he inscribed on the registry the name *David* followed by *Snell* followed by dash and ending with *Orkney*. Beneath, he added, "And friends."

The manager watched the pen, fascinated, and once more recalled his position in all this. "But, sir, I haven't said if we have space—"

"Oh, surely you must, for six miserable wanderers in sore need of respite from overfriendly airline stewardesses. One room would do it!"

"One?" said the manager, aghast.

"We wouldn't mind the crowd, would we, chums?" asked the older man, not looking at his friends.

No, they wouldn't mind.

Neither did I, scribbling away madly.

"Well," said the manager, uneasily fumbling at the registry. "We just happen to have two adjoining—"

"*Perfecto!*" cried David Snell-Orkney.

And, the registration finished, the manager behind the desk

and the visitors from a far place stood regarding each other in a prolonged silence. At last the manager blurted, "Porter! Front! Take these gentlemen's luggage—"

But just then the hall porter ran over to look at the floor. Where there was no luggage.

"No, no, none." David Snell-Orkney airily waved his hand. "We travel light. We're here only for twenty-four hours, or perhaps only twelve, with a change of underwear stuffed in our overcoats. Then back to Sicily and warm twilights. If you want me to pay in advance . . ."

"That won't be necessary," said the manager, handing the keys to the hall porter. "Forty-six and forty-seven, please."

"It's done," said the porter.

And like a collie dog silently nipping the hooves of some woolly, long-haired, bleating, dumbly smiling sheep, he herded the lovely bunch toward the elevator, which wafted down just at that precise moment.

I paused in my scribbling because . . . at the desk, the manager's wife came up, steel-eyed, behind him. "Are you mad?" she whispered wildly. "Why? Why?"

"All my life," said the manager, half to himself, "I have wished to see not one Communist but ten close by, not two Nigerians but twenty in their skins, not three cowboy Americans but a gross fresh from the saddle. So when six hothouse roses come in a bouquet, I could not resist potting them. The Dublin winter is long, Meg; this may be the only lit fuse in the whole year. Stand by for the lovely concussion."

"Fool," she said.

No, I think not, I thought.

As we watched, the elevator, freighted with hardly more than the fluff from a blown dandelion, whisked up the shaft, away.

• • •

It was exactly at high noon that a series of coincidences occurred that tottered and swerved toward the miraculous, and myself at the eye of the maelstrom.

Now, the Royal Hibernian Hotel lies half between Trinity College, if you'll excuse the mention, and St. Stephen's Green, which is more like it, and around behind is Grafton Street, where you can buy silver, glass, and linen, or pink hacking coats, boots, and caps to ride off to the goddamned hounds; or, better still, duck in to The Four Provinces pub for a proper proportion of drink and talk—an hour of drink to two hours of talk is about the best prescription.

It was high noon, and out of the Hibernian Hotel front who should come now but Snell-Orkney and his canary five, myself following and taking dictation, but telling no one.

Then there was the first of a dumbfounding series of confrontations.

For passing by, sore torn between the sweet shops and The Four Provinces, was Timulty himself.

Timulty, as you recall, when Blight, Famine, Starvation, and other mean Horsemen drive him, works a day here or there at the Kilcock post office. Now, idling along between dread employments, he smelled a smell as if the gates of Eden had swung wide again and him invited back in after a hundred million years. So Timulty looked up to see what made the wind blow out of the Garden.

And the wind, of course, was in tumult about Snell-Orkney and his uncaged pets.

Timulty, frozen to the spot, watched the Snell-Orkney delegation flow down the steps and around the corner. At which point he decided on sweeter things than candy and rushed the long way to the Provinces.

I walked briskly after, feeling like a stage manager at an animal fair.

Ahead of me, rounding the corner, Mr. David Snell-

Orkney-plus-five passed a beggar lady playing a harp in the street. And there, with nothing else to do but dance the time away, was my taxi driver, Mike himself, flinging his feet about in a self-involved rigadoon to "Lightly o'er the Lea." Dancing, Mike heard a sound that was like the passing of warm weather from the Hebrides. It was not quite a twittering nor a whir, and it was not unlike a pet shop when the bell tinkles as you step in and a chorus of parakeets and doves starts up in coos and light shrieks. But hear he did, above the sound of his own shoes and the pringle of harp. He froze in mid-jig.

As David Snell-Orkney-plus-five swept by, all tropic-smiled and gave him a wave.

Before he knew what he was doing, Mike waved back, then stopped and seized his wounded hand to his breast. "What the hell am I waving for?" he cried to me as I arrived. "I don't know them, *do* I?"

"Ask God for strength!" I said as the harpist flung her fingers down the strings.

Drawn as by some strange new vacuum cleaner that swept all before it, Mike and I followed the Team down the street.

Which takes care of two senses now, the sense of smell and the use of the ears.

It was at the *next* corner that Nolan, bursting from The Four Provinces pub with an argument pursuing, came around the bend fast and ran bang into David Snell-Orkney. Both swayed and grabbed each other for support.

"Top of the afternoon!" said David Snell-Orkney.

"The back side of something!" replied Nolan, and fell away, gaping to let the circus by. I could see in his eyes that he had a terrible urge to rush back in to report upon this fell encounter with a feather duster, a Siamese cat, a spoiled Pekingese, and three others gone ghastly frail from under-eating and overwashing.

The six stopped outside the pub, looking up at the sign.

Lord, I thought. They're going *in*. What will *come* of it? Who do I warn first? Them? Or the bartender?

Then the door opened. Finn himself looked out. Finn, come into town to visit his cousin, and now ruining the occasion by his very presence! "Damn," said Nolan, "that spoils it! Now we won't be allowed to describe this adventure. It will be Finn this, Finn that, and shut up to us all!"

There was a long moment when Snell-Orkney and his cohorts looked at Finn. Finn's eyes did not fasten on them. He looked above. He looked over. He looked beyond.

But he *had* seen them, this I knew. For now a lovely thing happened.

All the color went out of Finn's face.

Then an even lovelier thing happened.

All the color rushed back into Finn's face.

Why, I thought, he's . . . *blushing*!

But still Finn refused to look anywhere save the sky, the lamps, the street, until Snell-Orkney trilled, "Sir, which way to St. Stephen's Green?"

"Jesus," said Finn, and retreated. "Who knows *where* they put it *this* week!" and slammed the door.

The six went on up the street, all smiles and delight, and Nolan was all for heaving himself through the door when a worse thing happened.

Garrity, the elevator operator from the Royal Hibernian Hotel, whipped across the sidewalk from nowhere. His face ablaze with excitement, he ran into The Four Provinces to spread the word.

By the time Nolan and I were inside, and Timulty rushing in next, Garrity was all up and down the length of the bar, passing Finn, who was suffering concussions from which he had not as yet recovered.

"It's a shame you missed it!" cried Garrity to all. "I mean, it was the next thing to one of the fiction-and-science fillums they show at the Gayety Cinema!"

"How do you mean?" asked Finn, shaken out of his trance.

"*Nothing,* they weigh!" Garrity told them. "Lifting them in the elevator was throwing a handful of chaff up a chimney! And you should have *heard.* They're here in Ireland for"— he lowered his voice and squinched his eyes—"for *mysterious reasons!*"

"Mysterious?" I prompted.

"They'll put no name to it, but mark my declaration, they're up to no good! Have you ever seen the like?"

"Not since the great fire at the convent," Nolan said. "I—" But the word "convent" seemed one more magic touch. The doors sprang wide at this. Father Leary entered in reverse. That is to say, he backed into the pub, one hand to his cheek, as if the Fates had dealt him a proper blow unbewares.

Reading the look of his spine, the men shoved their noses in their drinks until such time as the father had put a bit of the brew into himself, still staring as if the door were the gates of Hell ajar.

"Beyond," said the father, at last, "not two minutes gone, I saw a sight as would be hard to credit. In all the days of her collecting up the grievances of the world, has Ireland indeed gone mad?"

The priest's glass was refilled. "Was you standing in the blast of The Invaders from the Planet Venus, Father?"

"Have you seen them, then, Finn?" the father said.

"Yes, and do you guess them bad, Your Holiness?"

"It's not so much bad or good as strange and *outré,* Finn, and words like *rococo,* I should guess, and *baroque* if you go with my drift."

"I lie easy in the tide, sir."

"When last seen, where heading?" I asked.

"On the edge of the green," said the priest. "You don't imagine there'll be a bacchanal in the park now?"

"The weather won't allow, beg your pardon, Father," said Nolan, "but it strikes me, instead of standing with the bag in our mouth and not eating oats, we should be out on the spy—"

"You move against my ethics," said the priest.

"A drowning man clutches at anything," I said, "and ethics may drown with him if *that's* what he grabs instead of a life belt."

"Off the Mount," said the priest, "and enough of the Sermon. What's your point?"

"His point is, Father," panted Nolan, "we have had no such influx of honorary Sicilians since the mind boggles to remember. For all we know, at this moment, they may be reading aloud to Mrs. Murphy, Miss Clancy, or Mrs. O'Hanlan in the midst of the park. And reading aloud from *what*, I ask you?"

" 'The Ballad of Reading Gaol?' " guessed Finn.

"You have rammed the target and sunk the ship," Nolan grouched, maddened that the point had been plucked from him. "How did we know these imps out of bottles are not selling real-estate tracts in a place called Fire Island? Have you *heard* of it, Father?"

"The American gazettes come often to my table, man."

"Well, do you remember the great hurricane of nineteen-and-forty-six, when the waves washed over Fire Island there in New York? An uncle of mine, God save his sanity and sight, was with the coast guard there, which evacuated the entirety of the population of Fire Island. It was worse than the twice-a-year showing at Fennelly's dressworks, he said. It was more terrible than a Baptist convention. Ten thousand men came rushing down to the stormy shore carrying bolts of drape material, cages full of parakeets, tomato- and tangerine-colored sport coats, and lime-colored shoes. It was the most tumultuous scene since Hieronymus Bosch laid down his palette after he painted Hell for all generations to come. You do not easily evacuate ten thousand Venetian-glass boyos with their great blinky cow eyes, and their phonograph symphonic records in their hands, and their rings in their ears, without tearing down the middle. My uncle, soon after, took to the heavy drink."

"Tell us *more* about that night," said Kilpatrick, entranced.

"More, hell," said the priest. "Out, I say. Surround the park. Keep your eyes peeled. And meet me back here in an hour."

"That's more like it," cried Kelly. "Let's *really* see what dread thing they're up to!"

The doors banged wide. They flew back. I fended them off and the directionless mob on the sidewalk, and the priest used his compass. "Kelly, Murphy, you around the north side of the park. Timulty, you to the south. Nolan, Clannery, and Garrity, the east; Moran, MaGuire, Kilpatrick, the west. Git!" But somehow or other in all the ruction, Kelly and Murphy wound up at The Four Shamrocks pub, halfway to the green, and fortified themselves for the chase, and Nolan and Moran each met their wives on the street and had to run back to the Provinces, and MaGuire and Kilpatrick, passing the Grafton Street Cinema and hearing Deanna Durbin singing inside, cadged their way in to join Doone, who I knew was spending the afternoon there.

So it wound up with just two, Garrity on the east and Timulty on the south side of the park, looking in at the visitors from another world. I joined Timulty, who, in concentration, refused conversation.

After half an hour of freezing weather, Garrity stomped up to us and cried, "What's *wrong* with the fiends? They're just *standing* there in the midst of the park. They haven't moved half the afternoon. And it's cut to the bone is my toes. I'll nip around to the hotel, warm up, and rush back to stand guard with you, Tim, and you, Yank!"

"Take your time," called Timulty in a strange sad wandering philosophical voice, as the other charged away.

Ignoring me, Timulty walked into the park and sat for a full hour watching the six men, who, as before, did not move. You might almost have thought, to see Timulty there, with his eyes brooding and his mouth gone into tragic crease, that he was some Irish neighbor of Kant or Schopenhauer, or had just read something by a poet or thought of a song that declined his spirits. And when at last the hour was up and he had gathered his thoughts like a handful of cold pebbles, he turned and made his way out of the park to me, just as Garrity ran back to pound his feet and swing his hands. But before he could explode with questions, Timulty pointed in and said, "Go sit. Look. Think. Then *you* tell *me*."

Everyone at The Four Provinces looked up sheepishly when I opened the door and beckoned Timulty in. The priest was still off on errands around the city, and after a few walks about the green to assuage their consciences, all had returned, nonplussed, to intelligence headquarters.

"Timulty!" they cried. "Yank! Tell us! What? What?"

Timulty took his time walking to the bar and sipping his drink. Silently, he observed his own image remotely buried beneath the lunar ice of the barroom mirror. He turned the subject this way. He twisted it inside out. He put it back wrong-side-to. Then he shut his eyes and said:

"It strikes me as how . . ."

Yes, said all silently, about him.

"From a lifetime of travel and thought, it comes to the top of my mind," Timulty went on, "there is a strange resemblance between the likes of them and the likes of us."

There was such a gasp as changed the scintillation, the

goings and comings of light in the prisms of the little chandeliers over the bar. When the schools of fish-light had stopped swarming at this exhalation, Nolan cried, "Do you mind putting your hat on so I can knock it off!?"

"Yeah! Put it on, knock it off!" cried everyone.

"Hush," I said.

"Consider," Timulty calmly said. "Are we or are we not great ones for the poem and the song?"

Another kind of gasp went through the crowd. There was a lame burst of approval. "Oh, sure, we're *that*!" "My God, is *that* all you're up to?" "We were afraid—"

"Hold it!" Timulty raised a hand, eyes still closed.

And all shut up.

"If we're not singing the songs, we're writing them, and if not writing, dancing them, and aren't *they* fond admirers of the song and the writing of same and the dancing out the whole? Well, just now I heard them at a distance reciting poems and singing, to themselves, in the green."

Timulty had something there. Everyone had to paw everybody and admit it.

"Do you find any *other* resemblances?" asked Finn heavily, glowering.

"I do," said Timulty, with a judge's manner.

There was a still more fascinated indraw of breath and the crowd drew nearer, as I took notes in a fever.

"They do not mind a drink now and then," said Timulty.

"By God, he's right!" cried Murphy.

"Also," intoned Timulty, "they do not marry until very late, if ever at all! And—"

But here the tumult was such he had to wait for it to subside before he could finish:

"And they—ah—have very little to do with women."

After that there was a great clamor, a yelling and shoving

about and ordering of drinks, and someone invited Timulty outside. But Timulty wouldn't even lift one eyelid, and the brawler was held off, and when everyone had a new drink in him and the near-fistfights had drained away, one loud clear voice, Finn's, declared:

"Now would you mind explaining the criminal comparison you have just made in the clean air of this honorable pub?"

Timulty sipped his drink slowly and then at last opened his eyes and looked at Finn steadily and said, with a clear bell-trumpet tone and wondrous enunciation:

"Where in all of Ireland can a man lie down with a woman?"

He let that sink in.

"Three hundred twenty-nine days a damn year it rains. The rest it's so wet there's no dry piece, no bit of land you would dare trip a woman out flat on for fear of her taking root and coming up in leaves—do you deny that?"

The silence did not deny.

"So when it comes to places to do sinful evils and perform outrageous acts of the flesh, it's to Arabia the poor damn-fool Irishman must take himself. It's Arabian dreams we have, of warm nights, dry land, and a decent place not just to sit down but to lie down on, and not just lie down on but to roister joyfully about on in clinches and clenches of outrageous delight."

"Ah, Jaisus," said Finn, "you can say *that* again."

"Ah, Jaisus," said everyone, nodding.

"That's number one." Timulty ticked it off on his finger. "Place is lacking. Then, second, time and circumstances. For say you should sweet-talk a fair girl into a field, eh? in her rain boots and slicker and her shawl over her head and her umbrella over that and you making noises like a stuck pig half over the sty gate, which means you've got one hand in her bosom and the other wrestling with her boots, which is as far as you'll damn well get, for who's standing there behind you, and you feel his sweet spearmint breath on your neck?"

"The father from the local parish?" offered Garrity.

"The father from the local parish," said everyone, in despair.

"There's nails number two and three in the cross on which all Ireland's males hang crucified," said Timulty.

"Go on, Timulty, go on."

"Those fellows visiting here from Sicily run in teams. *We* run in teams. Here we are, the gang from Finn's pub, are we *not?*"

"Be damned and we are!"

"*They* look sad and are melancholy half the time and then spitting like happy demons the rest, either up or down, never in between—and who does *that* remind you of?"

Everyone looked in the mirror and nodded.

"If we had the choice," said Timulty, "to go home to the dire wife and the dread mother-in-law and the old-maid sister, all sour sweats and terrors, or stay here for one more song or one more drink or one more story, *which* would all of us men choose?"

Silence.

"Think on that," said Timulty. "Answer the truth. Resemblances. Similarities. The long list of them runs off one hand and up the other arm. And well worth the mulling over before we leap about crying Jaisus and Mary and summoning the guard."

Silence.

"I," said someone, after a long while, strangely, curiously, "would like . . . to see them closer."

"I think you'll get your wish. Hist!" I said, not too dramatically, considering the situation.

All froze in a tableau.

And far off we heard a faint and fragile sound. It was like the wondrous morning you wake and lie in bed and know by a special feel that the first fall of snow is in the air, on its way down, tickling the sky, making the silence to stir aside and fall back in on nothing.

"Ah, God," said Finn, at last, "it's the first day of spring. . . ."

And it was that too. First the dainty snowfall of feet drifting on the cobbles, and then a choir of bird song.

And along the sidewalk and down the street and outside the pub came the sounds that were winter *and* spring. The doors sprang wide. The men reeled back from the impact of the meeting to come. They steeled their nerves. They balled their fists. They geared their teeth in their anxious mouths, and into the pub like children come into a Christmas place and everything a bauble or a toy, a special gift or color, there stood the tall thin older man who looked young and the small thin younger men who had old things in their eyes. The sound of snowfall stopped. The sound of spring birds ceased.

The strange children herded by the strange shepherd found themselves suddenly stranded as if they sensed a pulling away of a tide of people, even though the men at the bar had flinched but the merest hair.

The children of a warm isle regarded the short child-sized and runty full-grown men of this cold land, and the full-grown men looked back in mutual assize.

Timulty and the men at the bar breathed long and slow. You could smell the terrible clean smell of the children way over here. There was too much spring in it. Even I backed off a bit.

Snell-Orkney and his young-old boy-men breathed swiftly as the heartbeats of birds trapped in a cruel pair of fists. You could smell the dusty, impacted, prolonged, and dark-clothed smell of the little men way over there. There was too much winter in it.

Each might have commented upon the other's choice of scent, but—

At this moment the double doors at the side banged wide and Garrity charged in full-blown, crying the alarm:

"Jesus, I've seen everything! Do you know where they are *now*, and what *doing?*"

Every hand at the bar flew up to shush him.

By the startled look in their eyes, the intruders knew they were being shouted about.

"They're still at St. Stephen's Green!" Garrity, on the move, saw naught that was before him. "I stopped by the hotel to spread the news. Now it's your turn. Those fellows—"

"Those fellows," said David Snell-Orkney, "are here in . . ." He hesitated.

"The Four Provinces," said Heeber Finn, looking at his shoes.

"The Four Provinces," said the tall man, nodding his thanks.

"Where," said Garrity, gone miserable, "we will all be having a drink instantly."

He flung himself at the bar.

But the six intruders were moving also. They made a small parade to either side of Garrity and just by being amiably there made him hunch three inches smaller.

"Good afternoon," said Snell-Orkney.

"It is and it isn't," I said, carefully, waiting.

"It seems," said the tall man surrounded by the little boy-men, "there is much talk about what we are doing in Ireland."

"That would be putting the mildest interpretation on it," said Finn.

"Allow me to explain," said Mr. David Snell-Orkney.

"Have you ever," he continued, "heard of the Snow Queen and the Summer King?"

Several jaws trapped wide down.

Someone gasped as if booted in the stomach.

I have, I thought, but go on.

Finn, after a moment in which he considered just where a blow might have landed upon him, took a long, slow sip of his ale with scowling precision and, with the fire in his mouth, replied, carefully, letting the warm breath out over his tongue:

"Ah... *what* Queen is that again, *and* what damned King?"

The men at the bar leaned forward, in favor of storytelling anytime; then caught themselves and leaned back.

"Well," said the tall pale man, "there was this Queen who lived in Iceland, who had never seen summer, and this King who lived in the Isles of Sun, who had never seen winter."

"Ya don't say?" said Nolan.

Finn scowled at Nolan. "He will, if he has a *chance!*"

The men muttered at Nolan, who tucked in his head.

Snell-Orkney said: "The people under the King almost died of heat in the summers.... And the people under the Snow Queen almost died of ice in the long cold winters. But both monarchs had deep compassion for their people and decided they could not allow their suffering any longer. So in the autumn of one year the Snow Queen followed the cry of geese going south—to fair weather. And the Sun King followed the hot winds blowing north until they were cooled. In the quiet of a forest, they saw one another. She was a woman all white as the snows of forever, a drift of eternity, the blizzards of Time, the moonlight on glaciers and wind blowing the frail curtains of a window in winter. White. All white!"

The men at the bar murmured at this description.

"As for the Sun King?" Snell-Orkney smiled. "He was all

fire, all warm and all blazing and as bright as the fires of whole forests aflame. Self-consumed in his burning conflagrations of yearning! The Sun King indeed. The King of the Sun!

"They grew nearer. And looking into each other's eyes, they fell in love. And were married. And every winter, when the cold killed people in the north, all of the Snow Queen's people moved south, and lived in the mild island sun. And in the summer, when the sun killed the people in the south, all of the Sun King's people moved north, to be refreshed and cooled. So there were no longer two nations, two peoples, but *one* race, which commuted from land to land with the changing of the weathers and the shifting of the seasons, forever and forever." Snell-Orkney paused.

The men were spelled. They looked around at each other. They muttered. The mutter grew. They stirred. Then Nolan began to applaud. Garrity picked up. So did Finn and Timulty, and all the rest, until it really seized them and they gave glad cries. I joined them.

It was a true standing ovation, in which Snell-Orkney stood drenched in their approval. He shut his eyes shyly and gave a small bow of his head.

Then, quite suddenly, each man discovered his own hands beating the air. The men became self-conscious of their applause. The applauding died down as each slowed the beat of his palms. They glanced around in wonder, to find themselves approving of those that they had, not long ago, doubted. The men studied each other's hands, but at last Finn blurted:

"Ah, what the hell!"

And he gave more applause, as did the men. It rang the rafters. It exploded. It concussed as all cried: Sure, what the hell! ... Yeah! ... Who gives a damn! ... Well done!

The thunder died. Snell-Orkney stood there, blushing, as Timulty said:

"God, if you only had a brogue, what a teller of tales you would make!"

Aye! . . . Sure! . . . Right! said all.

"Would you *teach* me the brogue, sir?" asked Snell-Orkney.

Timulty hesitated. "I . . . well . . . ah, God! Why not! Yes! If you're goin' ta shoot off your mouth, best do it right!"

"Many thanks," said Snell-Orkney.

Finn interrupted, hesitantly. "Somewhere along the line we have missed the point of your dear story. I mean, the *reason* you told us about the Queen and the King and all that."

"How silly of me," said Snell-Orkney. "We are the Sun King's children. Which means that we have not seen autumn in five years, or seen a snowflake melt, or felt a winter wind, or heard a windowpane crack with frost. We hardly know a cloud when we see it. We are parched for weather. We must have rain, or possibly, snow, or perish—right, chums?"

"Oh, right, yes, right," said all five in a sweet chirruping.

Outside, there was a pulse of light, thunder, sounds of possible rain, promises of snow.

Finn nodded, pleased. "God listens real *close*."

To which the men added vociferously: Oh, you'll get plenty of rain . . . Lots . . . You'll drown . . . Prepare to swim.

Snell-Orkney went on: "We have followed summer 'round the world. We have lived in the warm and the superwarm and the hot months in Jamaica and Nassau."

"Port-au-Prince," said one of the chums.

"Calcutta," said a second.

"Madagascar, Bali," said a third.

"Florence, Rome, Taormina!" added the fourth.

"But finally, just yesterday, we heard, on the news, this is one of those years in Dublin with exceptional snow. Where in all the world, we said, would we most like to see snow?

So we said, Let's go north, we must have cold again. We didn't quite know what we were looking for, but we found it in St. Stephen's Green."

"The *mysterious* thing?" Nolan burst out, then clapped his hand to his mouth. "I mean—"

"Your friend here will tell you," said the tall man.

"*Our* friend? You mean—Garrity?"

Everyone looked at Garrity.

"As I was going to say," said Garrity, "when I banged in the door. They was in the park, standing there . . . *watching the autumn leaves* fall off because the trees were loaded with *ice*!"

"Is that *all*?" cried Nolan, dismayed.

"It seemed sufficient unto the moment," said Snell-Orkney.

"*Are* there any leaves left up at St. Stephen's?" asked Timulty. "And are the damn trees covered with snow!?"

Nobody seemed to know. We all stood still.

"Hell," said Timulty numbly, "it's been twenty years since I *looked*."

"Me? Twenty-five years," said Garrity.

"Thirty!" admitted Nolan.

"The most incredible treasure in all the world," said Snell-Orkney. "A few touches of scarlet and amber and rust and wine, the relics of time, the husks of old summer, somehow left on the branches. But the trees themselves! The branches, the boughs cloaked in sheaths of ice, costumed in frost, burdened with snow that blows away in plumes, whispering! Ah, dear!"

All were enchanted. "Aw, now . . . sure . . . well . . . ," they muttered.

"He speaks deep," whispered Nolan.

"Drinks all around!" cried Snell-Orkney, suddenly.

"He's touched *bottom*," said Timulty.

The drinks were poured and drunk.

"Now, where *are* them damned trees?" cried Nolan.

Yeah ... By God ... Right! said all.

And not ten minutes later we were all up at the park, together.

And well now, as Timulty said, did you ever see as many damned leaves left on a tree as there was on the first tree just inside the gate at St. Stephen's Green? No! cried all. And what, though, about the *second* tree? Well, it was not so many leaves as it was frost and sheaths of ice and snow, that as you watched just lifted and blew in spirals and whirls down into the men's faces. And the more they looked, the more they saw it was a wonder. And Nolan went around craning his neck so hard he fell over on his back and had to be helped up by two or three others, and there were general exhalations of awe and proclamations of devout inspiration as to the fact that as far as they could remember, there had never *been* any goddamn leaves or snow on the trees to begin with, but now they were there! Or if they had been there, they had *never* had any color, or if they *had* had color, well, it was so long ago ... Ah, what the hell, shut up, said everyone, and look!

Which is exactly what Nolan and Timulty and Kelly and Garrity and Snell-Orkney and his friends and I did for the rest of the declining afternoon. For a fact, autumn had taken its colors out, but winter had truly arrived to cover the park white on white. Which is exactly where Father Leary found us.

But before he could say anything, three out of the six summer invaders asked him if he would hear their confessions.

And the next thing you know, with a look of great pain and alarm the father was taking Snell-Orkney & Co. back to see the stained glass at the church and the way the apse was put together by a master architect, and they liked his church so much and said so out loud again and again that he cut way down on their Hail Marys and the rigmaroles that went with.

But the top of the entire day was when one of the young-old boy-men back at the pub asked what would it be? Should he sing "Mother Machree" or "My Buddy"?

Arguments followed, and with polls taken and results announced, he sang *both*.

He had a dear voice, all said, eyes melting bright. A sweet high clear voice.

And as Nolan put it, "He wouldn't make much of a son. But there's a great daughter there somewhere!"

And all said "Aye" to that.

And Snell-Orkney and his pals prepared to leave.

But seeing this, Finn raised a great hand to prevent.

"Hold on! You have improved the weather in and out of the park and the pub. Now we must hand back some of the same to you!"

"Oh, no, no," was the protest.

"Yes!" said Finn. "Men?"

"Finn!" they responded.

"Shall we show them a sprint?"

"A sprint?" There was an onslaught of jubilation. "Yes!"

"A sprint?" said Snell-Orkney and his chums.

29

"There's no doubt of it, Doone's the best." Added Finn: "Anthem sprinter, that is."

"Devil take Doone!"

"His reflex is uncanny, his lope on the incline extraordinary, he's off and gone before you reach for your hat."

"Hoolihan's better anytime."

"Time, hell. *Now?* Before the tall gent with the pale face and his congregation get away?"

Or, I thought, before everything shuts at once, in a few hours, meaning spigots, accordions, piano lids, soloists, trios, quartets, pubs, sweet shops, and cinemas. In a great heave like the Day of Judgment, half Dublin's population would be thrown out into raw lamplight, there to find themselves wanting in gum-machine mirrors. Stunned, their moral and physical sustenance plucked from them, the souls would wander like battered moths for a moment, then wheel about for home.

But now here I was listening to a discussion the heat of which, if not the light, reached me and Snell-Orkney's crew at fifty paces.

"Doone!"

"Hoolihan!"

Timulty charted my face then glanced at Snell-Orkney and said: "Are you wondering what we're up to? Are you much for sports? Do you know, for instance, the cross-country, the four hundred, and such man-on-foot excursions?"

"I've witnessed two Olympic Games." said Snell-Orkney.

Timulty gasped. "You're the rare one. Well, now, what do you know of the special all-Irish decathlon event which has to do with picture theaters?"

"The anthem sprint you have just mentioned," said Snell-Orkney.

"Hold on," I finally said. "*What* kind of sprint?"

"A-n-t-," spelled Finn, "h-e-m. Anthem. Sprinter."

"Since you came to Dublin," Timulty cut in, "I know that you, being a fillum man, have attended the cinema."

"Last night," I said, "I saw a Clark Gable film. Night before, an old Charles Laughton—"

"Enough! You're a fanatic, I know, as are all the Irish. If it weren't for cinemas and pubs to keep the poor and workless off the street or in their cups, we'd have pulled the cork and let the isle sink long ago. Well." He clapped his hands. "When the picture ends each night, have you observed a peculiarity of the breed?"

"End of the picture?" I mused. "Hold on! You can't mean the *national* anthem, can you?"

"*Can* we, boys?" cried Timulty.

"We can!" cried all.

"Any night, every night, for tens of dreadful years, at the end of each damn fillum, as if you'd never heard the baleful tune before," grieved Timulty, "the orchestra strikes up for Ireland. And what happens *then?*"

"Why"—I fell in with it—"if you're any man at all, you try to get out of the theater in those few precious moments between the end of the film and the start of the anthem."

"You've nailed it!"

"Buy the Yank a drink!"

"After all," I said casually, "after a few times the anthem begins to pale. No disrespect meant," I added hastily.

"And none taken!" said Timulty. "Or given by any of us patriotic IRA veterans, survivors of the Troubles and lovers of country. Still, breathing the same air ten thousand reprises makes the senses reel. So, as you've noted, in that God-sent three- or four-second interval, any audience in its right mind beats it the hell out. And the best of the crowd is—"

"Doone," said Snell-Orkney. "Or perhaps Hoolihan. Your anthem sprinters!"

Everyone smiled, proud of his intuition.

"Now," said Timulty, his voice husky with emotion, his eyes squinted off at the scene, "at this very moment, not one hundred yards down the slight hill, in the comfortable dark of the Grafton Street Theatre, seated on the aisle of the fourth row center, is—"

"Doone," I said.

"The man's eerie," said Hoolihan, lifting his cap to me.

"Well . . ." Timulty swallowed. "Doone's there, all right. He's not seen the fillum before—it's a Deanna Durbin brought back by the asking—and the time is now . . ."

Everyone glanced at the wall clock.

"Ten o'clock!" said the crowd.

"And in just fifteen minutes the cinema will be letting the customers out for good and all."

"And?" I asked.

"And," said Timulty. "And! If we should send Hoolihan, here, in for a test of speed and agility, Doone would be ready to meet the challenge."

"You people don't go to the cinema just for an anthem sprint, do you?" asked Snell-Orkney.

"Good grief, no. We go for the Deanna Durbin songs and all. But if Doone, for instance, should casually note the entrance of Hoolihan, here, who would make himself conspicuous by his late arrival just across from Doone, well, Doone would know what was up. They would salute each other and both sit listening to the dear music until *finis* hove in sight."

"Sure." Hoolihan danced lightly on his toes, flexing his elbows. "Let me at him, let me *at* him!"

Timulty peered close at me. "Lad, I observe that the details of the sport have bewildered you. How is it, you ask, that full-grown men have time for such as this? Well, time is the one thing the Irish have plenty of lying about. With no jobs at hand, what's minor in your country must be made to look major in ours. We have never seen the elephant, but we've learned a bug under a microscope is the greatest beast on earth. So while it hasn't passed the border, the anthem sprint's a high-blooded sport once you're in it. Let me nail down the rules!"

"First," said Hoolihan reasonably, "knowing what they know now, find out if these gents want to bet."

Everyone looked at Snell-Orkney and me to see if their reasoning had been wasted.

"Yes," we said.

All agreed we were better than human.

"Designations are in order," said Timulty. "Here's Fogarty, exit-watcher supreme. Nolan and Clannery, aisle-superintendent judges. Clancy, timekeeper. And general spectators O'Neill, Bannion, and the Kelly boys, count 'em! Come on!"

I felt as if a vast street-cleaning machine, one of those brambled monsters all mustache and scouring brush, had seized me. The amiable mob floated Snell-Orkney and associates and myself down the hill toward the multiplicity of little blinking lights where the cinema lured us on. Hustling, Timulty shouted the essentials:

"Much depends on the character of the theater, of course!"

"Of course!" I yelled back.

"There be the liberal freethinking theaters, with grand aisles, grand exits, and even grander, more spacious latrines. Some with so much porcelain, the echoes alone put you in shock. Then there's the parsimonious mousetrap cinemas, with aisles that squeeze the breath from you, seats that knock your knees, and doors best sidled out of on your way to the men's lounge in the sweet shop across the alley. Each theater is carefully assessed, before, during, and after a sprint, the facts set down. A man is judged then, and his time reckoned good or inglorious, by whether he had to fight his way through men and women en masse, or mostly men, mostly women, or, the worst, children at the flypaper matinees. The temptation with children, of course, is to lay into them as you'd harvest hay, tossing them in windrows to left and right, so we've stopped that. Now mostly it's nights here at the Grafton!"

The mob stopped. The twinkling theater lights sparkled in their eyes and flushed their cheeks.

"The ideal cinema," said Fogarty.

"Why?" I asked.

"Its aisles," said Clannery, "are neither too wide nor too narrow, its exits well placed, the door hinges oiled, the crowds a proper mixture of sporting bloods and folks who mind enough to leap aside should a sprinter, squandering his energy, come dashing up the aisle."

I had a sudden thought. "Do you ... handicap your runners?"

"We do! Sometimes by shifting exits when the old are known too well. Or we put a summer coat on one, a winter coat on another. What else? Now, Doone, being fleet, is a two-handicap man. Nolan!" Timulty held forth a flask. "Run this in. Make Doone take two swigs, big ones."

Nolan ran.

Timulty pointed. "While Hoolihan, here, having already gone through all Four Provinces of the pub this night, is amply weighted. Even all!"

"Go now, Hoolihan," said Fogarty. "Let our money be a light burden on you. We'll see you bursting out that exit ten minutes from now, victorious and first!"

"Let's synchronize watches!" said Clancy.

"Synchronize my back-behind," said Timulty. "Which of us has more than dirty wrists to stare at? It's you alone, Clancy, has the time. Hoolihan, inside!"

Hoolihan shook hands with them all, as if leaving for a trip around the world. Then, waving, he vanished into the cinema darkness.

At which moment, Nolan burst back out, holding high the half-empty flask. "Doone's handicapped!"

"Fine! Clannery, go check the contestants, be sure they sit opposite each other in the fourth row, as agreed, caps on, coats half buttoned, scarves properly furled. Report back to me."

Clannery ran into the dark.

"The ushers, the ticket taker?" Snell-Orkney wondered.

"Are inside, watching the fillum," said Timulty. "So much standing is hard on the feet. They won't interfere."

"It's ten-thirteen," announced Clancy. "In two more minutes—"

"Post time?" I said.

"You're a dear lad," admitted Timulty.

Clannery came hotfooting out.

"Ready! In the proper seats and all!"

" 'Tis almost over! You can tell—toward the end of any fillum the music has a way of getting out of hand."

"It's loud, all right," agreed Clannery. "Full orchestra and chorus behind the singing maid now. I must come tomorrow for the entirety. Lovely."

"*Is* it?" said all.

"What's the tune?"

"Ah, off with the tune!" said Timulty. "One minute to go, and you ask the tune! Lay the bets. Who's for Doone? Who Hoolihan?" There was a multitudinous jabbering and passing back and forth of small change.

I held out four shillings.

"Doone," I said.

"Without having seen him sprint?"

"A dark horse."

"Well said!" Timulty spun about. "Clannery, Nolan, inside, as aisle judges! Watch sharp there's no jumping the *finis*."

In went Clannery and Nolan, happy as boys.

"Make an aisle, now. Yank, you and Snell and Orkney over here with me!"

We rushed to form an aisle between the two closed main
entrance-exit doors.

"Fogarty, lay your ear to the door!"

This Fogarty did. His eyes widened.

"The damn music is *extra* loud!"

One of the Kelly boys nudged his brother. "It will be over
soon. Whoever is to die is dying this moment. Whoever is to
live is bending over him."

"Louder still!" announced Fogarty, head to the door panel,
hands twitching as if he were adjusting a radio. "There!
That's the grand ta-ta that comes just as THE END jumps on
the screen."

"They're off!" I murmured.

"Hush!" said Timulty. "There's the anthem! Tenshun!"

We all stood erect. Someone saluted.

But still we stared at the door.

"I hear feet running," said Fogarty.

"Whoever it is had a good start before the anthem—"

The door burst wide.

Hoolihan plunged to view, smiling such a smile as only
breathless victors know.

"Hoolihan!" cried the winners.

"Doone!" cried the losers, myself and Snell-Orkney.
"Where's Doone?"

For, while Hoolihan was first, a competitor was lacking.

"The idiot didn't come out the wrong door?"

We waited. The audience shuffled off and was gone.

Timulty ventured first into the empty lobby.

"Doone?" he called.

Silence.

"Could it be he's in *there*?"

Someone flung the Gents' door wide. "Doone?"

No echo.

"Good grief," cried Timulty. "It can't be he's broken a leg and lies on the aisle slope with the mortal agonies?"

"That's it!"

The island of men, heaving one way, changed gravities and heaved the other, toward the inner door, through it, and down the aisle, Snell-Orkney, chums, and myself in hot pursuit.

"Doone!"

Clannery and Nolan were there to meet us and pointed silently down. I jumped in the air twice to see over the mob's head. It was dark in the vast theater. I saw nothing.

"Doone!"

Then at last the mob bunched near the fourth row on the aisle. I heard their boggled exclamations, staring at Doone.

He was still seated in the fourth row, his hands folded, eyes shut.

Dead?

None of that.

A tear, large, luminous, and beautiful, fell on his cheek. Another tear, larger and more lustrous, emerged from his other eye. His chin was wet. It was certain he had been crying for some while.

We peered into his face, circling, leaning.

"Doone, are ya sick?"

"Is it fearful news?"

"Ah, God," cried Doone. He shook himself to find the strength, somehow, to speak.

"Ah, God," he said at last, "she has the voice of an angel."

"Angel?"

"That one up there." He nodded.

We turned to stare at the empty silver screen.

"Is it Deanna Durbin?"

Doone sobbed. "The dear dead voice of me grandmother come back—"

"Your grandma's behind!" exclaimed Timulty. "She had no such voice!"

"And who's to know, save me?" Doone blew his nose, dabbed at his eyes.

"You mean to say it was just the Durbin lass kept you from the sprint?"

"Just!" cried Doone. "Just! Why, it would be sacrilege to bound from a cinema after a recital like that. You might as well jump across the altar during a wedding, or waltz about at a funeral."

"You could've at least warned us it was no contest." Timulty glared.

"How could I? It just crept over me in a divine sickness. That last bit she sang—'The Lovely Isle of Innisfree,' was it not, Clannery?"

"What else did she sing?" asked Fogarty.

"What *else* did she sing?" cried Timulty. "He's just lost us half our day's wages and you ask what *else* she sang! *Gah!*"

"Sure, it's money runs the world," Doone agreed, seated there. "But it is music that holds down the friction."

"What's going on there?" cried someone above.

A man leaned down from the balcony, puffing a cigarette. "What's all the rouse?"

"It's the projectionist," whispered Timulty. Aloud: "Hello, Phil, darling! It's only the Team! We've a bit of a problem here, Phil, in ethics, not to say aesthetics. Now, we wonder if, well, could it be possible to run the anthem over?"

"Run it over?"

There was a rumble from the winners, a mixing and shoving of elbows.

"A lovely idea," said Doone.

"It is." Timulty, all guile, called up, "An act of God incapacitated Doone."

"A tenth-run flicker from the year 1937 caught him by the short hairs is all," said Fogarty.

"So the fair thing is"—here Timulty, unperturbed, looked to heaven—"Phil, dear boy, also is the entire last reel of the Deanna Durbin fillum still there?"

"It ain't in the ladies' room," admitted Phil, smoking steadily.

"What a wit the boy has. Now, Phil, do you think you could just thread it back through the machine there and give us the *finis* again?"

"Is that what you *all* want?" cried Phil.

There was a hard moment of indecision. But the thought of another contest was too good to be passed, even though already-won money was at stake. Slowly everyone nodded.

"I'll bet myself, then," Phil called down. "A shilling on Hoolihan!"

The winners laughed and hooted; they looked to win again. Hoolihan waved graciously. The losers turned on their man.

"Do you hear the insult, Doone? Stay awake, man!"

"When the girl sings, damn it, go deaf!"

"Places, everyone!" Timulty jostled about.

"There's no audience," said Hoolihan. "And without them there's no obstacles, no real contest."

"Why"—Snell-Orkney blinked around—"let's *all* of us be the audience."

"Snell-and-Orkney," said Timulty, "you're a genius!"

Beaming, everyone threw himself into a seat.

"Better yet," announced Timulty, up front, "why not make it teams? Doone and Hoolihan, sure, but for every Doone man or Hoolihan man that makes it out before the anthem freezes him on his hobnails, an extra point, right?"

"Done!" cried everyone.

"Pardon," I said. "There's no one outside to judge."

Everyone turned to look at me.

"Ah," said Timulty. "Well. Nolan, outside!"

Nolan trudged up the aisle, cursing.

Phil stuck his head from the projection booth above.

"Are ya clods down there ready?"

"If the girl is and the anthem is!"

And the lights went out.

I found myself seated next in from Doone, who whispered fervently, "Poke me, lad, keep me alert to practicalities instead of ornamentation, eh?"

"Shut up!" said someone. "There's the mystery."

And there indeed it was, the mystery of song and art and life, if you will, the young girl singing on the time-haunted screen.

"We lean on you, Doone," I whispered.

"Eh?" he replied. He smiled ahead. "Ah, look, ain't she lovely? Do you hear?"

"The bet, Doone," I said. "Get ready."

"All right," he groused. "Let me stir my bones. Oh, no! Jesus save me."

"What?"

"I never thought to test. My right leg. Feel. Naw, you can't. It's dead, it is!"

"Asleep, you mean?" I said, appalled.

"Dead or asleep, hell, I'm sunk! Lad, lad, you must run for me! Here's my cap and scarf!"

"Your cap . . .?"

"When victory is yours, show them, and we'll explain you ran to replace this fool leg of mine!"

I clapped the cap on, tied the scarf.

"But look here—" I protested.

"You'll do brave! Just remember, it's *finis* and no sooner! The song's almost up. Are you tensed?"

"God, I *think* so!"

"It's blind passions that win, boy. Plunge straight. If you step on someone, don't look back. There!" Doone held his legs to one side to give clearance. "The song's done. He's kissing her—"

"The *finis*!" I cried.

And leaped into the aisle.

I ran up the slope. I'm first! I thought. I'm ahead! There's the door!

I hit the door as the anthem began.

I slammed into the lobby—safe!

I won! I thought, incredulous, with Doone's cap and scarf like victory laurels upon and about me. Won for the Team!

Who's second, third, fourth?

I turned to the door as it swung shut.

Only then did I hear the shouts and yells inside.

Good Lord! I thought, six men have tried the wrong exit at once, someone tripped, fell, someone else piled on. Otherwise, why am I the first and only? There's a fierce silent combat in there this second, the two teams locked in mortal wrestling attitudes, asprawl, akimbo, above and below the seats—that *must* be it!

I've won! I wanted to yell, to break it up.

I threw the door wide.

I stared into an abyss where nothing stirred.

Nolan came to peer over my shoulder.

"That's the Irish for you," he said, nodding. "Even more than the sprint, it's the muse they like."

For what were the voices yelling in the dark?

"Run it again! Over! That last song! Phil!"

"No one move. I'm in heaven. Doone, how *right* you were!"

Nolan passed me, going in to sit.

I stood for a long moment looking down along all the rows

where the teams of anthem sprinters sat, none having stirred, wiping their eyes.

"Phil, darling?" called Timulty, somewhere up front.

"It's done!" cried Phil.

"And *this* time," added Timulty, "*without* the anthem."

Applause.

The dim lights flashed off. The screen glowed like a great warm hearth.

I looked back out at the bright sane world of Grafton Street, the pub, the hotels, shops, and night-wandering folk. I hesitated.

Then, to the tune of "The Lovely Isle of Innisfree," I took off the cap and scarf, hid these laurels under a seat, and slowly, luxuriously, with all the time in the world, moved in past Snell-Orkney and his canary five and quietly sat myself down . . .

30

And suddenly it was time to leave.

"But great God!" Timulty said. "You just arrived!"

"We found what we came for and said our say and watched your amazing sprint, for which much thanks. There's no need to stay," announced the tall sad happy old young man. "It's back to the hothouse with the flowers . . . or they wilt overnight. We are always flying and jumping and running. We are always on the move."

The airport being fogged in, there was nothing for it but the birds cage themselves on the Dún Laoghaire boat bound for England, and there was nothing for it but the inhabitants of Finn's and myself should be down at the dock to watch them pull away late in the evening. There they stood, all six, on the top deck, waving their thin hands down, and there stood Timulty and Nolan and Garrity and the rest of us waving our hands up. And as the boat hooted and pulled away, the keeper-of-the-birds nodded once and winged his right hand on the air, and all sang forth: *As I was walking through Dublin City, about the hour of twelve at night, I saw a maid, so fair was she . . . combing her hair by candlelight.*

"Jesus," said Timulty, "do you *hear?*"

"Sopranos, every *one* of them!" cried Nolan.

"Not Irish sopranos, but real *real* sopranos," said Kelly. "Damn, why didn't they *say?* If we'd known, we'd have had a good hour of *that* out of them before the boat."

Timulty nodded and added, listening to the music float over the waters, "Strange. Strange. I hate to see them go. Think. Think. For a hundred years or more, people have said we had none. But now they have returned, if but for a little time."

"We had none of *what?*" asked Garrity. "And *what* returned?"

"Why," said Timulty, "the fairies, of course, the fairies that once lived in Ireland, and live here no more, but who came this day and changed our weather, and there they go again, who once stayed all the while."

"Ah, shut up!" cried Kilpatrick. "And listen!"

And listen we did, nine men on the end of a dock as the boat sailed out and the voices sang and the fog came in, and they did not move for a long time until the boat was far gone and the voices faded like a scent of papaya on the mist.

By the time we got back to The Four Provinces it had begun to snow, which soon turned to rain.

31

The night of the long knives.

Or one long knife—the guillotine.

If only I had known, as the heroes in mystery novels used to say.

When it was over, I was reminded of Elijah at the gang-plank or myself in Beverly Hills in the bookshop buying my portable Melville and hearing that strange woman's prophecy of doom: "Don't go on that journey."

And my naive response, "He's never met anyone like me before. Maybe *that* will make the difference."

Yep. Sure. The difference being it took a bit more time to prepare the pig's head for the hammer, the razor at the throat, and the hanging on the tender-hook.

Lenin referred to dumbclucks like me as "useful idiots."

Which is to say the image of Chaplin—remember?—crossing a street as a lumber truck passes and drops a warning red flag off the load. Chaplin picks it up and runs after the truck, to warn them they've lost the flag. Instantly, a mob of Bolshevicks rounds the corner behind him, unseen, as Chaplin stands waving the flag after the truck. Enter the cops. Who promptly seize Chaplin, trample the red flag, and beat the hell out of him before throwing him in the hoosegow. The mob, of course, escapes. So . . .

There I am, in Dublin, with a red flag, waving it at John. Or there I am in the Place de la Concorde as the Bastille wagons park and I offer to help folks up the guillotine steps. Only when I reach the top do I realize where I am, panic, and come down in two pieces.

Such is the life of the innocent, or someone who kids

himself he is innocent. As someone once said to me: "Let's not be *too* naive, shall we?"

I wish I had heard and followed that advice on that night in a Chinese restaurant somewhere in the fogs and rains of Dublin.

It was one of those nights when the prophet Elijah did not prevent me—nor did I prevent myself—from drinking too many drinks and spilling too many beans in front of Jake Vickers and his Parisian lady and three or four visitors from New York and Hollywood.

It was one of those nights when it seemed you can't do anything wrong. One of those nights when everything you say is brilliant, honed, sharpened to a razor edge of risibility, when every word you speak sends the house on a roar, when people hold their ribs with laughter, waiting for your next shot across their bows, and shoot you do, and laugh they do, until you are all bathed in a warm love of hilarity and are about to fall on the floor writhing with your own genius, your own incredible humor raised to its highest temperature.

I sat listening to my own tongue wag, aim, and fire, damn well pleased at my own comic genius. Everyone was looking at me and my alcohol-oiled tongue. Even John was breaking down at my wild excursions into amiable insult and caricature. I imagined I had saved up tidbits on everyone at the table, and like those handwriting experts we encounter on occasion in life who read more in our hairlines, eyebrows, ear twitchings, nostril flarings, and teeth barings than are written in our Horatio stars or inked on plain pad with pencil, guessed at the obvious. If we do not give ourselves away in our handwriting or clothes or the percentage of alcohol on our breaths, our breathing does us in or the merest nod or shake of the head as the handwriting expert sniffs our mouthwash, or our genius. So lining up my friends one after another, against the stockade wall, I fired fusillades of wit at their habits, poses, pretensions, lovers, artistic outputs, lapses in taste, failures to arrive on time, errors in observation, and on and on. Most of it, I would hope, gently done with no scars to bandage later. So I drilled holes in masks, poured sulphur in, and lit the fuse. The explosions left darkened faces but no lost digits. At one point Jake cried, "Someone stop him!"

Christ, I wish they had.

For my next victim was John himself.

I paused for breath. Everyone stilled in their explosive roars, watching me with bright fox eyes, urging me to get *on* with it. John's next. Fix *him*!

So there I was with my hero, my love, my great good fine wondrous friend, and there I was reaching out suddenly and taking his hands.

"Did you know, John, that I, *too*, am one of the world's great hypnotists?"

"Is that so, kid?" John laughed.

"Hey!" everyone cried.

"Yep," I said. "Hypnotist. World's greatest. Someone fill my glass."

Jake Vickers poured gin in my glass.

"Go it!" yelled everyone.

"Here goes," I said.

No, someone inside me whispered.

I seized John's wrists. "I am about to hypnotize you. Don't be afraid!"

"You don't scare me, kid," John said.

"I'm going to help you with a problem."

"What's that, kid?"

"Your problem is—" I searched his face, my intuitive mind. "Your problem is, ah."

It came from me. It burst out.

"*I* am not afraid of flying to London, John. I do not fear. It is *you* that fears. You're afraid."

"Of what, H.G. ?"

"You are afraid of the Dún Laoghaire ferry boat that travels over the Irish Sea at night in great waves and dark storms. You are afraid of that, John, and so you say *I* am afraid of flying, when it is you afraid of seas and boats and storms and long night travels. Yes, John?"

"If you say so, kid," John replied, smiling stonily.

"Do you want me to help you with your problem, John?"

"Help him, help him," said everyone.

"Consider yourself helped. Relax, John. Relax. Take it easy. Sleep, John, are you getting sleepy?" I murmured, I whispered, I announced.

"If you say so, kid," said John, his voice not so amused but half amused, his eyes watchful, his wrists tense under my holding.

"Someone hit him over the head," exclaimed Jake.

"No, no," laughed John. "Let him go. Go on, kid. Put me under."

"Are you under, John?"

"Halfway there, son."

"Go further, John. Repeat after me. It is not H.G. who fears flying."

"It is not H.G. who fears flying—"

"Repeat, it is I, John, who fear the damned black night sea and fog on the ferry from Dún Laoghaire to Folkestone!"

"All that, kid, all that. Agreed."

"Are you under, John?"

"I'm sunk, kid."

"When you wake you will remember nothing, except you will no longer fear the sea and will give up flying, John."

"I will remember nothing." John closed his eyes, but I could see his eyeballs twitch behind the lids.

"And like Ahab, you will go to sea with me, two nights from now."

"Nothing like the sea," muttered John.

"At the count of ten you will waken, John, feeling fine, feeling fresh. One, two . . . five, six . . . ten. Awake!"

John popped his pingpong eyes wide and blinked around at us. "My God," he cried, "that was a good sleep. Where was I? What happened?"

"Cut it out, John!" said Jake.

"John, John," everyone roared. Someone punched me happily in the arm. Someone else rumpled my hair, the hair of the idiot savant.

John ordered drinks all around.

Slugging his back, he mused on the empty glass, and then eyed me, steadily.

"You know, kid, I been thinking—"

"What?"

"Mebbe—"

"Yes?"

"Mebbe I *should* go on that damned ferryboat with you, ah, two nights from now . . .?"

"John, John!" everyone roared.

"Cut it out," shouted Jake, falling back, splitting his face with laughs.

Cut it out.

My heart, too, while you're at it.

How the rest of the evening went or how it ended, I cannot recall. I seem to remember more drinks, and a sense of overwhelming power that came with everyone, I imagined, loving my outrageous jokes, my skill with words, my alacrity with responses. I was a ballet dancer, comically on balance on the high-wire. I could not fall off. I was a perfection and a delight. I was a Martian love, all beauteous bright.

As usual, John had no cash on him.

Jake Vickers paid the bill for the eight of us. On the way out, in the fog-filled rainy street, Jake cocked his head to one side, closed one eye, and fixed me with the other, snorting with mirth.

"You," he said, "are a *maniac*!"

That sound you hear is the long whistling slide of the guillotine blade rushing down through the night . . .

Toward the nape of my neck.

The next day I wandered around without a head, but no one said. Until five that afternoon. When John unexpectedly came to my room at the Royal Hibernian Hotel.

I don't recall John's sitting down after he came in. He was dressed in a cap and light overcoat, and he paced around the room as we discussed some minor point to be revised before I sailed off for England, two days later.

In the middle of our Ahab/Whale discussion John paused and, almost as an afterthought, said, "Oh, yeah. You'll have to change your plans."

"What plans, John?"

"Oh, all that bullshit about your coming to England on the ferryboat. I need you quicker. Cancel your boat ticket and fly with me to London on Thursday night. It'll only take an hour. You'll love it."

"I can't do that," I said.

"Now, don't be difficult—"

"You don't understand, John. I'm scared to death of airplanes."

"You've told me that, kid, and it's time you got over it."

"Maybe sometime in the future, but, please forgive me, John, I can't fly with you."

"Sounds like you're yellow, kid."

"Yes! I *admit* it. You've *always* known that. It's nothing new. I am the damnedest shade of yellow you ever saw."

"Then get over it. Fly! You'll save a whole day at sea."

"God," I moaned, falling back in my chair. "I don't *mind* being at sea all night. The ferry leaves around ten p.m. It doesn't get across to the English port until three or four a.m., an ungodly hour. I won't sleep. I might even be seasick. Then I take the train to London, it gets in Victoria at seven thirty in the morning. By eight fifteen I'll be in my hotel. By eight forty-five I'll have had a quick breakfast and a shave. By nine thirty I'll be at your hotel ready to work. No time lost. I'd be busy on the white whale as soon as you—"

"Well, screw that, son. You're coming on the airplane with me."

"No, no."

"Yes, you are, you cowardly bastard. And if you don't—"

"What, what?"

"You'll have to stay in Dublin!"

"What?" I yelled.

"You won't get your vacation. No final weeks in London."

"After seven *months*?!"

"That's right! No vacation."

"You can't *do* that!"

"Yes, I can. And not only that, Lorry, our secretary, she won't get *her* vacation. She'll be trapped here with you."

"You can't do that to Lorry. She's worked twenty-four hours a day, seven days a week for six months!"

"Her vacation's canceled unless you fly with me."

"Oh, no, John! John, no!"

"Unless you change color, kid. No more yellow."

I was on my feet.

"You'd really do *that* to her? Because of *me*?"

"That's the way it is."

"Well, the answer is no."

"What?"

"You heard me. Lorry goes to London. I go to London. And we go any damn way I please, as long as I don't interfere with our writing, my finishing, the script. I'll travel all night, and be on time at your room at Claridge's Friday morning. You can't fight that, argue that, I'll be there. I'm going on the ferry. You can't force me into flying on any goddamn plane."

"What?"

"That's it, John."

"Your final word?"

"The ferry for me. The plane for you. That's it."

John whirled, flung an invisible cape or scarf about his neck, and stormed out of the room, stalking, striding, making an exit like Tosca about to leap off the castle wall. The door slammed.

I fell down in my chair in horrible despair.

"Christ!" I yelled at the wall. "You damned fool! What have you *done*!"

For the next day and a half John refused to talk to me. We were at a place in the script where a vacation seemed convenient if not absolutely necessary. I was about forty pages from the end, and we were taking a breather, but only breath went back and forth between us. When I entered a room, John would about face and talk only to the other people present. At lunch or dinner or traveling around Dublin in a car or cab, he laughed and joked with Jake but addressed not a word or a glance at me. I did not exist. I was the rejected lover, the forever-to-be-forgotten and never-forgiven wife. The wonderful marriage had turned sour. I was to be repaid for my hypnotic magic act, though I did not immediately guess at this, with stones, rocks, and old razor blades. But not even that. He did not pick up and hurl anything at me. I had simply melted into thin air. I was not in the room. If his gaze swiveled, it sliced right through me, like an X-ray, and rushed on to some far point. I half expected to hear him speak of me in the past tense.

After a day of this, I took Jake Vickers aside in the lounge room of the Royal Hibernian.

"Jake," I whispered, for John was heading into the dining room nearby with five or six friends. "What the hell is going on?"

"Whatta you mean?"

"Am I or am I not here? When's John going to speak to me again!?"

Jake laughed quietly. "It's all a joke."

"Joke?" I cried. "Joke!"

"Pretend not to notice."

"Pretend!" I did everything except sing soprano.

"Keep your voice down. If he hears you getting hysterical it'll make him happy. Then you're really in for it."

"Christ, I'm in for it already. I can't take this! Does he know I'm going on the ferryboat, in spite of him?"

"I think so. You've ruined his joke, do you see?"

"He threatened Lorry, too. Is she going to fly with him?"

"Yeah, she's going."

"Thank God. He said he was going to penalize her, make her stay here, cancel her vacation—"

"She's going. Relax."

"I would, if I could get this iron anchor out of my stomach."

"Play it cool. Ignore him, too. Don't look at him. He's got to see, finally, you don't care, you're not riled."

"You're asking me to be Laurence Olivier."

"Act it out, anyway, buster," said Jake.

I acted. I laughed. I chatted with everyone. I even had the nerve to say out loud how great John thought my script was, so far. But John spooned his soup and buttered his bread and cut his steak, staring off at the ceiling or at his friends, while my gut settled in cement.

And then, the miracle happened that finished the script and got John to talk to me again.

32

It was seven o'clock in the morning.

I awoke and stared at the ceiling as if it were about to plunge down at me, an immense whiteness of flesh, a madness of unblinking eye, a flounder of tail. I was in a terrible state of excitement. I imagine it was like those moments we hear about before an earthquake, when perhaps the dogs and cats fight to leave the house, or the unseen, unheard tremors shake the floor and beams, and you find yourself held ready for something to arrive but you're damned if you know what.

I sat up quickly, put my legs down, my feet to the floor, arose, walked to the mirror over my typewriter and announced:

"I am Herman Melville!"

And sat down, still staring at myself to fix my self-portrait in place, and began to type, half the time not watching my fingers, keeping that young man old in a night in focus, in place, I did not want him to escape.

Believing that, I sat at the typewriter, and in the next seven hours wrote and rewrote the last third of the screenplay plus portions of the middle. I did not eat until late afternoon, when I had a sandwich sent up, and which I devoured while typing. I was fearful of answering the telephone, dreading the loss of focus if I did so. I had never typed so long, so hard, so fast, in all the years before that day and all the years since. If I wasn't Herman Melville I was at least, oh God, his Ouija board, and he was moving my planchette. Or his literary force, compressed all these months, was spouting out my fingertips as if I had twisted the faucets. I mumbled and muttered and mourned and yelled through the morning, all through noon, and leaning into my usual naptime. But there was no tiredness, only the fierce, steady, joyful, and triumphant banging away at my machine with the pages littering the floor—Ahab crying destruction over my right shoulder, Melville bawling construction over the left.

At last the metaphors were falling together, meeting up, touching, and fusing. The tiny ones with the small ones, the smaller with the larger, and the larger with the immense. Episodes separated by scenes and pages were rearranging themselves like a series of Chinese cups, collapsing and then expanding to hold more water, or in this case, by God, wine from Melville's cellar. In some cases I borrowed paragraphs or entire chapters from back of the book to move front, or scenes from the middle to the half-rear or scenes tending toward midway to be saved for finales to larger scenes.

What nailed it fast was hammering the Spanish gold ounce to the mast. If I hadn't fastened on that for starters, the other metaphors, like pilot fish and minnows and shark followers and sharks, might not have surfaced to swim in the bleached shadow of the Whale. Capture the big metaphor first, the rest will rise to follow. Don't bother with the sardines when Leviathan looms. He will suction them in by the billions once he is yours.

Well, the gold coin, small as it seems, is a very large symbol. It embodies all that the seamen want, along with what Ahab insanely desires above all. He wants the men's souls, and while his soul is dedicated to the destruction of Moby Dick, he is wildly wise to know and use the gold ounce as summons and reward. Therefore, the ship's maul and the pounded nail and the bright sun-symbol of power and reward banged to the mast with the promise that gold will pour from Moby Dick's wounds into their outreached cupping hands. Their religious fervor for minted gold runs in the invisible traces of Ahab's equally religious fervor for the true wounds and the true blood of the Beast.

The men do not know it, but the sound they hear of the maul striking the coin's fastening nail is their sea-coffin lid being hammered flat shut.

When Ahab shouts that the first man up who spies the Whale will earn this ounce, a man scrambles to obey.

No sooner up than he falls into the sea.

No sooner fallen than his body is eaten by the tide, which is to say, he returns not. The sea is hungry. And the sea is owned by the White Whale. You cannot buy or beggar it.

No sooner is the man lost than the tides are becalmed, the sails fall like the loose skin of a dying elephant. The ship is fastened to the hot sea like the gold coin forever nailed to the mast.

In the calm, the men begin to fade and die. Exhausted with waiting, with the gold coin on the mast beating on them like a true solar presence, the morale of the ship disintegrates.

In the long and terrible quiet of many days, Queequeg throws the bones that tell his death and goes to have a coffin built. So in the long silences of heat and waiting we hear his coffin being sawed and nailed and the whisper as the shavings fall from the proud feather that is the symbol of his tribal power on the shaven lid.

Queequeg says goodbye to his friend and spells himself into a death trance. How to save him? How to bring him out of his terrible catatonic state?

Melville offers no solution.

One moment Queequeg is frozen and lost by his own secret will, the next he is up and about.

Only one thing, I reasoned, could break the spell. Love. That banal thing: friendship. If Ishmael were threatened with death, would not Queequeg, from the depths of his own inner hiding places, spring forth, summoned by possible murder? It seemed the strong, and thus the proper, solution. Let the men then, in the first case, threaten dying Queequeg. Ishmael intervenes when he sees a sailor cutting a new tattoo in Queequeg's stolid flesh with a knife. Thus Ishmael proves his love, his friendship. Now, when the sailor turns on Ishmael and would cut his throat, what's more reasonable than to assume that Queequeg, having secretly seen their friendship proven by Ishmael not a minute before, would shake himself free from his self-suiciding trance and thrust between murderer and his bedmate? The answer is a resounding Yes.

And in the moment of Queequeg's seizing the sailor to bend him across his knee and murder him, why then, would this not be a perfect time for, at last, oh, my Lord, yes, at last, the arrival of the White Whale!?

Again, yes.

And the whale is sighted and shouted to view. Moby Dick heaves in sight, as Ahab pounds across the deck and the men gather at the rail to stare at the great white wonder, and Queequeg, in this moment of delivery, cannot possibly return to his self-nailed coffin, as Ahab cries to the men to row, row, and row again, out of this silence, this stillness, this damned and becalmed sea.

The men row out, following Moby Dick, and they row into a wind!

Good Grief, the lovely wind.

And I had rowed there, all in a single day.

Starting with the coin on the mast and the wind at last in the high limp sails and Moby Dick leading them off across around the world.

What followed, as metaphor, seemed inevitable in that single day of writing.

Ahab dares to row out of the calm.

So? The typhoon arrives to punish him for his sin!

And with it the certain destruction of the *Pequod*, and Saint Elmo's fires, which ignite the masts and Ahab's harpoon. "It but lights our way to Moby Dick!" cries the captain.

Ahab defies the storm and thrusts his fist down along the harpoon, shouting, "Thus, I put out the fire!"

The Saint Elmo's fires are destroyed and the storm dies.

And the stage is set for the final lowerings for Moby Dick.

So I kept hammering away with the sailor falling from the mast, the sea becalmed, the arrival of the Whale, the almost- deaths of Queequeg and Ishmael, the lowering, the pursuit, the harpooning, the roping of Ahab to the Beast, the plunge, the death, and Ahab arisen, dead, beckoning from the side of the Whale for his men to follow, follow . . . into the deep. And all the while hungry and bursting with the need to bound off to the bathroom and back quickly phoning for sandwiches and, at last, six, seven hours later, midafternoon, falling back in my chair with my hands over my eyes, sensing I was being watched and looking up at last to see old Herman still there but exhausted, fading to a ghost and gone and then I telephoned John and asked could I come out?

"But," said John, "you sound funny. Doesn't sound like you."

"It's not. It's him."

"Who?"

"Never mind. It's over."

"What's over?"

"Tell you when I get there."

"Move your ass, kid, move your ass."

An hour later I threw the forty new pages in his lap.

"Who was that on the phone?" he joked.

"Not me," I said. "Read."

"Go out and chase the bull around the field."

"If I did I'd kill him, I feel so good."

"Go have a drink, then."

I did.

Half an hour later, John came into the study with a bewildered look, as if he had been kicked in the face.

"Jesus," he said. "You were right. It's finished. When do we start shooting?"

"Tell me, John," I said.

"Did old Herman whisper in your ear?"

"Shouted."

"I hear the echoes," John said. "Goddamn."

"By the way," he said, as an afterthought. "About our trip to London?"

"Yes?" I stiffened, eyes shut.

"Take the ferryboat," said John.

33

Half a year older, I came into Finn's a day later, with rain bringing me to the door and rain waiting to take me away.

I set my luggage down by the bar, where Finn leaned over to blink at it, as did Doone and Mike and all the rest.

"Is it going away you are?" said Finn.

"Yes."

The inhabitants of Finn's turned and did not drink from their glasses, large or small.

"A remarkable thing happened," I said. "It was a surprise."

"The sort of thing that is always welcome here." Finn laid out a Guinness. "Let us in on it?"

"After all these hours and days and weeks and months, I got out of bed yesterday morning," I said, "walked to the mirror, stood there and looked at myself, ran to my typewriter and typed steadily for the next seven hours. At last, at four in the afternoon, I wrote '*Finis*' and called Courtown House and said it's over, it's through, it's finished. And found a taxi and came out to throw the forty pages in himself's lap. And we opened a bottle of champagne."

"Here's another," said Finn, and popped a cork.

He poured it for all and filled my glass.

"At this very moment," Doone asked, as everyone waited, "are you that one who moved your hand and did the scenes?"

"Am I Herman Melville?"

"That's the one."

"No," I said. "He was waiting to visit and could not stay. I was gathering him up all those days and months, reading and re-reading, to make sure he got into my bloodstream or nerves or behind my eyes or whatever. He came because I called. Spirits like that don't stay. They give of themselves and go."

"It must have been quite a feeling," said Doone.

"No way to describe it. You'll see it on the screen someday."

"God willing," said Finn.

"Yes," I said, nodding. "God willing."

"Well, here's to Herman Melville inside or out of this young man," said Doone.

"Herman Melville," said all.

"Well, now," said Finn, "it's goodbye?"

"Will you ever come back?" asked Doone.

"No," I said.

"A realist," said Finn.

"It's just," I explained, "I live so far off and I don't fly. And chances are I'll never work in Ireland again. And if too much time passes, I wouldn't want to come back."

"Aye," said Timulty, "and all of us old or dead or both and no sight worth seeing."

"It has been," I said, nursing a final glass, "the greatest time of my life."

"You *have* improved the weather around here," said Doone, tenderly, wiping his nose.

"And for the hell of it," said Mike, "let's pretend that someday you'll return, and by that time, think of the stuff we'll have saved up to tell, and you the richer for it."

"Aye," said all.

"That's most tempting." I smiled. "Dare I say I will miss all of you?"

"Aw, the hell," said Finn quietly.

"Damn," said some others, looking at me like a son.

"Before you go," said Finn. "On the Irish, now. Have you crossed our T's and dotted our I's? How would you best describe . . . ?"

"Imagination," I said quietly.

Silence. They waited.

"Imagination," I went on. "Great God, everything's wrong. Where *are* you? On a flyspeck isle nine thousand miles north of nowhere!! What wealth is there? None! What natural resources? Only one: the resourceful genius, the golden mind, of everyone I've met! The mind that looks out the eyes, the words that roll off the tongue in response to events no bigger than the eye of a needle! From so little you glean so much; squeeze the last ounce of life from a flower with one petal, a night with no stars, a day with no sun, a theater haunted by old films, a bump on the head that in America would have been treated with a Band-Aid. Here and everywhere in Ireland, it goes on. Someone picks up a string, someone else ties a knot in it, a third one adds a bow, and by morn you've got a rug on the floor, a drape at the window, a harp-thread tapestry singing on the wall, all starting from that string! The Church puts her on her knees, the weather drowns her, politics all but buries her ... but Ireland still sprints for that far exit. And do you know, by God, I think she'll *make* it!"

I finished my champagne and then went about shaking each hand and buffing each arm with a gentle fist.

"Goodbye, Timulty."

"Lad."

"So long, Hannahan."

"Boy."

"Mr. Kelly, Mr. O'Brien, Mr. Bannion."

"Lad." "Yank." "Boyo."

"Mr. Doone, keep sprinting."

"I'm on me toes."

"Mr. Finn, keep pouring."

"The well will never run dry."

At the door I turned to see them as in a picture lined up there. I was glad they did not come along to see me out. It was as in the old cinema scenes. I looked at them, and they at me.

"God speed you, Yank."

"God bless you, Mr. Finn."

They waved, I waved, and went out the door.

Mike got behind the wheel of the 1928 Nash.

"Pray that it starts," he said.

We prayed. It did. We drove off down the road toward the Irish Sea and the port, away from 1918 and 1922 and 1929 and 1945 and 1953, and I did not look back as Finn's vanished in the past. I saw with wet eyes that, God, the hills were green. Oh, yes, the hills were *green*.

A NOTE ABOUT THE AUTHOR

Ray Bradbury has published some twenty-seven books—novels, stories, plays, essays, and poems—since his first story appeared when he was twenty years old. He began writing for the movies in 1952—with the script for his own *Beast from 20,000 Fathoms*. The next year he wrote the screenplay for *It Came From Outer Space*. In 1953 he lived in Ireland writing the script of *Moby Dick* for John Huston. In 1961 he wrote the narration spoken by Orson Welles for *King of Kings*, and the short animated film *Icarus Montgolfier Wright*, based on his story of the history of flight, was nominated for an Academy Award. Films have been made of his "Picasso Summer," *The Illustrated Man*, *Fahrenheit 451*, and *Something Wicked This Way Comes*. Since 1985 he has adapted his stories for his own half-hour show on USA Cable television.